BOOKS BY

Carrie Carr
====================

Destiny's Bridge

Faith's Crossing

Hope's Path

Love's Journey

Strength of the Heart

The Way Things Should Be

Something to Be Thankful For

Diving into the Turn

Carrie Carr

Yellow Rose Books

Nederland, Texas

Copyright © 2006 by Carrie Carr

All rights reserved. No part of this publication may be reproduced, transmitted in any form or by any means, electronic or mechanical, including photocopy, recording, or any information storage and retrieval system, without permission in writing from the publisher. The characters, incidents and dialogue herein are fictional and any resemblance to actual events or persons, living or dead, is purely coincidental.

ISBN 978-1-932300-54-3

First Printing 2006

9 8 7 6 5 4 3 2 1

Cover design by Katherine Smith

Published by:

Yellow Rose Books
4700 Highway 365, Suite A, PMB 210
Port Arthur, Texas 77642

Find us on the World Wide Web at
http://www.regalcrest.biz

Printed in the United States of America

Acknowledgements:

I want to thank the folks who worked so hard to make this book possible: Lori, for helping me make a vague idea into a story, and for being there with an encouraging word when I would stumble, as well as her talents for editing; Jane, for her editing skills and patience; Katherine Smith for the fantastic cover; and last, but most definitely not least, Cathy - for allowing me to continue to live my dreams.

For my Mom, who has been, and always will be, my hero and inspiration.

And, for my Jan, the love of my life, and my heart and soul. Always and forever, my love.

Chapter One

THE DINGY MOTEL room was mostly dark, and the only sounds that could be heard were the guttural moans of two people in the throes of passion. Two sets of clothes, strewn about the room in no particular order, led up to the king-sized bed. Boots, one pair scuffed and dusty and the other bright red, lay by the door next to a well-worn pair of jeans and petite red knit slacks. The shirts tossed on a nearby chair were about as unevenly matched: a ratty, denim shirt half-covered by a red soft silk with a scattering of rhinestones on it. The tiara on the red western hat sparkled in the dim light from the neon sign outside, and the ragged brown felt hat next to it seemed poor in comparison.

"God, baby. Yes." A woman, straddling her lover, swayed her hips, her head thrown back. Heavily teased, dark hair cascaded around her shoulders. Her body glistened in the faint light from the flashing motel sign that sliced through gaps in the paneled curtains. One hand from the body beneath her slid up her torso, the short nails raking at the woman's skin. She rocked again, and the person below moaned as well. The callused hand squeezing her breast was the woman's undoing. She gasped and fell forward, spent. After a moment, she slid off to one side and rolled over onto her back. "You're good at that, Shelby Fisher."

"Haven't had any complaints, yet." Rising to a sitting position, Shelby reached for the cigarettes on the nightstand and pulled one from the pack. "You want one?" Her own short hair, dark and in disarray, barely touched her neck. She propped herself up against the headboard and took a long drag on the cigarette.

Still out of breath, Shelby's bed partner shook her head. "No, I can't. It might darken my teeth." She got up from the bed and walked into the bathroom, well aware of the appreciative glance she received.

"I never could understand rodeo queens—more concerned

about how they look than how they feel." Shelby took another deep drag, watching in a disinterested gaze the smoke rings that floated around her head.

Chapter Two

ONE TANNED HAND snaked out from under the covers to turn off the alarm clock before its shrill buzzing could start. Rebecca Starrett yawned and stretched, excited about the day ahead. She sat up and brushed her hand through her hair, then swung her legs over the side of the bed and hurried to the bathroom. Glancing out the window while brushing her teeth, she noticed the bright central Texas sky and decided that it would be a wonderful day.

Today she would load up her horse, Patches, in a borrowed trailer and compete for the first time in the local rodeo. At twenty-six, she'd probably be the oldest 'new' rider there, but Rebecca didn't care. The one thing that mattered was that her dream would come true today, and nothing would ruin it. She hurried through her morning routine so that she could take care of her chores. Her thick, red hair fought with the heavy brush as she tried to bring some order to it, so it took Rebecca a little longer than usual to head downstairs.

Rebecca lived in an apartment above stables where she took care of other people's horses in return for room and board for Patches. She worked full-time at the small western wear store in town and considered herself lucky to have found the job at the store and lodgings at the stable. Although her parents lived nearby, she wanted to be on her own, and this arrangement allowed for that. Her life was just like she liked it.

It didn't take long to feed the other horses, and then she was at the stall where Patches quartered. "Good morning, girl. We've got a big weekend planned." Rebecca rubbed the velvety nose of her best friend. The horse had been a gift from her father when she was twenty-three, when she had expressed a desire to learn to barrel race. "Do you think we're up to it?" The mare seemed to be, and Rebecca just hoped she was, as well.

THE INDOOR ARENA was empty except for a few performers milling around. Early matinees wouldn't begin for a couple more hours, and most of the performers were putting last minute touches to equipment and taking care of animals. The dust wasn't too bad yet, and Shelby was thankful for that. By the early evening, the noise and dirt would be heavy in the air. She slapped her leather bull rider's glove against her thigh and kept an eye out for someone in particular. As she passed a few other women, she nodded to them. "Ladies." Her eyes continued to scan the area, and she didn't pay much attention to the circle of women she'd just ambled by.

Tittering and a few grumblings could be heard. One voice in particular stood out from the rest. "That Shelby thinks she's God's gift to women."

"From what I've heard, that's not too far off," another high-pitched voice added. All heads swiveled to watch the bull rider move away, and more lewd comments were whispered.

Two cowboys, one older and as well worn as his saddle, the other one, more handsome than smart, leaned against the arena gate watching the scene. Bemused, the older one said, "I don't know why, Rob, but women flock to that gal like flies to a pile of manure."

Rob Sanger shook his head. "I don't understand it myself, Henry. Maybe it's that damned quiet way of talking she has. Women seem to love it." He spit a stream of tobacco into the dirt, then studied the passing form of the bull rider. She was slim and the denim jeans she wore fit her like a second skin. "Or, more'n likely, it's that tight little ass she has." Rob laughed, although his smile didn't quite reach his eyes. This was the third rodeo in a row where he had seen Shelby Fisher this year, and he was tired of her beating his score every time. Although the women didn't compete with the men, it didn't stop some of the guys from picking on Rob when her score was higher. "Damned unnatural. Women don't belong in rodeos. They should be at home, cooking, cleaning, and having kids. Like my mom did." He glared at her retreating form until it disappeared toward the barn adjacent to the arena.

The air in the barn held a strong smell of hay and manure, although the stalls were cleaned out two to three times a day. The few people present were busy with their own animals and tack. After checking a few stalls, Shelby finally saw who she had been looking for. She walked up behind her target, and put her arms around the buxom woman. "Hey, beautiful."

Natalie fought off the arms and spun around. "What do you think you're doing?" She quickly looked around to see if anyone had noticed what Shelby had done. Satisfied no one had seen, she patted her fluffed hair to make sure it was still in place. Her hair was teased out as wide as her shoulders, and she had used so much hairspray to get it in that condition, there wasn't much that could budge the mess. Her expensive green outfit was just as gaudy as the red one she'd worn the night before. "Keep your hands off me, Shelby."

"I thought you said you enjoyed last night."

"We can't be seen together. It would ruin me." Natalie Wheeler was the rodeo queen, and she didn't want any kind of scandal to cause her to lose the tiara that she wore so proudly upon her western hat. The honor had cost her father a lot of money, especially since she was older than the runners up. "Last night was fun, but that's all it was. I thought you understood that."

Shelby's jaw clenched. She should have known better. Some things never changed, and she had yet to find anyone that was different from what her father had warned her about. She couldn't understand what Natalie's problem was. They'd enjoyed a night of what she thought was mind-blowing sex, and here the woman acted as if they didn't even know each other. Shelby decided she'd never understand the rest of her gender. She struggled to keep from yelling at the woman before her and tried to save face the only way she could. "It might have been fun for you, but I've had better." When Natalie raised her hand to slap her, Shelby inclined her head in the direction of a pair of boys who were cleaning nearby stables. "Uh-uh. Wouldn't want your adoring public to know you're not only a whore, but a bitch, too." She tipped her dusty brown hat at Natalie and edged by her. "Have a nice ride, tonight, Your Majesty."

Shelby stomped ahead, turned past some stalls halfway through the barn and slammed into another woman. They both fell back onto the sawdust covered floor. Shelby picked up her hat which had fallen off in the collision. "Why don't you watch where you're going?" She stood and dusted her hat against her leg, and was suddenly eye-to-eye with an angry redhead.

"Me? You're the one whose hat was so low that she probably couldn't see her damned feet," the redhead snapped. She was almost the same height as Shelby's five feet, eight inches, but where the bull rider was thin, this woman was much more curvaceous. "I think you owe me an apology."

Still mad at Natalie, Shelby crammed the hat back onto her head and pulled the brim low over her face. "Okay, fine. I'm sorry you're such a klutz." Shelby sidestepped the upset woman and continued on her way.

"Why, that, that—"

"Bitch," a woman who ran up to her supplied. "I saw what happened, Rebecca. Are you okay?"

Rebecca wiped the hay from her clothes and was thankful she didn't land in a pile of something more fragrant. "I'm fine, Paula. Pissed as hell, but fine. Who does that woman think she is?" She had already changed into her 'rodeo' outfit, and used her hands to brush off her bright blue spandex jeans. The white silk shirt she wore didn't seem to have any stains on it, and Rebecca decided that the woman who ran into her better be thankful for that fact.

"That was Shelby Fisher. No one really likes her, unless they're in bed with her. Then, I hear, they just tolerate her long enough to enjoy the ride." Paula helped brush off the back of Rebecca's shirt and pants. "Not that I have any practical experience, mind you. My husband would kill me if I even thought about it." She shook her head. Only five years older than Rebecca's twenty-six, nothing Paula Fay Winger heard or saw surprised her anymore. Curious as to what her friend thought, she couldn't help but add, "She's really kind of cute, when she's not being such an evil bitch."

"Paula!" Rebecca wasn't sure what shocked her more, the way Paula casually talked about the sexual escapades of Shelby Fisher, or the fact that no one seemed to mind that there was a lesbian 'carrying on' right in front of them.

"Well, it's true. I heard one of the other girls talk about her. They say when she's cleaned up and not hiding under that hat, she can be almost attractive." She stood by while Rebecca rubbed hard at her saddle and gear for the third time that day. "You're going to wear all the leather off if you keep that up."

Embarrassed, Rebecca stopped. "I know. I can't help it. This is my first rodeo, and I want to look good." She'd been practicing for years and had gotten the entry money she'd needed from her parents. The hard part was to get up her nerve to compete. Rebecca checked all her gear again, then placed it carefully back where it belonged. "And as for Ms. Grump, I don't care how attractive she is under that hat. She's rude, crass, and just plain mean. And I'm not looking for a quick jump in the sack with some old dusty rodeo rider, anyway." *Especially a woman. Have all these people gone mad?*

"Suit yourself. But I kind of like that dangerous type. Just ask Buddy."

"Ah, right." Rebecca was barely able to hold off her laughter at the thought of the cherubic Buddy being dangerous. Paula's husband was the least dangerous person Rebecca had ever met.

He was short, pot-bellied, and had the friendliest smile in the world. His balding head didn't help his case much, either. Since Paula was the short, dumpy type, they were a match made in rodeo heaven. "You just keep living that dream, Paula."

When Rebecca had arrived at the barns a few days previously, the gregarious couple practically adopted her. Paula and Buddy had both taken Rebecca under their wing, helping her to become familiar with the rodeo grounds and the other participants. Paula felt a certain duty to make certain their charge was taken care of. And that meant warning Rebecca against the likes of Shelby Fisher.

Rebecca was older and a lot less naïve than she looked. She was ready for a little excitement in her otherwise dull life, and hoped that this rodeo was it.

THE AFTERNOON PRELIMINARIES were rarely well attended, and the arena was only about one-quarter full for the first matinee. More people would be coming in for the evening show. The excited voices of children intermingled with those of their parents, who could be caught bragging about their first experiences at the rodeo. People who otherwise didn't know one end of a boot from another could be found dressed to the nines, wearing brand new denim jeans and starched western shirts, topped off with cowboy hats that usually still had the price tags inside.

Shelby stood behind the arena fence, her arms draped over the metal bars and one boot braced against the bottom rail. No matter how often she witnessed it, the opening of the rodeo always brought her a small thrill and reminded her of the times when she had stood in this very spot with her father. He would point out the more outrageous outfits in the stands, and they'd both share a quiet laugh at how people dressed. It was days like this when Shelby missed him the most.

She pushed away from the fence and shook her head. Thinking about people long gone wouldn't make them come back, and she knew that if she wanted to get a decent meal and give it time to settle, she'd better do it now. Shelby decided to just grab something from concessions, because she didn't feel like going out to her truck and search an unfamiliar town for an eatery. She spied a hot dog vendor who was completing a transaction with a woman dressed in a flashy blue outfit.

The vendor looked up as Shelby approached. "I'll be right with you." He finished counting the woman's change.

"Take your time, I'm not in that big of a hurry."

With her food in her hand, the other woman turned around and looked into the rider's eyes. "You?"

"Yeah?" Shelby didn't recognize the redhead, but from the way she was acting, they'd obviously met. "Should I know you?" She made a cursory glance down the voluptuous body. Far from being overweight, the woman had curves in all the right places. At first, Shelby wondered if she might know the woman from a one night stand, but she would have remembered holding a body like this one.

"You don't, huh?"

"I don't think I do, but I'd like to."

"I can't believe your attitude," she huffed.

Shelby watched her leave, enjoying the way the blue pants clung to the woman's form. "Nice."

The vendor couldn't agree more. "You got that right." Then he realized he was talking with a woman and looked almost ill. "What can I get for you, ma'am?"

"Chili dog, hold the onions." Shelby gave him the three dollars he asked for, and started for the back pens where the bulls were kept. She had no interest in watching the first event, which was the team roping, and wanted one more look at the bull she had drawn. She almost choked on her hot dog when she heard a woman laugh.

"Losing your touch, Shel?" Dressed in creased jeans and a matching western denim shirt, the woman stepped forward. She was about the same height as Shelby, but a lot more muscular. With her shortly cropped, blonde hair and small breasts, most people mistook Andrea Graham for a man. "I hope you do better with the bulls than the ladies."

Shelby edged past her competitor. Andrea was years younger than she and was forever bragging there wasn't a woman she couldn't have. "Scared, Graham?" She continued to eat her hot dog as she walked, and wasn't surprised when Andrea hurried to catch up.

"Are you asking if I'm scared of you, or the bulls? 'Cause either one of you ain't worth worrying about." She spat off to the side. Thinking it made her look better to the ladies, Andrea was never without a dip of snuff between her lower lip and gums. "I'll ride both of them better than you this time."

"Mmm." Shelby continued to chew her hot dog, hoping Andrea would give up and go find someone else to torment.

The walk to the back pens kept Shelby on edge as Andrea continued to taunt her about everything from her choice in women to the fact that she still drove around in her father's old truck and travel trailer. The last comment finally got a rise out of

Shelby, who spun on her heel and threw the remainder of her hot dog at Andrea's feet. "Shut your fucking mouth, Graham, or so help me, I'll shut it for you."

"You and who else?" Tilting her Stetson back on her head, Andrea leaned forward, obviously hoping Shelby would take the first swing. "Your old man's been dead for a long time, and I heard that your momma was a whore."

Before Shelby could launch her attack, a pair of strong arms wrapped around her and held her back. "Let me go!"

"Cool down, Shelby." Henry glared over the angry woman's shoulder. "Andrea, you're up early, so you'd better go get your equipment." He waited until she was gone before he released his grasp and stood by passively as Shelby vented.

"Goddamn it, Henry! Why'd you go putting your nose in where it doesn't belong? I've had about all I can stand of that bitch." Shelby glared up at the older man as she tucked in her shirt which had come loose during her attempt to free herself from his grasp.

"I don't blame you none, girl. But all that would've done is get you tossed out of the rodeo, and I know you don't want that."

Shelby grudgingly agreed, but that didn't make her feel any better. She still needed to lash out at someone, and Henry was the closest target. "I'm a grown woman, and I don't need a keeper."

"No, you don't. But I was a good friend of your father's, and I figured he wouldn't mind if I kept my eye on you a bit." He looked down at the remains of the partially eaten chili dog that littered the floor near the indoor pens. "You've got time to go get you another one, if you want. Things don't kick off here for at least another hour."

Shelby shook her head. "I've lost my appetite." She stepped by Henry and strode out into the open air.

AFTER COOLING OFF, Shelby decided to go through the barns and check out some of the other animals. She had just passed an empty stall when a hand grabbed her by the back of her belt. "Whoa!"

A smiling woman stepped out of the shadows of the stall. Another one of the queen's court, her blonde hair was teased high, and the bright pink stretch jeans and top matched her boots and hat. "Hey there, Shelby. Where are you off to?"

"Hi, Jessica." Shelby's response was deliberately cool. She had heard from some of the rodeo people that Jessica tended to be on the possessive side, and she didn't want any part of it. "I'm going to watch the opening parade."

Jessica tugged harder on Shelby's belt, pulling her into the stall. "I only have one question for you."

"What's that?"

"Is all royalty your type, or just the queen?" She had seen Shelby and Natalie enter the old motel together the evening before, and hoped it was the ammunition she needed to get what she wanted, namely Shelby.

Shelby slapped at Jessica's hands as Jessica tried to unbutton Shelby's shirt. "I don't know what you're talking about." Her shirt was soon opened, and it didn't take Jessica any time at all to unzip Shelby's pants and pull them down around her ankles. "I don't think...."

"You don't have to think, baby. Just let me take care of you," Jessica breathed, dropping to her knees in front of the bull rider. She tugged Shelby's underwear down slowly, savoring the moment.

For her part, Shelby had to stretch her arms across the rail beams of the vacant stall to keep from falling down while Jessica pleasured her. After she slammed her head against the wood, it took her a couple of minutes to get her bearings. With shaky hands, Shelby pulled up her underwear and pants and buttoned her shirt.

Jessica wiped her own mouth, pleased with herself. She was unbuttoning her own blouse when Shelby stopped her.

"Sorry, darlin', but I've got to go." Shelby patted Jessica on the ass as she walked shakily out of the stall. "Thanks, though."

"Damn you, Shelby!" Jessica yelled.

Shelby let out a snort of laughter and hustled away, unaware they'd had an audience the entire time.

STEPPING FROM THE shadows, the rodeo clown pulled his hat lower over his face and followed Shelby at a discreet distance. He had been on his way back from his trailer when he'd heard the noise in the stall, and the sight of the two women together was almost more than he could stomach. *The way that bull rider allowed that other woman to put her mouth on her is against everything I've ever been taught in church.* An acid-like taste filled his mouth, and Fred spat on the ground.

Fred had once been a popular bull rider, but no one knew that about him since he'd changed his name and gone on the smaller rodeo circuit where no one would know him or the things he'd done. His new career left him bitter and usually at least marginally drunk and longing for the glory days of his youth.

"How's it going, Fred?" one of the wranglers asked, slapping the painted clown hard on the back. "Looks like we have a mess of kids near the front rows, so at least you'll have a good audience for the matinee."

Fred tightened the belt on his well-worn, brightly-colored chaps. "Just great. One of them will probably puke a hot dog on me or something." He strode by the pens and made his way to where he could watch the Grand Parade and sip on a flask of whiskey.

Shelby stood behind the chutes with the others, and yet she was removed from them. She never felt a kinship with the people she met on the circuit. Some she saw more than others, and some were just locals who tried their hand at rodeoing. When she went outside for another cigarette, she saw Natalie near the door flirting with several of the cowboys. Once the men left, Shelby ambled over. "Making the rounds, aren't you?"

"Shelby, go away," Natalie hissed, looking around. "Someone could see us talking."

"Yeah. That's a great crime these days, isn't it?" As much as she hated to admit it, Shelby felt something for Natalie, and the persistent denial of their brief relationship hurt.

When a young stable hand brought Natalie's horse to her, she instantly became the Rodeo Queen. "Thank you, handsome," she said to the boy. "I bet you're going to break some hearts when you grow up," she told him, her voice syrupy sweet. The boy reddened, but grinned as he took off.

Natalie turned her attention back to Shelby. "If I mean anything to you, just go away. This could be my only shot at fulfilling my greatest dream." She put her foot up into the stirrup and climbed onto the saddle.

Shelby grabbed the horse's halter. "Dammit, Natalie. You chase me all over the place, finally get me to agree to sleep with you..."

"Sssh!"

But Shelby wasn't finished. "...and then kick me aside like yesterday's trash." Her voice had risen, and the people around them turned and were now looking their way. "I'm not going to stand for this, Natalie. No one makes a fool of me."

Natalie jerked hard on her horse's reins, breaking Shelby's hold . "Fuck you, you little bull riding tramp. You're dirt, and you'll always be dirt." She kicked the animal hard and almost ran over Shelby as she guided her horse toward the ring.

FOCUSING HER THOUGHTS, Rebecca put the finishing touches on her tack. Her horse was all saddled up. She could hear the other riders around her gossiping and almost felt sorry for whomever it was they were talking about.

"...charmed the pants right off her. As a matter of fact, her husband caught them in the hay trailer," one woman exclaimed. "They claimed it was some sort of Oriental massage, but what kind has both people naked, I ask you?"

Rebecca rolled her eyes. *Don't these women have anything better to do with their time?* Then a name came up that caught her attention.

"She's been traipsing around too long, if you ask me. That Shelby Fisher needs to settle down somewhere. Just how long can a person ride those monstrous bulls? And why would a lady want to?" a women asked.

"She's not a lady like we are," another answered, and they all laughed knowingly.

Inching closer, Rebecca was stunned by the topic of conversation the so-called "ladies" were pursuing.

"It's a shame, really. The rodeo used to be good family fun. Now, so many of those kind of people are here, it's hard to tell the men from the women." The rest of the women agreed. "And," the speaker who was apparently emboldened, said in a louder voice, "I think we should find a way to get that Shelby off the circuit, for good!"

"Amen," the others chorused.

The ringleader pointed toward the Rodeo Queen's departing back, then glanced sidelong over at Shelby. "Looks like she bit off more than she could chew this time. Our queen won't let someone like that pester her."

Rebecca watched as Shelby adjusted her hat and squared her shoulders. The bull rider held her head up high and made her way outside again. Rebecca thought about riding over to see if Shelby was okay, but after their previous encounters, thought better of it. After all, the woman was a pain in the ass, wasn't she?

Chapter Three

THE GRAND ENTRY Parade was announced. That's what they called it, but Paula secretly joked about it being the Grand Pain in the Patootie, because it took her away from her preparation time for the barrel racing events that took place first in the evening. Paula looked around for Rebecca, and was relieved when she raced up beside her, her horse in tow. "Is everything okay?" Paula asked.

"Sure. I was just afraid I'd miss my big entrance," Rebecca said. Patches jangled her bridle and snorted while her mistress looked around at the half-empty stands. "Early birds are bustling with excitement, aren't they?"

Paula laughed. "Not. It's good practice for you, though. And, it'll help you see if your horse can handle the noise in a covered arena."

"Noise?" Rebecca's eyes widened. She hadn't thought of that before. *What if I get out there and fall off Patches? What if we both freeze up? What if—*

"Are you okay?"

Rebecca tried to peer through the throng of riders ahead of them to see the arena. "I didn't even think about the noise factor. Do you think I'll look like an idiot?"

"I doubt that very seriously. But just to be on the safe side, ride here between me and Therese." Then she addressed the woman on her left. "Therese, this is my friend Rebecca. It's her first rodeo."

A quiet woman with dark hair and eyes dipped her head to acknowledge Rebecca. "It's very nice to meet you, Rebecca. Don't let Paula scare you. I've never seen anyone get thrown during the Grand Parade."

"Thanks. Nice to meet you, too." Rebecca stuck her tongue out at Paula, who laughed heartily. Rebecca made a face back and said, "I'm telling Buddy on you." She watched the non-riding participants—the rodeo clowns and the bull and bronc riders — go to the front of the line. *I wonder if Shelby had time to get up there?* Then she wondered why she even cared. She'd only spoken to the woman twice, and both times left a bad taste in her mouth.

HAVING BEEN IN enough Grand Entries in her day, Shelby opted to skip the matinee version. She needed her bull riding gear and decided to go back to her trailer before it got too hot outside. Her father had bought the old travel trailer when she was born, and it had been old then, but now it was what she called a dump on wheels. But it was cheaper than a hotel room every night, and it had been the only real home she'd ever known.

Shelby's mother, Vivian, had been a Rodeo Queen and barrel racer. In a moment of bad judgment, she fell for Ted Fisher's good looks and charm. Nine months later, she had a daughter of her own, but was disowned because she'd had the child out of wedlock, so Shelby never knew her mother's family.

Vivian sold her horse and belongings to survive, while Ted, a bull rider, bought the trailer so they could keep up with the circuit. They married, and then spent most of their time drinking, fighting, and making up. When Shelby was six, Vivian hooked up with a carnival worker at one of the county fairs they were at, and wasn't seen or heard from again. Ted didn't force Shelby to go to school and had taken his daughter with him on the circuit. When she was twelve, his drinking and riding got him gored by a bull and killed.

That moment changed Shelby's life as she knew it. Not only was she a witness to the horrible accident, but she was sent to live with Ted's sister. Nadeen Fisher was an old maid who lived a boring life in a small, boring town outside of Lubbock, Texas. When Shelby turned sixteen, much to her aunt's dismay, but with her grudging permission, she took her father's truck and trailer and went to ride in the rodeo.

Now Shelby sat in the old trailer and looked around for her spurs. They were purely for show since she never raked the bull, but the kids loved seeing someone dressed the part, and Shelby enjoyed the attention. She picked up her chaps and bull rope, then lit another cigarette. Sitting on the bed, she looked at the dismal shape of the trailer. It was clean, but it made last night's cheap motel look like a four-star establishment. For not the first time in her life, she found herself wondering what she was doing there.

WHAT AM I doing here? The butterflies in Rebecca's stomach became full-fledged hawks the moment the riders in front of her moved forward. She had only ridden in small playdays to prepare herself for this moment, and she felt faint as she, Paula, and Therese crossed the threshold to the arena to a smattering of applause. The smaller venue she was used to didn't have such crowds, even as small as today's was. She was grateful that the playdays gave her the opportunity to hone her skills, even though, at the moment, she was overwhelmed.

As Rebecca felt all the blood drain out of her face, Paula leaned over and said, "Wave and act like you've done this before, hon. They'll never know the difference. You're lucky it's a small turnout. This is a good way to break in."

The horses moved along at a sedate pace, and by the time they were halfway around the arena, Rebecca felt more comfortable. She craned her neck left and right, looking at the men and women who walked along the front of the line but she couldn't spot Shelby.

"Are you looking for someone in particular?" Paula teased. "I thought she wasn't your type."

"She's not! And for your information, I think she's obnoxious." Rebecca didn't even like women, at least not in that way. At least she didn't think so. She spent so much time with the horses, though, that her dating experience was limited to one boy in high school and a few single dates after she graduated. Since Somerville was so small, it was more like going out with a brother than a real date, so she didn't have much to go by. "But, you're right, I don't see her anywhere."

Paula leaned to the side and waved at a group of school children causing a few of the girls to squeal with excitement. She turned back to eye Rebecca. "She's most likely getting ready for the bull riding competition. Some of the prelims are coming up. I see you're feeling a bit better."

Rebecca was feeling much more comfortable now and was waving at the crowd just as enthusiastically as Paula was. "I am, thanks. Nothing to it."

Once the Grand Entry had made its circuit, all the performers went back behind the threshold. Next up were the queen and her court. The lights of the arena dimmed, and a rider emerged from each side, one carrying a United States flag, the other a Texas flag. They raced down the sides of the arena at a full gallop and crisscrossed at the end. When they stopped, they were ready for the queen and her procession.

The spotlight flooded the arena and hit Natalie in all her splendor. The incandescent green outfit could be seen from every seat in the arena, which was exactly how Natalie wanted it. She waved, then kicked her horse into a full gallop. Rebecca noted how the Rodeo Queen leaned forward, bringing some excitement to the usually dull routine. Halfway through her run, the saddle slid from the snorting animal. Natalie pitched off to the side. She tried to hold on to the reins, but let go to grab at the saddle, which continued to twist to the inside.

Rebecca thought Natalie would just fall from the saddle, but the rodeo queen's boot caught in the stirrup. She was dragged around the arena, her horse still at a full run. A flurry of movement came from all sides. Six clowns raced out onto the dirt. Many other people, including Shelby, hurried out to stop the frantic horse.

One of the clowns managed to grab hold of the reins and drag the horse to a standstill. The lights went up to the stunned silence of horrified onlookers. Two more clowns grabbed at the stirrup and dislodged Natalie's foot.

Battered and bleeding, Natalie pointed an accusing finger at Shelby. "Keep that bitch away from me," she gasped.

An ambulance rolled into the arena, and a man and a woman jumped from the vehicle just as it stopped. The paramedics moved everyone away and checked the extent of the Rodeo Queen's injuries, strapped her to a backboard, and loaded her into their van.

One of the clowns who had helped catch the horse stepped forward. "Her cinch strap was cut," he announced.

Everyone looked at Shelby.

"What?" Shelby looked from one person to another. "You don't actually think I had anything to do with that, do you?"

"Well," one of the girls in the court reminded her, "you were seen arguing with her earlier today."

Rebecca looked on in shock. *She was. I saw it.* But, unlike so many around her, she didn't want to accuse anyone without proof so she kept her mouth shut.

"Let's worry less about that and pray that poor Natalie recovers okay," Paula reminded everyone.

Agreements were murmured, and the performers went back to their duties.

"Ladies and gentlemen," the announcer said. "While our lovely queen is going to be just fine, in order to give her time to get back on her feet, our runner up, the lovely Jessica Anders, will be the reigning queen for the remainder of the rodeo." The announcement was followed by light applause.

Rebecca found a good place to watch the first round of calf roping. Although she had no skill in the sport, it fascinated her to watch man, or woman, versus the animal. She stepped to the side and jostled another person who had moved to stand next to her.

"Amazing, aren't they?" Rebecca asked. "I can barely walk and chew gum at the same time, much less ride and toss a rope."

From the corner of her eye, she noticed Shelby examining her.

"Is this your first?" Shelby asked. "Rodeo, I mean?"

Rebecca almost jumped. They were the first non-threatening words she had heard from the woman, and she realized that Shelby had a nice voice. Soft, with a slight accent that said she was a native Texan. "As far as participating, yes, it is. Although I've done a lot of small playdays for practice." She watched as a contestant jumped from his horse and flipped a calf over, tying its feet almost immediately. "I probably sound like an idiot to you, though. My name's Rebecca."

"I'm Shelby, and you don't sound like an idiot at all. Everyone has to start somewhere."

"Oh? Did you start out in playdays, too?"

Shelby laughed. "Hell, I was born on a bull, I think. No, darlin', I've been eating rodeo dust my entire life." An announcement boomed over the PA system and Shelby tipped her head. "I think they're calling the racers to draw numbers."

"Oh, shit." Rebecca began to leave. "Thanks."

"For what?"

Rebecca looked down at the ground shyly. "For, well, just thanks." She hurried off, leaving a smiling Shelby behind.

SHELBY THOUGHT ABOUT going back to her trailer for a nap, but decided to stay and see how Rebecca fared in her first ever rodeo event. *She'll probably be nervous as hell, and I'm sure a friendly face in the audience couldn't hurt.* Shelby had to laugh at that. She was anything but a friendly face. *But, she's pretty enough to warrant a little extra attention.*

Shelby eyed the woman appreciatively from the distance. Unlike a lot of the women at the rodeo, Rebecca wasn't wearing a lot of makeup, and she had her red hair pulled back in a ponytail. Her forehead had a slight crease where her hat had been, and her blue eyes were clear with excitement. *Not too bad. Easy on the eyes.*

The fair and rodeo would last a month, and Shelby bet herself she could have the woman in her bed by the end of the week, if she so desired. *She already wants me, I can tell.*

REBECCA HAD DRAWN number eight. She didn't know if drawing that position made her more relieved or more anxious. Many of the women who would be racing before her had been riding the same circuit for years, and some were nowhere as old as she, so she didn't have near the experience they had. However, when the announcer called her name, everything else shifted out of focus, and she saw only the first barrel in the cloverleaf pattern.

Urging Patches to the first barrel on the right, she leaned in as they went to the inside of the barrel. Diving into the turn, Rebecca and the horse moved as one, lightly touching the barrel but leaving it standing. Her adrenaline pumping, Rebecca didn't feel the loss of her hat as she and Patches went for barrel number two. Hooking to the right of it, they spun and easily made the turn, racing for the third and final barrel at the top of the cloverleaf design. Taking the right-hand side again, the barrel wobbled slightly, but it didn't fall. Horse and rider were back to the starting point before it stilled.

The announcer read out the top five contestants, and Rebecca was thrilled to have placed at number four. There were two more heats in the event, so she knew that the standings could quickly change. She was leading Patches back to the barn for a good rubdown, when a horrible crash came from behind the pen area. She hurried toward the sound to see what had happened.

Three men were helping Rob to his feet. Nearby, a giant light fixture had fallen so hard that not only had it shattered into pieces, but it had left a dent in the hard dirt. "That was a bit too coincidental for me," Rob snarled. "I checked all the fixtures myself yesterday. There was nothing wrong with that one."

Rebecca looked around for Shelby, who was conspicuously absent. Keeping her thoughts to herself, she led Patches to her assigned area of the barn. Shelby was there, sitting on a bale of hay, a broad smile on her face.

"You did really well," Shelby called out. "Congratulations."

"Thanks." Rebecca pulled off her saddle, and switched Patches' bridle for a blue halter.

"Want some help?"

Rebecca looked at the woman sitting so close to her. "No, that's okay. I'm used to doing this." She gathered up a brush and began a gentle stroking, letting the familiar routine relax her.

Shelby stood up and dusted off the seat of her jeans. "Anyway, I just wanted to let you know I enjoyed watching you ride." She headed for the exit.

"Wait." Rebecca cursed herself for her rudeness. She waited

until Shelby turned around, holding a pack of cigarettes in one hand. "Thanks."

"You're welcome." Tipping her hat, Shelby left the barn.

What an enigma you are, Shelby Fisher. I don't know whether to be afraid of you, or intrigued by you.

OUT IN THE bright sunshine, Shelby adjusted the tilt of her hat to protect her eyes from the glare of the sun. She expelled a breath and puzzled for a moment about whether she would make any headway on her bet with herself about Rebecca, after the reaction she'd just gotten from Rebecca. She lengthened her stride and headed for her trailer, hoping to calm her rapidly beating heart.

Shelby normally didn't watch the barrel racing, but she decided that if all of them were half as good as Rebecca and her horse, then she'd have to start paying better attention. *Yeah, right. You're just hot for her. Don't lie to yourself.* She was almost to her trailer when Andrea called out to her.

"That fresh meat just keeps getting better and better, doesn't it?" Andrea Graham leaned against a horse trailer nearby. She was wearing her customary tank top, which showed her muscles. She wouldn't put her denim shirt on until right before it was time to ride.

Shelby turned as Andrea came strolling up. "You leave her out of your petty little games, Andy. She's too good for the likes of you." *And me.* But she couldn't admit out loud that she liked what she saw, too. Her advance was abruptly halted by a strong hand on her forearm.

"Oh, I don't know. Maybe we should let the little lady decide for herself." Andrea pulled Shelby closer. "Or are you afraid she'll choose me?"

"You're the last person I'm afraid of," Shelby ground out, jerking her arm free. "But I also know you like them more experienced, and I think you'd be sorely disappointed." She hoped she could keep a predator like Andrea away from Rebecca, who, in Shelby's opinion, seemed naïve for her age.

Andrea laughed. "Right. And you're saying this because you're just such a nice person? Or maybe you want her for yourself." She followed Shelby to the run-down trailer. "Haven't you gotten rid of this thing yet? I figured it would have collapsed by now."

Glad that the topic had changed, Shelby felt on more even ground. "Don't even start about my trailer, Graham. At least I don't have to live out of hotel rooms."

"Don't you mean you can't afford to live out of hotel rooms? When are you going to admit that you're a has-been and give it up? How many bones did you break last year, old woman?" Andrea was almost ten years Shelby's junior, and rubbed the age difference in her face every chance she got.

She's got a point. Bull riding is a young person's sport. Or, at least a sport for someone who's good at it. I'm neither, really. Shelby unlocked her trailer door with a sigh. She reached into her pocket and pulled out a quarter and tossed it to Andrea. "Here. Go buy yourself an ice cream, compliments of an old woman." Then Shelby closed the door in Andrea's face.

PAULA FOUND REBECCA sitting on the bale that Shelby had vacated earlier. "You did so great!" She beamed as she came to stand next to Rebecca and put a hand on her shoulder. "I bet your folks will really be proud of you."

"I guess. Maybe they'll be here for tomorrow night's ride. There was just no way they could afford to take off work to watch me, but they both sent their love. That's okay too, because I'd rather them see the finals, anyway." Rebecca allowed her thoughts to drift away.

"Are you all right? They're not giving you a hard time about all of this, are they?"

Rebecca picked at the straw. "No, nothing like that. They've been extremely supportive. I'm just a bit confused, that's all."

"Oh. Well, if I can help, let me know. Buddy says that I'm almost as good a listener as I am a talker—and you know how much I love to talk."

"Thanks." Rebecca glanced around to make sure they wouldn't be overheard. "Is Shelby Fisher everything people say she is? I've had a couple of run-ins with her, and I can't quite figure her out."

Paula gave the question some thought before answering. "Well, if they say she used to be a pretty good bull rider, then the answer is yes. But too many years of drawing the tough rides have been hard on her."

Still looking around for eavesdroppers, Rebecca asked, "What about personally?"

"What are you asking about?"

Rebecca faced her friend. "I've heard that she goes through women pretty easily. Not that it matters, but I spent a little time with her earlier today, and she seemed almost nice to me."

"She can be. I've never had any problems with her, but then again we run in different circles. I can't tell you what I don't know. But, if you want, we can go make Buddy take us out to dinner before the bull riders compete. Unless you'd rather get something at the fair."

"No, that's a great idea." Rebecca stood from her seat and hugged Paula. "Thanks for being such a good friend."

"You're welcome." Paula hooked her arm in Rebecca's and looked around. "Let's go find that handsome man of mine."

Chapter Four

THE REST OF the matinee went according to the program. Shelby drew a bull named Diablo's Pet, and mentally prepped herself for the ride. She was about to go to the chute area when she felt a light touch on her arm.

Rebecca smiled shyly. "Good luck."

It felt good to have someone say that to her, especially since she couldn't actually remember anyone ever saying it. "Thanks." Shelby put on her gloves and adjusted her chaps. "Are you going to watch?"

"Do you mind if I do?"

Shelby grinned. "The best spot is over where we watched the calf roping earlier. Just stay off the fence and you'll be perfectly safe."

"Thanks."

Shelby tipped her hat and sauntered to the chutes.

Rebecca watched her leave and was embarrassed when she realized she was checking out Shelby's butt. *Well, it does fit in those jeans nicely. No one can fault me for noticing that.* She hurried over to the spot Shelby had designated, her excitement evident to everyone around her.

"What's the matter?" Rob asked. "Haven't you ever seen bull riding before?" He eyed her curiously before casting a glance toward Shelby, then examined her again.

Ignoring him, Rebecca squeezed between two older men to get a better view of the area. She smiled at them and was rewarded with a pat on the shoulder and smiles from both.

Rob nodded at one of the men, who vacated his spot so that Rob could sidle up next to Rebecca. His voice was low and gravelly. "If you know what's good for you, you'll stay away from Shelby. She's bad news."

"I'm fully capable of taking care of myself," Rebecca assured him. "So, if you'll excuse me, I'd like to be left alone to enjoy the event." She turned away from the bronc rider.

Two men nearby chuckled. One of them said, "Look how

that sweet-looking woman cut Rob off at the knees while still being nice."

"Yup, Rob don't like that kinda treatment from women."

Stifled laughs passed through the group. Rob stormed away, and Rebecca resumed her place between the two older cowboys.

"I'm afraid you made an enemy of that one, miss," one of the older men said. "He's not used to anyone standing up to him or telling him no."

Rebecca looked over her shoulder. "Then he'd better leave me alone, or it'll be a new learning experience for him." Just then, Shelby's name was announced. She tensed and focused her attention back to the floor of the arena. *Here she goes.*

It took a full minute or two for the bull to be calmed enough to get the chute open. Each second that ticked by made Rebecca more nervous. She was glad she was in a group of other rodeo people. If she'd had to wait alone, she might not have been able to wait it out.

When the chute finally opened, the massive black bull leaped into the air, tossing its rider up with it. Shelby managed to hang on but almost lost her grip when Diablo suddenly spun to the left. She had been expecting a right turn, and she was hanging on for her life as the bull changed direction, this time adding another leap.

Shelby's hat fell, and it must have obscured her vision as it did, because it looked like she never saw the bull toss his head back. He hit her right between the eyes, and her head jerked back.

A collective gasp rose from the sparse crowd as Shelby dangled from the bull. Two riders on horseback raced in to help free her. Shelby and the bull had been close enough to Rebecca that she very clearly saw the blow, and she couldn't believe that Shelby was still mounted. But she clung to the saddle horn on her rescuer's horse while the rider helped her from the bull. Then Shelby dropped to her feet and waved to the crowd, indicating that she was okay.

Rebecca was shaking. Although Shelby hadn't made her time, it had still been one of the most exciting and terrifying things Rebecca had ever seen in her life. She edged her way through the crowd, back to where the ambulance was parked and was only a few feet behind Shelby when she saw her fend off a paramedic.

"I NEED TO check you out." The paramedic kept talking, trying to get Shelby to stay still long enough for them to treat the cut on her forehead.

"I'm fine, dammit."

"You don't look fine," Rebecca said. "You look like you could use at least a bandage or something."

"No one asked you," Shelby bit off. She thought of the ride, of the roaring around her, the way the bull jerked her about, and how it had only taken two seconds before all she could see was dirt. She had known that Rebecca was out there somewhere, watching, and Shelby had wanted to make the full ride, if only to impress her. *Jesus Christ! My mind shouldn't have been occupied with something other than the two thousand pound animal I was tied to. Shit!*

The paramedic frowned and spoke to Rebecca. "She could probably use some stitches and an X-ray."

"Yeah, yeah, whatever," Shelby said as she allowed him to lean in and check her over. He cleaned the wound and applied butterfly closures and a gauze bandage. "Change the gauze at least once a day, and if it looks infected, have your doctor check it. And don't be tearing off that gauze when I'm not looking. It'll help to deter infection."

"Thanks," she said, and he looked back her, surprised at her change of demeanor.

Someone handed Shelby her hat, and she placed it on her head, although further back than normal. She decided to stop being such a bitch, and tried to turn and smile for Rebecca, but the movement hurt her head. "Sorry I didn't stay on. I never expected that bastard to come out away from my hand like that. But you should watch some of the other guys. It's really good when they cover their bull."

Rebecca frowned. "What?"

"You know, stay on for the entire ride. Something I can't seem to do lately." It had been close to a year since Shelby had made any money at all, and her savings were almost depleted. She'd either have to win something at this rodeo, or find something else to do. Or she'd end up stuck staying with her aunt again. She could always find work flipping hamburgers or doing farm work long enough to pad her account again. But anything other than winning were options that Shelby didn't want to even consider.

"Are you going back to watch?" Rebecca asked, concern etched all over her face.

"For a little bit, probably. Have to keep an eye on the competition," Shelby kidded. She hopped from the back of the ambulance with a wave to the attendant. "Thanks, Joe. I owe you one."

He stripped off his rubber gloves and shook his head. "Staying in once piece for a change would be a nice start."

Shelby ignored the jab and headed back to the chutes. "I volunteered earlier to help for a bit, so if you've got something else to do...."

"No. I think I'll go back to my spot and watch."

Shelby watched her leave, wondering if Rebecca's sudden attention meant her interest in Rebecca was mutual.

SHELBY JOINED A few others on top of the chute as a bull was prepared. She almost wished she could have followed Rebecca to watch, since the rider Shelby would be assisting was none other than Andrea. The cowboys crowded around and did their assigned jobs without much talk, since they'd been doing it most of their lives. Henry was the flank man, or the person who pulled a leather strap across the bull's flank to enhance the natural bucking motion of the animal. He gave Shelby a nod as she helped him.

"Well, lookee here. Grandma's got a boo-boo," Andrea said as she settled onto the bull. She kept one leg on the wall of the chute while the bull fought the confines. "Why don't you just find a nice rocker, and sit back and let me show you how it's done?" Her skin-tight shirt showed muscles that rippled, and the denim jeans she wore looked as if they'd split if she moved wrong.

"Why don't you worry about yourself, and just leave me the hell alone?" Shelby snapped. "You've still got a ride to make, you know." She decided that no matter how much she needed the extra money, she wouldn't help around the chutes any more than she had to. The small rodeos were always in need of an extra hand and willing to pay for it. Putting up with the likes of Andrea was getting to be just too much for her nerves.

Andrea grinned and blew her rival a kiss. "Piece of cake." She pulled her white felt hat down tight and nodded, signaling for the chute to be opened.

Her 'piece of cake' went well, until the bull slammed sideways into the fence in an attempt to dislodge its rider. Unable to break free from her rope, Andrea screamed. The bull's second charge into the fence knocked her from her seat. By the time the rodeo hands got her off the bull, Andrea's face was covered in blood and she was unconscious. Her arm holding the rope was bent at an unnatural angle, and a splinter of bone appeared through a rip in her shirt.

Once again, an ambulance rushed into the arena. Although it

appeared to be only Andrea's arm that was damaged, they weren't taking any chances with other possible injuries. While the other contestants looked on from their positions around the arena, the paramedics quickly loaded Andrea into the back of the ambulance and drove off to the hospital.

Shelby stood unmoving at the chute, watching the tail lights of the vehicle until it was out of sight. She pulled her last cigarette from the pack and placed it in her mouth, her shaky hand the only outward sign of her distress.

THE BULL RIDING had been the final event for the matinee. Rebecca listened as the arena director announced that it was in the best interests of all to postpone the rest of the rides until the evening show. No one complained, although some could be heard grumbling about the "coincidences" that had happened.

Rebecca had watched the ride from her usual place, glad to be in between the same men she had found before. The announcer had said the woman's name was Andrea Graham. When Andrea's ride went bad, Rebecca felt what little food there was in her stomach attempt to escape. She wanted nothing more than to find a nice quiet place to get her nerves back under control and decided the best place for that would be with Patches, so she headed back toward the barn.

On her way, she noticed a solitary figure moving away from the arena. Rebecca changed her course, intent on intercepting her. She wasn't sure why she was so concerned about the surly bull rider, but there was just something about the loneliness in Shelby's eyes that kept Rebecca moving.

Shelby was walking away from the chutes, and it was clear to Rebecca that she was ignoring the conversations around her. More than once she heard Shelby's name mentioned, and it occurred to Rebecca that some of the men were apparently taking Shelby's rivalry with Andrea into consideration.

"Is that Andrea Graham a friend of yours?" Rebecca asked as she caught up. The bloody ride had upset her terribly, but at the moment she was more concerned with what Shelby was feeling, if Shelby would let her in.

"No." Shelby continued to walk.

"But that was a terrible thing. The bull was just vicious."

"Yeah, that's how it is sometimes."

Rebecca was taken aback by Shelby's 'matter of fact' tone. "I can tell you weren't good friends with her at all then."

Shelby glanced at her, eyes narrowed. "As much as I dislike her, I never want to see another person come to any harm. The next time it could just as easily be me." She turned away and picked up her pace.

"That's true. Thank God you weren't hurt more than you were earlier." Rebecca continued to follow after Shelby. "Is there anything I can do?"

"Just leave me alone, okay?"

"But I thought—"

"You and I aren't friends and we never will be. Just go back to your perfect little world, and leave me the hell alone." Once out in the warm night, Shelby lit her cigarette. *The old Shelby would have just seduced her and been done with it. I'm tired of the old Shelby. And I don't know why, but Rebecca's different. I don't want to do that to her.*

Rebecca hurried to get in front of Shelby. "I understand that you're upset about your friend, but don't take it out on me."

"I told you, that bitch is not my friend." She kept moving, and several drags later, she finished the cigarette. Shelby tossed it ahead and crushed it beneath her boot. They continued walking though the parking lot until they were where most of the performers kept their "homes." Shelby had never been so glad to see her trailer in her life. She stopped and pulled out her keys.

"But you're both—"

"What?"

"You know—you're, uh..."

"You can't even say the word, huh? Lesbians? Yes. We're lesbians. And we're both bull riders. But she likes to compete for more than scores, if you know what I mean." Shelby opened her trailer door, leaned in, and felt around on the counter for more cigarettes. She opened the pack and in seconds had another lit one between her lips. Tossing the match aside, she took a drag and on the exhale said, "As a matter of fact, she was talking about *you* earlier today."

"Me? But I'm not a lesbian!"

Shelby laughed. "Right. And I'm not a has-been. Darlin', the way you've been eyeing every woman around here, I'd say you're either in serious denial, or you're lying to me."

"I'm not lying," Rebecca said. Then she realized what option that left her. "Not that I'm in denial, either. I've dated a few men." Even to her ears the excuse sounded lame. *Wouldn't I know something like this? Why is she giving me such a hard time?* "I'm not lying," she repeated.

"I rest my case." With that, Shelby laughed so hard she started coughing. "Ow! You're making my head hurt."

Rebecca stormed away with Shelby's laughter ringing in her

ears. *I can't be a lesbian. I've never had those kinds of thoughts. Not really.* She continued to walk back toward the barns, her mind spinning with the new revelation.

If it were true, then certain aspects of her life finally clicked into place. All those crushes on other girls while she was growing up popped into her mind. Then she thought of her best friend when she was a pre-teen, and how much it hurt to lose that friendship years later.

Tonya moved in up the street from where Rebecca was raised. Both girls were eleven at the time. They had the same interests and tastes in music and clothes, and neither could understand why all the girls in their class found boys so attractive. Even when Tonya moved away right before high school, they vowed to stay in touch.

They did, for a while. Tonya even came to spend the summer with Rebecca and her family when the girls were seventeen. But then something happened that ruined their childhood bond. Rebecca caught Tonya smoking marijuana in the guest bathroom and told her that she wouldn't allow that to happen around her baby brother. Tonya agreed to keep it out of the house, but the next day, Rebecca caught her again. Although it nearly killed her to do it, Rebecca made good on her threat and had Tonya kicked out of the house.

Thinking back to that day, Rebecca felt the pain as if the wound were fresh. They'd never spoken again, and she lost more than a friend. She'd never allowed another person close to her heart since.

TWO DAYS LATER, Rebecca was going over Patch's last-minute grooming details when Paula showed up with someone. Rebecca looked up from her work and said, "Hi."

Paula motioned for the man to step up beside her. "Rebecca, I'd like you to meet Cleve Winters. He's a friend of Buddy's and another roper. We just ran into each other, and I didn't know if you two had met."

"No, we haven't." Rebecca wanted to use the brush she held to whack Paula in the head. *I hate it when people try to play matchmaker.* "It's nice to meet you," she said to the short man with brown hair and eyes. "Have you known Buddy and Paula long?"

"Quite a few years. As a matter of fact, it was Buddy who taught me how to rope," Cleve said.

"That's great." Rebecca turned back to Patches and began to brush, even though the horse's coat already gleamed. She felt her face flame with irritation and glanced over at Paula. By the expression on Paula's face, Rebecca could tell that Paula knew she had made a mistake.

"Cleve, would you mind helping me find my wayward husband?" Paula asked. "It's lunch time, and he's got the money."

"I'll do better than that. Why don't you let me buy your lunch?" Cleve offered. Addressing Rebecca, he asked, "How about it, Rebecca? Would you care to join us?"

Damn. How do I get out of this? "That's very sweet of you, but I really want to make sure everything is perfect for my ride. Maybe next time?"

"Allrighty then." He winked at her. "I'll hold you to it." Paula led him away, and he appeared to be listening intently as she chattered about the rodeo.

Rebecca heaved a sigh of relief. The last thing she wanted to do was get involved with someone at the rodeo. *But you're already involved, aren't you? Or at least you wish you were.* Angry that her thoughts betrayed her, Rebecca smacked the brush against her horse's side and went back to grooming poor Patches.

Chapter Five

THE NEXT TWO nights the rodeo went off as planned. The workers and contestants all relaxed, and some of them got together for a friendly game of cards. They set up a table behind the pens, and someone brought in three or four bottles of alcohol.

Men of all ages were gathered around the makeshift table, some already quite drunk, while others were well on their way. Bawdy jokes were followed by drunken tales of conquests, as some bragged while others learned.

"Well, Rob, are you going to join us, or what?" Henry asked. He noticed how the younger man had been sulking around the area for a while, and figured he was just too shy to join in without being invited.

"Sounds good to me." Rob sat down next to another man, who was a bit younger than him. "Well, I know everyone else at the table, but I don't believe we've been introduced. I'm Rob. What do you do 'round here?"

The other man shook his hand. "Cleve Winters. I'm a roper, but I'm hoping you won't hold that against me," he said.

"Nah. We're pretty good about that," Henry assured him. "As long as you don't win too many hands, that is."

"Then I'm perfectly safe." Cleve flashed a ready smile to his new friends while listening to their stories. Cleve liked the camaraderie of the men around him and was glad he had been invited to join them. Rob poured him a drink of whiskey, which he downed quite easily.

"Slow down there, Cleve," Henry warned. "You'll want to be able to last more'n a hand or two."

Cleve laughed. "No problems there. I've been drinking for years, and it's never affected me yet." He swallowed another shot and gasped. "Although this stuff is a bit stronger than what I'm used to."

Standing in the shadows, Shelby listened to the men play

cards for a while. She took a small sip from the bottle of beer she held, not wanting to be hung over the next morning, like most of the men would be. At times she wished she had done something different with her life, but she didn't know what that something would be. Standing there watching the men get increasingly drunk, she thought back to the time she met her only other living relative, or at least the only relative who would have anything to do with her.

As if the shock of losing her father wasn't enough, being placed with someone she didn't even know was more than the twelve year old could handle. Almost from the very beginning, Shelby fought her "confinement," and ran away at least half a dozen times.

Nadeen Fisher tried everything she could to make Shelby feel welcome in her home, even going so far as attempting to home-school the youngster. When that didn't work, she was forced to send Shelby to the local high school where her differences made her stand out. Many days the girl would return from school so upset she'd go up to her room without dinner.

Shelby barely made the grade in school, and only then because of her aunt's insistence. She dropped out when she was sixteen, and, until recently, she never looked back. But now she was remorseful. She knew that people like Rebecca and Paula and even the flighty girls in the queen's court all had high school diplomas. They would certainly have nothing to do with her outside of the rodeo arena, and that thought hurt.

After draining the bottle of beer, Shelby tossed it in a nearby trash bin and lit another cigarette. She took another bottle from the six-pack carton at her feet and twisted the top from it. She felt her life was an old beat up vehicle, and someone had wrecked the car.

INSIDE THE BARNS adjacent to the pens, Rebecca locked up her gear for the night. The area was quiet, and even Patches seemed content to stand nearby with her eyes closed. The stall was open, but Rebecca wasn't worried about her horse leaving. Patches had always been an easy-going ride and had never given her any trouble. She added clean hay to the floor of the stall while her horse stood outside of it, apparently asleep.

Drunken singing could be heard from nearby, and Rebecca frowned. Although she didn't drink and never understood the appeal, she wasn't anyone's mother. They could drink if they pleased. So, she went back to her work until she heard a shuffling noise outside the stall.

"There ya are. I've been lookin' fer you," a drunken cowboy slurred.

Rebecca looked up. "Now you've found me. Why don't you go and sleep it off? You're going to feel it tomorrow as it is."

"I'd rather feel you, sweet thang."

Suddenly Rebecca was afraid. This wasn't just a friendly drunk. Slightly taller than Rebecca, his slight frame swayed. She picked up the broom she had been using and held it out in front of herself. "Don't make me hurt you, Cleve. You seem like a sweet guy."

Cleve moved in closer, "You like me and you know it."

"Yes, I do. But not in that way." Rebecca looked around desperately for help, but the barn seemed empty except for the two of them.

"Are you another one of those fags? 'Cause if you are, I can fix that." Cleve squeezed at his crotch. "Rob says all they need is a good man."

Great. He's been getting lessons in love from Rob. "Cleve, go into one of the empty stalls and sleep this off. Believe me, in the morning you'll be thankful you did."

He stepped closer and grabbed at Rebecca with one hand, the broom with the other. He tossed the broom behind him. His thick fingers tangled in the V of her shirt and buttons popped. She screamed, and he pressed her back against the stall, mumbling, "I'm sorry. Buy you 'nother one." When he leaned in and nuzzled his face in to kiss Rebecca on the neck, she screamed again, this time in his ear.

"Shhh! Not so loud!"

Rebecca tried to push him away. "Get off!" she said, her voice half-muffled in his shirt. His panting sickened her. "Cleve! Stop!" She tried to bring her knee up, but she was pinned against the hard, wooden wall.

"Just let me," he grunted as he pressed into her. "Yeah, loosen up, baby. You just let ol' Cleve—"

Rebecca heard a whump, and Cleve dropped to his knees before her. She looked up, eyes wide, to see Shelby wielding the discarded broom. Since Cleve was already off balance, Shelby tossed the broom aside, then grabbed Cleve by the collar of his shirt and slammed his head into the wall on the right. He slumped to the ground, moaning.

Stepping over Cleve's semi-conscious form Shelby took a closer look at Rebecca. "Are you all right?"

"I'm fine. I don't know why he did that, but thank you." Rebecca tried to pull the tattered pieces of her shirt together, but failed.

"Come away from that asshole." Shelby took Rebecca's arm and led her aside, then removed her outer shirt and draped it over Rebecca's shoulders, leaving herself in a white tee shirt. "Sorry it's not very clean. I might've worked up a sweat helping out around the arena and barns."

Rebecca forced back tears as she slipped her arms through the sleeves. "This is just fine, Shelby. Thank you so much." She swallowed her tears and let Shelby adjust the collar.

A group of men showed up as Shelby was helping Rebecca with her shirt. Fred Tanner, out of his clown makeup, grabbed Shelby and jerked her out of the stall. "Get away from her, you pervert! Can't you leave decent people alone?"

"Go to hell, Fred," Shelby shouted back, fighting against his hold.

Rebecca stood frozen in place with her fingers on the last button to Shelby's shirt. She opened her mouth to speak, but before she could say anything, Tanner shook Shelby. Since he was much bigger, he had no problem holding the struggling bull rider.

"Maybe we should teach her a lesson," another man said. "She could be the one causing all the problems around here."

Tanner sneered. "She very well could be. We should—"

"You stupid idiots!" Rebecca pulled Fred's hands away from Shelby, and he looked at her with surprise. "You should all shut up and leave us both alone. She helped me. Or maybe you didn't notice the guy lying on the ground," she shouted, pointing at Cleve. "He's the one guilty of assault. Not her!"

Some of the men grumbled, but they quieted. They helped Cleve to his feet and took him away, while Fred continued to stare daggers at Shelby. "This isn't over, Fisher. I'll have my eye on you."

Shelby didn't back down. "Why don't you watch yourself and your little cronies? Stupid men and booze never mix." Shelby didn't look at Rebecca again until they had all left. Then she asked, "Do you need a ride home?"

"No, I have my car." Rebecca buttoned the top button of Shelby's shirt, which fit surprisingly well, except for being slightly tight against her breasts. She was glad they were about the same size, although Shelby appeared much larger to her. *Maybe it's just because of that swagger she has. It should be registered as a lethal weapon.* "Thank you again for your help."

Shelby looked down at the hay-strewn floor. "I'm sure you'd have beaten him to death with that broom, but I'm glad I was around."

"Me, too."

They both stood quietly for a moment, neither ready to leave. "I'm glad he didn't get you on the ground. Your shirt's ripped, but your boots and jeans are still nice."

Shelby looked down at her clothes and Rebecca followed her gaze. Shelby's clothes were definitely old and worn, and suddenly Shelby appeared embarrassed by it. "I'll get your shirt back to you as soon as I can."

"No matter. Whenever is fine. At least let me walk you to your car."

"Thanks. But then you'll have to walk back alone." Rebecca knew for all her bravado, Shelby wasn't any more able to take care of herself than she was.

"Don't worry. If they get me under a light, they'll let me go," Shelby lightly said as they walked out into the evening.

Rebecca stopped. "I don't think that's funny. You shouldn't put yourself in danger."

"Do you remember what I do for a living?" Shelby asked, walking dutifully beside Rebecca. "It's not the safest career."

"That's true. But you at least have some control over it." Rebecca stopped next to her Toyota Camry. "Here's my ride."

"Nice."

"Thanks. My parents bought it for me last year when I turned twenty-five." Opening the door, Rebecca studied Shelby's face. "Thank you again."

Shelby blushed. "You're welcome. Do you have someone you can stay with? I mean, after what happened tonight, is there someone at home you can talk to? Boyfriend maybe?"

"I'm staying with my parents. They have a house in town." On impulse, Rebecca leaned over and kissed Shelby on the cheek. "Now get back inside before I have to get rough with you."

"Yes, ma'am." Shelby waited until Rebecca's car cleared the parking lot before heading back to her trailer. Her hand stayed on her cheek where it had been kissed, and a silly smile played across her face.

THE NEXT MORNING, Shelby sat outside her trailer polishing her spurs when a man dressed in crisp western wear stopped in front of her. "Shelby Fisher?"

"Yeah?"

"I'm Martin Saunders, the Arena Director. I'd like to ask you a few questions, if I could."

Shelby studied the man for a moment. He looked harmless. But she'd been in the business long enough to know not to take things at face value. "I can't stop you. But I might not answer, either."

"Fair enough." He looked around for a place to sit and, not finding one, Saunders remained standing. "I hear you were a witness to what happened in the barns last night. I'd like to get your view on the entire matter."

Not wanting to say anything that could hurt Rebecca, Shelby stayed silent.

"I've already spoken to Miss Starrett. She gave me your name and told me where to find you." He stepped forward and squatted so that he was on the same level as Shelby and close enough so that they wouldn't be overheard. "All I want from you is what you saw."

"I really didn't see that much," Shelby started. "I was outside the barns and heard a scream, and when I came in, I saw Cleve had torn Rebecca's shirt and was trying to...." She was unable to continue.

"You saw him actually attack her? Not just come in after the fact?"

"That's right. The sorry bastard was all over her," Shelby said. "He's just lucky all I had was a damned broom."

Saunders held out his hand. "Thank you, Ms. Fisher. That's all I needed to hear."

THAT AFTERNOON, PAULA'S voice was heard over most of the barn. "I can't believe you didn't want to press charges. He deserves to be in jail, after what almost happened. I'm sorry I'm the one who introduced you two."

"But it didn't happen. Shelby was there," Rebecca reminded her. "Besides, I don't think that Cleve meant any harm. He was drunk and even apologized when he tore my blouse."

"That doesn't mean he won't do it again and maybe next time succeed. Damn it all, Rebecca. You've got to have more sense than that."

Rebecca stopped cleaning her saddle and glared at Paula. "I have plenty of sense. Enough not to jump to conclusions about someone without giving them a proper chance."

"Are you talking about Cleve? Or Shelby? Because right now, I think they're interchangeable. Shelby's been alone a lot of years, hon. You coming in overnight isn't going to change her, even if she wanted to. And I don't know that she does."

"Who says I'm trying to change her? I just want to be her friend."

Paula threw up her hands. "And I've been telling you, she's

not the type to have friends. I've been around quite a while, and even followed the same circuit before Buddy and I were married. She's a loner and a player. Don't fall for her charms."

"Charms?" Rebecca laughed. "Are we talking about the same person? She's the most surly and obnoxious person I've ever met."

"She can be, that's a fact. But I also know that most women around here would jump at the chance to be in her favor." *You included, I'd imagine.*

Rebecca gathered up the cleaning supplies and put them away. "I think I'm perfectly safe, Paula. All I wanted was to be her friend, but she obviously doesn't want that. So you have nothing to worry about."

I hope not. Because I'd hate to see you hurt by the likes of her. You're a pure soul, and don't deserve that kind of pain. "Well, forgive me for worrying, anyway. Must be the mothering instinct, since I never had kids of my own."

"You're forgiven," Rebecca assured her, moving to where Paula stood and giving her a hug. "As long as you realize I'm perfectly capable of taking care of myself."

"Oh, I realize it all right. But it won't stop me from worrying."

THE RODEO HAD long been over for the night, and the man at the end of the bar tossed back shots of whiskey as if they were water. His friend, sitting next to him, was in no better shape. "I know that bitch had something to do with it."

Cleve looked down into his half empty mug of beer and sighed. "I can't believe I was so stupid, Rob. I thought she liked me."

"All women are sneaky sluts. They want you to be interested, but the moment you are, they won't give you the time of day." Rob motioned to the bartender to bring him another drink.

"What about Carla, your girlfriend? You don't mean her too, do you?"

Rob turned his head and looked at Cleve as if he had two heads. "Of course I do. She's only with me because I'm good in bed, and I win my events and always have money. Don't let her fool you. If I stopped winning tomorrow, she'd leave me in an instant."

"That sucks." Cleve took another sip of his beer. "I really needed this rodeo, man. I was going to use the money to find my dad."

"Is he lost?" Rob downed another shot and grimaced as it warred with his empty stomach.

"Yeah. I don't know him that well, but I heard he's got a place somewhere around here in the Austin area. I haven't seen him since I was a kid. He did the rodeo circuit, too."

"Another winner, huh? Guess we all have stories like that." Rob stared down at his empty glass. After a few moments, he said, "Fisher's old man sucked at bulls. I heard that he was totally shit-faced when he rode that last time." Rob cracked open a peanut and ate it, leaving the shell on the bar in front of him with its fallen comrades. "Stupid-assed thing to do. They say he was almost gored in half."

"God, that's nasty." Cleve got the bartender's attention and ordered another round of drinks. "How old was Shelby?"

"Just a kid, from what I heard. She saw the whole thing, too." Rob accepted the new drink and quickly downed it. "Thanks." He wiped his mouth with his sleeve. "Guess that explains why she's so fucked up."

"I don't think there's much wrong with Shelby, 'cept she's queer," Cleve said under his breath. He felt it was morally wrong but didn't feel like talking about it. To Rob, he said, "I guess."

Rob belched, feeling the acid rising in his stomach. "I'm going to the john, then head back to the motel to give my old lady what she wants. You all right?"

"Yeah. I'll just finish this beer, and go. Thanks for listening, man." After the events of the day, Cleve decided a change in scenery was in order, and he resolved to start looking around the following morning for some idea as to where his father could be found.

EARLY THE NEXT morning, Shelby was busy shoveling out the pens when she heard her named called. She looked up to see a small blonde heading her way. "Carla, watch your step. It's pretty nasty in here."

"You don't know the half of it," Carla snarled. She stood close enough to Shelby to breathe her air. "Rob tells me that you got his friend Cleve kicked out."

"If you're asking if I answered a few questions from the arena director, then the answer is yes." Shelby went back to her work. She knew that Carla had always been jealous of the attention her boyfriend gave Shelby, who couldn't care less about him. Carla wasn't the only one who didn't understand why Rob was so fixated. Shelby wished he'd just stay away from her so that Carla would stop treating her like crap and calling her "dyke" behind her back.

"Rob's not happy."

"Tell Rob he can kiss my ass," Shelby said. She turned and leaned forward to shovel, but Carla suddenly rammed her. She hit the ground on all fours. Luckily, she missed landing in what she'd been shoveling. Shelby scrambled to her feet and turned around to glare at Carla. "I don't know what your major malfunction is, but you need to get over it."

Carla slapped Shelby, hard. "Fuck you, Fisher."

"You wish," Shelby countered. Her hands were clenched at her sides, and it took all of her restraint not to pound on the other woman. "Trouble is, you'd like it. And then where would your boyfriend be?"

"Bitch!" Carla stepped back, but slipped and fell into a pile of manure. "Shit!"

"How about that. You finally got something right." Shelby picked up her shovel and leaned it against the pen, then climbed through the horizontal bars of the fence.

"What was that all about? Are you okay?" Rebecca had witnessed the entire scene, and Shelby blushed with embarrassment.

"I'm not the one covered in shit," Shelby said, although the entire exchange had left her feeling dirty, especially now that she knew that Rebecca had seen it. She decided to take a walk on the fair grounds, hoping to calm herself.

The only way Shelby ever felt relaxed was when she was by herself. She was glad that the fair grounds were still quiet, with only the vendors and a few rodeo contestants milling around. Shelby slowed and lit a cigarette. Her thoughts were interrupted by Rebecca's voice.

"Those things aren't good for you."

"Neither is riding bulls," Shelby retorted as she wheeled around to face the Rebecca. She was in no mood to be mothered, especially by Rebecca. Shelby was glad that Rebecca pressed her lips together and put her head down, but she continued to follow Shelby as she checked out the fair grounds.

It wasn't long before Rebecca spoke up again. "So you were raised around rodeos?"

"Yeah." Shelby continued to walk, kicking at small rocks with her boots.

"What about your family? Don't they care?"

"They're dead. Not much they can say about it," Shelby said. "Well, my old man is, anyway. My mom probably is, too." She stopped and faced Rebecca. "Why the twenty questions?"

Rebecca looked down at her sneakers. "I was just trying to learn more about you."

Shelby reined in the urge to walk away. "You want to know about me? Fine. Let's walk, and I'll tell you all the gory details of my miserable life."

"If it's going to upset you, you don't have to tell me anything."

"I know, but you're not going to leave me alone until I do." They passed by the closed-up carnival rides where very few people were stirring. "My mother was a Rodeo Queen and barrel racer who should have learned to say no where my dad was concerned. That's how I got here. They ended up living in that trailer I use now, until Mom left when I was six." Her voice told of the pain the desertion still caused. "I'd go with dad to the rodeos, at least until he died on a bull when I was twelve." Shelby lit another cigarette.

"That's horrible. But—"

"Then I was sent to live with his sister, until I was sixteen. She was nice, but boring."

Rebecca touched Shelby's arm, but pulled her hand back when Shelby jerked away. "And you've been doing this ever since?"

"Yeah. It's not much, but it's all I know."

"I'm sorry."

Shelby looked at the woman standing beside her. She could tell that Rebecca felt bad asking her about her life. *If she was looking for some romantic ideal, she certainly didn't find it.* "Me too. So if you don't mind, can I just please—"

Shelby's words were cut off by a loud rumble that came from the rodeo arena. Men's shouts and women's screams echoed in the cool morning air. Shelby and Rebecca looked at each other then ran back to see what the problem could be.

When they got to the arena, they could see the problem: the retaining walls of the pens had collapsed, and now all the bulls usually housed within were running all over the place. Men were putting the pens back together, as others worked to wrangle the cattle. The more experienced ropers were trying to get their horses saddled, while other men were using blankets to try and herd the frightened animals back to their pens.

Shelby grabbed Rebecca by the arm. "Come on! I think you'll be safe in the stands, until they're all rounded up."

Rebecca resisted Shelby's attempt to lead her away. "Shouldn't I help?"

"Have you ever been around a scared, two-thousand pound animal?"

"No."

"Then get your ass up there!" Shelby yelled. "I don't want to have to worry about you, as well as these damned beasts." She lifted Rebecca over the pipe fence.

"I don't appreciate being manhandled like...Shelby! Look out!"

Shelby glanced over her shoulder and saw a mottled brown bull charging. Without hesitating, she instinctively jumped up and climbed the fence, raising her legs. Her heart in her throat, Shelby gave Rebecca a shaky smile. "Thanks."

"You're welcome. Be careful with the rest of them, okay?"

Shelby took off after the bulls. She knew that most of them weren't trying to hurt anyone, but they were all running scared. The sooner they were herded back into the pens, the better it would be for them, and for everyone else.

WATCHING SHELBY HELP round up the frightened animals showed Rebecca another side of the bull rider. Where some of the cowboys were rough with the bulls, Shelby showed an almost reverent attitude toward them.

Rebecca didn't know she was the focus of someone else's attention until Therese sat down beside her. "She's dangerous, that one."

"Who?"

"You know who I'm talking about," Therese stated quietly.

Rebecca turned so that she could see Therese's face. "Shelby? I don't think she's dangerous at all."

Leaning back in the plastic stadium seat, Therese shook her head. "I didn't take you for a fool, Rebecca. But she'll chew you up and spit you out, then step on you."

"Are you speaking from experience?"

"No. For some reason, Shelby has never pursued me. And that's just what it is when she wants someone. A hunt. Don't let her slow southern drawl fool you. She's a viper."

The half laugh that escaped Rebecca's throat sounded almost bitter. "Trust me. I'm not being pursued by her. She barely gives me the time of day."

"Maybe. But she can make a woman want her so easily. She's hard to deny. And even harder to forget, once she's discarded you." Therese's eyes were almost threatening.

"How do you know so much about her?"

Therese stood and brushed off her jeans. "Let's just say a friend of mine wasn't as lucky as we are, and leave it at that."

ONCE THE BULLS were all rounded up, Rebecca went in search of Shelby. She found her by the barn door, smoking a cigarette. "Where were you? I was worried." She hated the way her voice sounded, but she couldn't help it. The pleading tone was against her nature.

"We finished, and I thought I'd grab a quick smoke before the matinee started." Shelby took a long drag and looked around at the parking lot, which was quickly filling up. "Saturday's are always good matinees. You should hear some great cheering during your ride today."

Rebecca was secretly pleased that Shelby seemed to be keeping up with her schedule, but it concerned her that she looked so withdrawn and worn out. She didn't know how to bring that up. Shelby didn't appear to want to talk at all. Brightly, she asked, "Are you going to watch?"

"I'll try, but I've got some other stuff I have to do to earn my keep around here. As you've seen, I'm not much of a bull rider."

"Is there anything I can help you with?"

"No." Shelby backed up a step, and she kept her head down. Not knowing what else to say, Shelby lit another cigarette as Rebecca stood waiting.

Rebecca accepted Shelby's abrupt manner. "I need to give Patches a little bit of my time. She's going to think I've deserted her in this strange place." She took a step forward, then swallowed and turned on her heel. *That was close. I almost gave her a hug. I need to get my emotions under control, where Shelby is concerned.*

REBECCA'S NEXT RIDE was consistent with her first, and she ended up in fifth place behind Therese and Jessica, who placed second and fourth, respectively. The woman who was in first, Debbie, was a local who kept to herself. She did come up to Rebecca after her ride, however.

Debbie looked over Rebecca slowly. "Nice run."

"Thanks."

Debbie was tall, with brown hair and dark eyes, and she obviously enjoyed what she saw in Rebecca. Her swagger showed that she thought more of herself than others did. Only the lines in her face gave away her true age, somewhere between thirty and forty. The smirk she wore was almost more than Rebecca could stand, but she stopped taking care of Patches long enough to talk. She studied the woman, who would be considered handsome, in her own way. *She's not as pretty as Shelby.* That thought startled her. *Since when have I started thinking about how other women look? This rodeo is messing with my mind.*

"I haven't seen you here before. Are you new?"

"Yeah. But I've been doing some of the local playdays for a few years, now."

"That's great. I love to see 'new blood' come in. Once I retire my horse, I think I'll follow him. I'm Debbie, by the way."

"Rebecca. And, for the record, I think you have plenty of years left in you." The woman seemed friendly enough, but there was something about her that just didn't feel right to Rebecca. Maybe it was the way Debbie looked at her, like she was the last piece of chocolate cake on the platter.

"Thanks. Well, I'll leave you to your grooming. If there's anything I can do to help, just let me know, okay?" Debbie left, stopping to talk to others on her way out of the barn.

Rebecca turned back to Patches. "That was just strange."

"What was?"

Rebecca dropped her brush. "Damn, you scared me."

Shelby stood nearby, her hands in the front pockets of her jeans. "Sorry about that. I just wanted to congratulate you on another good ride."

"Thanks. But if I don't shed a few tenths off my time, Patches and I will be going home tomorrow." The thought saddened Rebecca more than she thought it should.

Shelby picked up the brush and handed it back to Rebecca. "I also came by to give you some good news. Because your event is a crowd favorite, the arena manager said they plan on taking the top six this time, instead of the usual three. So you've got a good chance."

"Really? That's great."

"Yep. So you just keep riding like you are, and you're a shoo-in for the finals tomorrow night."

Rebecca could barely contain her excitement. She patted her horse's neck. "I think we can handle that, can't we, Patches?" She looked back over at Shelby, who seemed embarrassed. "Thanks for letting me know."

"No problem." Shelby coughed nervously. "I guess I'll be going. I just wanted to keep you up to date." She turned and left, and Rebecca watched her amble away.

THE NIGHT PERFORMANCE went off without a hitch, though there was a lot of talk as the riders waited for something else disastrous to happen. More than one performer claimed the fair grounds were cursed. Because so many of the grumblings were aimed in her direction, Shelby was in a particularly foul mood. The draw didn't go in her favor, either. She drew another bull that was hard to ride. She was buckling her chaps on behind the pens when Rebecca came upon her.

"Do those actually do any good?" Rebecca asked.

"I don't think so, but it looks great for the crowd. And we do anything for the crowd, don't we?" Shelby put on her spurs. The round, loosely locked rowels were harmless, but made a nice jingling noise. She was tired of drawing the impossible bulls. "For the record, I don't use these, either. But a bull's hide is seven times thicker than humans, so he wouldn't feel it even if I did."

Rebecca shook her head. "I wasn't going to ask. I know you wouldn't purposely hurt something."

"Do you?" Shelby started to say something else, her dark eyes glittering dangerously, but she turned and walked off to the chutes instead.

The bull in the chute wouldn't be still, and Shelby hoped that she'd be able to stay on her required six seconds. Yes, it was less than the men's eight seconds, but that didn't make the ride any easier. She often felt that the organizers somehow padded the draw to even it out, but she didn't have any proof.

Shelby climbed on the bull and quickly got back up when it went wild again. She used the slats on the sides of the chute to balance on, and tried again to slowly lower herself onto the agitated animal. *At least it's a muley.* If worse came to worst, the hornless bull wouldn't be able to gore her, but it was still a dangerous ride.

After two or three tries at getting seated, Shelby was finally ready to go. With her left arm on the gate and her gloved right hand firmly holding the bull rope, Shelby nodded to the men at the gate. The bull leapt forward, and the time started.

The bull, Hank's Dinner, raced into the arena, then vigorously moved backward while simultaneously bucking to the left, for which Shelby was ready. She almost laughed at the move, until he spun quickly to the right, putting her "down in the well," which brought her low into the vortex of the spin. Stretched as far as she could, Shelby could only hang on and not touch the bull until the buzzer, and then wait for help.

At her dismount, the crowd cheered, and she was glad that she survived and had covered her bull. She waved with her left hand and used her right hand to pick up her hat, feeling the pull of the strained muscles. *That's going to be sore tomorrow. But it was worth it. I just hope that Rebecca saw me.* Shelby left the arena amid the cheers of the crowd.

The successful ride hadn't changed Shelby's mood much. She tried to tell herself to get over it, but knowing that Rebecca would be leaving in the next day or so depressed her more than she cared to admit. She thought about going to Patches' stall and waiting for Rebecca, but decided to quit seeing her. It would only hurt more when she moved on if she kept torturing herself with the contact. She went outside to have a cigarette instead, only to find that was where Rebecca was waiting.

"There you are! I was hoping you'd come out to your old haunt." Rebecca stepped forward into the light so that Shelby could see her.

"Here I am." She lit her cigarette and watched Rebecca closely. *What does she want from me? She has to have heard all the rumors by now. Plus some I don't even know and probably aren't true.*

Rebecca stepped closer and touched Shelby's right arm. "That was an incredible ride. When you got off, you looked like you were limping a little. You didn't hurt yourself, did you?"

Shelby shrugged the attention away. "I'm fine. It happens a lot in my line of business."

"Oh." Instead of dropping the subject, Rebecca forged on, bringing a half-smile to Shelby's face. "What would you do if you weren't doing this? I mean, I know you can't ride bulls forever."

"I guess I'd hire on as a wrangler or something. The rodeo's in my blood, and it's all I know."

"That's not true. You're good at a lot of things. Look at everything you do around here." Rebecca shivered slightly. A weather front earlier in the day had brought a pleasantly comfortable day, but a much cooler night. "I'm sure you could do whatever you set your mind to do."

"Then you just don't know me that well." Shelby started to walk away, but was stopped by a hand on her forearm. "What?"

"I thought we were becoming friends. What's happened to you?"

"Give me a break. I've seen a hundred of you on the circuit, and the story never changes." *It's time for a little tough love, for both our sakes. It was already too late to keep my heart from being broken. Maybe I keep Rebecca from breaking hers.*

Rebecca opened her mouth to speak, but was silenced by the stormy dark eyes inches away.

"You're just a kid, probably still in your teens." Shelby leaned in even closer, their breaths mingling in the cool night air. "You drive a small, safe sedan, probably still live at home and either had to borrow your daddy's rig, or someone brought you in order for you to compete."

Shelby ran a finger down the side of Rebecca's face, so tempted to give in to the desire that fueled her anger. "Kids like you are a dime a dozen on the circuit, Rebecca. They play cowboy, or cowgirl, then when the rodeo leaves their town, they go back to their safe little lives. Most of us follow the circuit, trying to make a living. We eat fast food when we can afford it and sleep in the cab of our trucks or the bottom of someone's trailer when we're broke." She leaned in and brutally covered Rebecca's mouth with her own, not surprised when her kiss was returned almost as rough. Hearing a noise somewhere close, she jerked back. "Go home, kid, and stay the hell away from bastards like me."

TOUCHING HER BRUISED lips with one hand, Rebecca watched Shelby go off into the night. Rebecca went into the barn. Therese was standing in her path, a knowing half-smile on her face. Rebecca rushed by her and went to Patches' stall, but Therese followed, then sat on the bale of hay nearby. "Are you okay?"

"I'm fine," Rebecca sniffled. "Is there something that you need?"

Therese hesitated, biting her lip. When she finally started to speak, her voice sounded sympathetic. "I worry about you, Rebecca. You haven't been here very long, and you don't know what that woman is capable of."

Remembering the kiss, Rebecca drew a shaky breath. *I think I have a pretty good idea. Damn, but she can kiss!* "Thank you, Therese, but I'm old enough to handle myself."

"It's just that they haven't caught whoever is behind all the accidents around here."

"Are you suggesting that Shelby is to blame?"

"Think about it." Therese came into the stall so they wouldn't be overheard. "She argued with Natalie, and you remember what happened. The overhead light in the pens fell and almost hit Rob, and we both know how well they get along." She stood, picked up an extra brush, and got on the other side of Patches, gently brushing the brown and white coat. "And don't forget about Andrea. She never gets hung up like she did, and Shelby was assisting in the chute."

Rebecca shook her head. "I don't believe it. Shelby is a gentle person. She'd never do any of those things on purpose."

Therese put the brush down. "Just think about it," Therese repeated. "And watch your back. You could be next."

SHELBY WENT INTO to her trailer. She locked the door behind her. She reached into the tiny refrigerator for a beer, opened it, and swallowed half of it before stopping to take a breath. Tossing her hat on the bed, she followed and lay back next to it, the half-empty bottle on her stomach. Tears burned her eyes, and for the first time since she was twelve, Shelby Fisher cried.

She remembered back to that horrible day when she'd stood with a friend of her dad's in her customary place to watch her father ride. She also remembered the talk of the other participants who gossiped amongst themselves that Ted Fisher's drinking would kill him one day. Most of them just didn't think it would be because he was stupid enough to get on a bull while drunk.

The bull came out, much like hers did tonight, and went into a spin. Ted was too uncoordinated to handle what was happening. His hand slipped just loose enough for him to be tossed forward and onto the sharp horns. Before they could get to him, the bull tried to toss him up in the air, which gutted him more. It wasn't an easy sight for anyone, especially his daughter. Every time she closed her eyes, she could still see the blood that drenched his body. The years hadn't lessened the pain of seeing her father die, although Shelby sometimes thought that he was the lucky one. *At least he's not still stuck in this life. I guess there's something to be said for that.*

Before Shelby knew it, she had been whisked off to live with her maiden aunt. The woman was kind, but she had no idea how to raise a child, especially one as wild and unruly as Shelby. At school, the other kids were merciless. Their tauntings about her clothes and the way she talked always embarrassed her.

When Shelby turned sixteen and decided to run off to re-join the rodeo, Nadeen gave her blessing. Shelby was glad her aunt loved her enough to let her go. As Shelby left that last day, Nadeen had smiled bravely and said, "I hope that this new life you crave will be what you need."

The thought of her aunt made Shelby realize she hadn't contacted the woman in over a year. She wondered what Nadeen was doing now, and if her aunt even missed her.

MEN'S BRONC RIDING was the final event of the evening, and half a dozen men were milling around waiting for it to begin. Shelby came in to join them and to observe. She'd had three beers and was more than a little relaxed. She stumbled, which caused them to laugh.

"Hey there, Fisher." Rob yelled, from his perch. "You taking up where your old man left off?"

"Actually, I came by after my *second place* ride to watch you fall on your arrogant face." Shelby joined three other riders on another piece of the pipe fencing.

"They only gave you second place because they felt sorry for your pitiful ass." Rob argued. He saw two women walk in from the barns. "Hey, isn't that your latest distraction?"

Shelby could see out of the corner of her eye that Rebecca had heard him also. "Shut up, Rob."

"You must really be bored, because she's not your usual type. But, then again, the pickings have been small this year." He laughed and glanced at the other men to gauge their reactions.

"You'd know all about small things wouldn't you?" Shelby asked, and the men around them laughed.

"Fuck off, Fisher." Rob gathered his gear and readied for his ride.

FROM WHERE SHE and Paula were standing, Rebecca heard the entire conversation between Rob and Shelby. She was still upset about the kiss and about the fact that Shelby seemed to have written off what she hoped was a budding friendship. Once she and Paula were back in the barns, she stopped her friend. "Can I ask you a question?"

"Sure. What's up?"

"I've heard some nasty rumors about Shelby."

"I was wondering when you'd ask questions. What kind of rumors?"

"Someone seems to think that she could be behind all the accidents around here. Do you think so? I don't think the Shelby that I've seen would do those things. I don't know what to believe."

"Shelby?" Paula thought about the question for a minute or two while they walked back to where their horses were. She finally stopped and met Rebecca's eyes. "I don't think so, but then again, I only see her a few times a year. For all I know, she could be off killing kittens the rest of the time."

Rebecca couldn't help but laugh. "That's a bit harsh, isn't it?"

"It got you to quit being so blasted serious." Paula took Rebecca by the arm and led her to the women's restroom. "What's brought on this kind of talk?"

"I just wanted to know, that's all." *I need to know.*

"Bull. There's more to it than that. Spill it." Paula leaned up against the closed bathroom door to keep the room to themselves. When Rebecca turned away from her and started checking herself in the bathroom mirror, she saw the look on Paula's face. Paula's eyes widened in surprise. "You haven't."

Rebecca continued to fluff at her hair, pulling it from its ponytail and then tying it back up. "What?"

"Don't tell me you've gone and fallen for her. Oh honey, no."

"No, of course not. I was just curious."

Paula walked over to the mirrors and stood in front of Rebecca. "She's not a bad person, but you're just looking at getting hurt."

The door opened, and Debbie and another woman walked in. "Hey girls. Imagine meeting you here," Debbie said. She looked at Rebecca. "Are you okay? You look a bit out of it."

"I'm fine, thank you." Rebecca stepped away from the sink area and moved past Debbie. "Good luck on your next ride."

"You, too." Debbie's eyes followed Rebecca and Paula, and a thoughtful look crossed her face.

HENRY WATCHED AS Rob cleaned his gear. "You're going to have to clear your head, boy, or you're going to miss the finals."

"If I do, it'll be that bitch's fault," Rob snarled. "She's always been a thorn in my side."

"Have you ever thought that it could go both ways? I'd be careful, if I were you."

Rob looked up from buckling his spurs. "What do you mean?"

Henry stepped in closer so they could speak without being overheard. "What's going on around here ain't accidents, boy. Someone's up to no good."

"Do you think that broad is bright enough to do stuff like that?"

"I don't know, but I'm just telling you to watch your back. We all need to be on special alert for anything out of the ordinary." Henry stepped back and nodded to a pair of men walking by. "Hi fellas. You comin' to the card game later tonight?" At their nods, he waved. "Great. See you then." He patted Rob on the back. "Just be careful."

"I will, Henry. Thanks."

Chapter Six

THE NEXT EVENING before the barrel racing event, Shelby sat in the stands and watched the clown act. Also known as barrelmen, it was the clown's job to help protect fallen riders and keep the crowds entertained between acts. As much as she hated Fred Tanner, the man was a professional when it came to his job. Children of all ages stood next to the fence, calling out to the painted men. Shelby wished she could remember being that carefree. But as a child, she had known the men behind the paint, so the aura was broken.

Fred's partner did some particularly clumsy stunt, causing them both to fall back over the barrel. The children laughed, and even Shelby found herself smiling.

"You should do that more often."

Shelby noticed Rebecca standing next to her. "Do what?"

"Smile." Rebecca gestured to the seat next to Shelby. "May I?"

"Sure, it's a free country."

Rebecca sat quietly for a minute or two, and Shelby could sense she was waiting for her to say something. When she remained silent, Rebecca leaned over to whisper in her ear, "Watch that little red-headed boy. I think he's having more fun teasing the girl next to him than watching the show."

"Must be the hair," Shelby said, earning her a light slap on the arm. "See what I mean?" She looked into Rebecca's face. "I'm sorry about last night. You didn't deserve to be treated like that."

"Why did you? Oh, and for the record, I'm twenty-six. Quite a bit older than a teenager." The words came out harsher than Rebecca planned.

Shelby looked at the arena floor, then back to Rebecca. "I was afraid we were getting too close."

"You don't like me? You sure have a funny way of showing it."

"No, I like you just fine. I was trying to scare you off, I guess."

"Why?"

Standing up, Shelby offered her hand to Rebecca. "Can we just take a walk? I'm getting tired of sitting."

"Sure." Rebecca allowed herself to be helped to her feet, and they started up the stairs to the exit.

THE MAIN CONCOURSE didn't have that many people milling about, so they had no trouble walked side by side. Rebecca could tell that Shelby was very careful not to make eye contact.

"What do you want from me? You've got to know that I'll be following the rodeo when it leaves."

Rebecca stopped. "Do I have to *want* anything from you? Maybe I just thought we could be friends. You look like you could use one."

"So this is a pity thing, is it?" Shelby glared at Rebecca. "For your information, I've been alone most of my adult life, and I like it like that. When I want company, I get it."

"You're impossible!" Rebecca started to turn leave away, but changed her mind and stood her ground. "Is it hard to share space with that huge ego of yours? Why does everything have to be about you?"

The words hung in the air, and Shelby didn't respond. Rebecca thought she appeared angry, but the bull rider didn't stalk off, so that was a good sign. Shelby stood, looking down at the dirt, clearly fighting to get her anger back under control. She glanced up, about to say something when Rebecca caught motion out of the corner of her eye.

An older couple approached. "Becca, sweetheart!" the woman gushed. "You look so cute in your rodeo outfit."

"Mom? Dad?" Rebecca embraced each of them separately, excited that her parents could make the evening and her final performance. "I'm so glad you're here."

Her father put an arm around her shoulders. "We wouldn't miss it for the world. I'm just sorry we couldn't be here for your other rides."

"I have someone I want you to meet—" But when she gestured to where Shelby had been standing a moment earlier, there was no sign of her. "A friend."

"Well, maybe we can meet this friend of yours later," her father offered. "Why don't you show us where Patches is? We've got a little time before we need to get to our seats."

Looking around the concourse, Rebecca sighed. "Sure," although all she wanted more than anything was to hunt down a certain person and give her a piece of her mind for running away.

SHELBY HURRIED OUT through the side door, trying not to draw attention to herself. Seeing Rebecca's parents had unnerved her more than she thought. The well-dressed couple was light-years away from Shelby's social circle, and she feared the disdainful looks they would have probably thrown her way. It gave her a good idea where Rebecca really came from, and made it even more clear how different they were.

She looked at the scratched plastic watch on her wrist and realized that the barrel racing events wouldn't start for another hour. As much as she wanted to watch Rebecca ride, another part of her knew she was just cruelly teasing herself. After tonight, Rebecca would have no reason to be at the fair grounds, and in another week or so Shelby would be moving on as well.

Shelby decided she needed a distraction, and smiled when she found her favorite type nearby. She headed off in that direction, hoping that no one would notice her.

REBECCA READIED HERSELF for the final ride. From the arena's threshold she watched as Therese and her horse took their turn, the roan animal handling the barrels with ease. Her own nerves were at an all time high, because she knew that somewhere Shelby was watching, and she wanted to look good and perform well.

After Therese rode past her, Rebecca heard her name being called. She pulled her hat down low over her eyes, patted Patches on the neck, then gently nudged the pony into action.

The first turn went well. Rebecca couldn't believe how fast Patches went, and soon they were at the second barrel. As they spun out of the turn, she felt the barrel make contact with her shin, and knew that she'd have a bruise on her leg tomorrow. But the barrel only rocked and didn't fall.

The final barrel loomed ahead, seeming farther away than ever before. Patches dove into the turn too sharply, causing the barrel to totter. Rebecca didn't have time to worry about it, as they were around it and racing for home. When she pulled up, she took time to look back, and saw that the barrel was still upright. "Yes!" she cheered, pumping one hand in the air.

Her final ride was her best performance, but it wasn't

enough for win, place or show. She placed fourth, but that was much higher than she expected. The purse that she won would more than pay for her time off work, and give her extra spending money as well.

She was on her way back to the barns, leading Patches, when Debbie, who had won first place, walked up to her. She held herself with an air that brought out the worst in everyone else around her, but her comment was kind. "That was an excellent ride."

"Thank you." Rebecca continued to walk, anxious to get away from the woman who made her so nervous. The predatory gleam in Debbie's eyes was almost as frightening as Cleve's when he'd accosted her in the stall. At least she knew where Cleve was coming from. This woman was much more duplicitous about it.

"I don't think I've ever seen a paint pony dive into the turns that well before. You must have really worked her hard to get her to do that."

Rebecca never slowed her pace. "Actually, she picked it up quite naturally. There wasn't a lot of training involved." *Please go away. I don't like you.* Rebecca fought off her natural instinct to run. *Maybe she'll step in some manure and disappear.*

Debbie didn't take the hint she wasn't welcome. Instead, she continued to walk alongside Rebecca. "Well, that's great. Sometimes the horses that are from strong purebred lines are the better ones to train, and they hold up better. I'm riding a horse from a line that my family has bred for generations."

Stopping, Rebecca spun around. "Are you insinuating that my horse isn't a purebred? I'll have you know that her lines can be traced farther back than your own."

"No offense, babe." Debbie held up her hands in a defensive gesture. "I just meant—"

"Never mind." Rebecca started walking again, glad that she was finally in the barns. "Thanks for the good wishes."

"You're welcome." Debbie backed away. "I see some friends I need to talk to. But, if you want to go out and do anything later, just look me up. I'll be around."

"Thanks." *Not! I'd rather be alone than spend any more time in your company, Miss Better Than Everyone Else.*

Paula met her at the stalls and wrapped her up in an exuberant hug. "That was just about the best ride I've seen from anyone in years! You and that little pony of yours practically flew."

"Thanks." Rebecca was still a little amazed about the ride as well. "I think Patches wanted to show off for my parents."

"Oh? Then they did make it? Is that them?"

Rebecca looked over her friend's shoulder. "Yes." She stepped out and waved to them, even though they'd already been to the stalls before. "Over here!"

Her mom and dad smiled and quickened their pace until they were in front of Patches stall with the other two women. Rebecca's mother hugged her then stepped back. "I don't think I took a breath the entire time you were out there, Becca. That was something else."

"Me either," her father said. "And I know I'll have a bruise where your mother's hand was attached to my leg." He looked at Paula and held out his hand. "I'm sorry, we haven't met. My name is Greg Starrett."

Rebecca quickly jumped in. "Forgive my lack of manners. This is Paula Fay Winger. She and her husband Buddy have been trying to help me stay out of trouble. Paula, this is my dad, and my mom, Kathy."

"Pleased to meet you both." Paula shook their hands. "Although I can't claim to help keep her out of trouble. She's done pretty well on her own."

Kathy agreed. "She's always been that way. Never given us any problems, unlike a lot of kids."

"Mom," Rebecca sighed, embarrassed.

"It's true. You got good grades, did your chores, and never got into any trouble."

Rattled by the conversation, Rebecca went into the stall and removed Patches' saddle and bridle. Part of her was glad the high stress of the competition was over, while another mourned the loss. She was so engrossed in brushing Patches she almost didn't hear her father's voice.

"Becca?"

"Yes?"

Greg stood just outside the stall and stared at his daughter. "Are you all right? You seem pretty quiet for someone who did so well in their first rodeo."

"I guess I'm just tired."

"That's a shame. I was going to take us all out to dinner at the Italian Garden restaurant. Paula and her husband were going to join us."

Rebecca didn't want to ruin everyone else's plans just because of her mood. "That sounds great. Let me finish with Patches, then I'll go get cleaned up."

Ten minutes later, Rebecca was with the excited group as they headed for her mother's SUV. The Tahoe would seat them all comfortably, and her mom enjoyed showing off the lush vehicle. Out of the corner of her eye, Rebecca spotted a solitary figure leaned up against the wall of the barns, a lit cigarette between her lips. She knew immediately who it was, and wished that Shelby was going with them for dinner.

SHELBY WATCHED THE group leave. She assumed they were going out to celebrate Rebecca's good finish, and part of her wanted to be among them. Angry at herself, she tossed the cigarette butt down and ground it out with her boot. "They'd never be comfortable around someone like me."

"Who, Fisher? Your useless mama?" Rob had stepped outside just in time to hear Shelby's comment. He'd had a couple of drinks, which usually caused him to think he had to harass someone. "I bet she was pretty good in the sack, though."

Shelby spun and heaved him against the wall. "Shut your fucking mouth, asshole! I ought to kill you for that." Her voice echoed around them. She was at least four to six inches shorter and forty pounds lighter, but that didn't stop her.

Rob laughed and roughly shoved her away from him. Shelby lost her footing and fell to the graveled ground. "From what I hear, you take after your whorin' old lady." Before she could scramble to her feet, he used his boot to hold her in place. "I just think it's funny that you've finally found a woman who won't fall to your charms. Maybe you're losing your touch." With a final stab of his foot, Rob backed away. "I'll see you tomorrow, has-been."

Watching him leave, Shelby looked around and noticed people eyeing her. "What the hell are y'all looking at?" she yelled, climbing to her feet. "Haven't you ever seen a person walking before?" She picked up her hat and dusted it off against her leg. "I hope he falls off tomorrow right after he leaves the chute." Her pride hurt, Shelby decided to turn in for the night.

ONCE BACK INSIDE the barn, Rob noticed someone waving to him. He changed the direction he was walking, and ended up near the stack of hay that was kept in one corner of the large barn. Looking around to make sure no one else saw them, he asked, "What do you want?"

The woman ran one of her painted nails down his chest. "That Fisher bitch gives you a lot of grief, doesn't she?" Her voice was sympathetic, while at the same time, extremely sexy.

"Yeah. But it's nothing I can't handle." Rob swallowed hard when one of her nails sneaked through his shirt and played with his chest. "What's it to you?"

"Have I ever told you how much bronc riders turn me on?" she asked, her hand continuing its path until she was rubbing him through his jeans.

Rob half-heartedly pushed the woman away. "I'm seeing Carla right now, you know." He didn't know why she was acting this way toward him, but was finding it harder and harder to resist her attention.

She rubbed him more vigorously. "So? You're not engaged, or anything, are you?"

"No. But, damn." His words came out in a half groan, as he felt himself being led behind the bales of hay. Before Rob could say anything else, she had unbuttoned his jeans and pulled them down slightly.

"I've wanted to do this for days," she admitted, right before taking him into her mouth.

Rob had no answer for her, except a few groans and grunts. He held her head, forgetting all about the rodeo, his girlfriend, and everything else.

Chapter Seven

THE FOLLOWING DAY the heat was back, hotter than before. More people flocked to the inside events, and fewer could be seen out on the fair midway where all the carnival rides and attractions lay.

Shelby spent more time than usual in the women's showers, glad that the arena was one of the newer ones. Her old trailer's shower had quit working years ago. All that was usable was the tiny sink in the kitchenette, and that only held water. She never could figure out how her parents had been able to live in such a small space. *It's probably why they drank and fought so much.* With her hair slicked back and her tee shirt sticking to her body from the cool water, she walked down the main concourse. She was surprised when she was accosted by Henry.

"There you are. Folks have been looking for you."

"Me? What for?" Shelby brushed by him to continue to her trailer. "As you can see, I was in the showers, for God's sake."

Henry fell in step beside her. "Bronc riding is coming up, and we haven't seen Rob since last night. Do you happen to know where he is?"

"Why are you asking me? We're not buddies. Hell, I don't even like the son of a bitch."

"I know that. But I also know there's been a lot of shit happening around here lately, and, well, folks have been talking."

Shelby stopped and faced him. "What have they been saying? Because frankly I'm getting a little tired of you beating around the bush."

"Some think you might have something to do with everything, since you happen to be at the scene of every crime."

"That's bullshit." Shelby started walking again, and they were soon out in the afternoon heat, where the performer's campers and trailers were. Two men were at Rob's trailer, trying to break in. "What's going on over there?"

"I don't know." Henry followed her until they were at the back of the crowd.

"I think I see his leg," someone yelled from the side, where he was looking in through a window.

Two burly men took turns at pounding at the door, until it finally gave way. One of them stepped into the trailer. "Get a doctor, he's unconscious!"

"Probably stone drunk," Shelby said to Henry. "I don't know what the big deal is."

One of the men in the crowd faced Shelby. "His door was jammed from the outside, and his windows were nailed shut. Someone was trying to get him out of the way."

Shit.

Shelby was glad that she and Henry had been at the back of the crowd. The older man quickly whisked her away for her own protection until they were back at the arena.

He looked around the vacant area to make certain they were alone. The one man who had seen them obviously didn't follow, and he was probably too interested in what was going on to tell anyone else. Henry didn't waste any time. "Answer me truthfully, girl. Did you do it?"

"Do what?"

"Don't play stupid, Shelby. It doesn't look good on you. Just answer me."

Shelby felt her face flush at the accusation. "If you mean did I do something to Rob, of course not! You know I hate the son of a bitch, but I'd never do something so underhanded."

"That's what I thought." Henry scratched his cheek. "Then we've got someone who's trying to make you look bad. Because each and every one of these so-called 'accidents' are set up to have you appear to be the culprit. Is there anyone who feels that bad about you?"

"Do you want the list alphabetically, or by age or gender?" Shelby asked. "I can name at least a dozen, right off the top of my head."

Henry couldn't help but chuckle at that remark. "You sound a lot like your old man. He was never one for being very diplomatic."

"Probably where I got it." Shelby leaned up against an empty pen where just yesterday a two-thousand-pound bull had been housed. "If someone's so pissed at me, why don't they just do one of their little nasty tricks to me? Why mess with everyone else?"

"I don't know. But I do know you'd better be extra special careful from here on out. Try not to piss anyone else off."

Shelby pushed off from her resting spot. "That's easier said than done." She patted Henry on the shoulder. "Thanks for the advice, though." She walked away, deep in thought. *Who would want to frame me?*

SEEING THE HORSE trailer reminded Rebecca that her part of the rodeo was over, and it made her blue. She led Patches to the back entrance, where the horse immediately loaded without a problem. "Good girl."

Mr. Lockneer, the man who owned the stables she lived above, closed the trailer door. "Don't feel bad. You'll score better next year," he assured her.

"It's not that. I guess I'm just not ready for it to be over."

"Well, maybe I can help with that." Lockneer made sure that Patches was properly secured before speaking. "Why don't I take your horse back out to the stables, and you can stay here in town with your family and enjoy the rest of the rodeo?"

She wanted to accept his offer, but felt bad about taking advantage of her employer's good nature. "That wouldn't be right, Mr. Lockneer. I only asked for the days off that I'd be competing. It's not fair for you to have to do my job."

Lockneer laughed. "I did it before I hired you, didn't I? Truthfully, Rebecca, it will give me an excuse to leave the house earlier and not have to listen to the missus talk about her bridge club."

"Well, if you're sure it wouldn't be an imposition—"

"Nonsense. All I ask if that you have fun while you're here." He patted her on the arm and climbed into the Ford F250 that was to pull the trailer.

Rebecca watched the truck and horse trailer drive out of sight. A sound behind her startled her.

"Did you hear the news?" Paula liked to share 'news' a lot.

"What's that?"

Paula pointed out to where the campers were. "They found Rob earlier, almost dead!"

"You've got to be kidding me. What happened to him?"

"He was locked up in his trailer and suffered severe heat prostration. The poor man!" Paula was on a roll, and was just getting started. "The ambulance attendant said that if he hadn't been found when he was, he'd have died for sure."

Rebecca frowned. "Surely it wasn't that bad. It's only late afternoon." She could see the heat waves coming from the graveled parking lot, but it didn't feel that hot to her.

"I think that part of the problem was he was already

dehydrated from drinking the night before. They found an empty bottle of Jack Daniels beside him, so there's no telling how much he drank. Luckily he's fine, now. He even refused to go to the hospital."

"That's not very smart."

"We are talking about Rob, you know." Paula leaned in closer. "But that's not the worst of it."

Rebecca was getting tired of the cloak and dagger routine. "Just tell me, please."

"They think that your new little friend Shelby might have something to do with it."

"Why?"

"Because of the circumstances. She was seen arguing with him last night. As a matter of fact, she was the last person who was seen with him, period." Paula pulled Rebecca into the barn area. "I'm so sorry I didn't seriously warn you about her, Rebecca. But I honestly didn't think she would be dangerous."

Pulling her arm free, Rebecca backed away from Paula. "Do you think so, too? Is there any real proof?"

Paula shushed her. "Quiet! If she's around somewhere, one of us could be next!"

Rebecca didn't care. "What have you been smoking? You know as well as I do that Shelby wouldn't hurt anyone."

"Tell that to everyone else," Paula told her, before walking away.

TIRED OF THE constant whisperings behind her back, Shelby kept to herself the remainder of the afternoon. By the time of the evening performance, all she wanted to do was finish her ride. Her draw was actually one of the more predictable bulls, and she figured she had a good chance of not only lasting the ride, but of winning a part of the purse.

She was fourth this evening, and waited patiently by as the other female riders took their turns. Only one was able to stay on the required six seconds, leaving her with even better odds, *if* she could stay on.

When Shelby started to climb over the chute, a couple of the men climbed down, leaving her with only two people to help her get ready for the ride. "Thanks, guys." It took longer than normal for her to get her bull rope just as she wanted it. With her left arm on the chute gate, Shelby nodded. The gate started to open, hung up, then opened all the way. Confused, the bull paused, spun out into the arena, and snorted his disgust with the way things were done.

Shelby hung on with all her might as the bull spun first one way then the other, then decided to leap up and pull his head way down. Just after the buzzer sounded, the bull flipped forward headfirst into the dirt. Shelby rolled underneath his massive bulk. The bull kept on moving, regained its footing, and trotted across the arena.

The crowd sat silent as Shelby lay motionless on the dirt floor of the arena. The clowns slowly maneuvered the bull out of the arena, but no one came out to see if the rider herself was injured. Finally, the ambulance drove out onto the dirt just as Shelby sat up. She looked around, and, realizing where she was, climbed shakily to her feet. The announcer stated that she was the second place winner, and the multitude that had been so quiet before was now on its feet, cheering her.

Embarrassed, Shelby raised her hand as she walked over and picked up her hat. She waved it in the air, and hurried out as quickly as her unsteady feet could carry her.

REBECCA HAD FOUND a seat close to the chutes to watch the bull riding event. She'd waited impatiently as the other riders took their turns, and was glad when most of them didn't last the required six seconds. When it had finally been Shelby's turn, Rebecca couldn't understand why it was taking so long for her to get ready. Then she noticed that the men who normally helped at the chutes climbed down and walked away.

Then the chute had opened, and Shelby had seemed to be doing well. But then Rebecca watched in horror as the bull rolled over. Shelby had lain still in the churned earth for a good ten seconds. Rebecca looked all around. Where was everyone? How come no one was helping the downed rider? She jumped from her seat and rushed to the pen area where a security guard stopped her.

"I'm sorry, Miss. You can't be back here." The big man looked apologetic, but wasn't moving. His uniform was that of a sheriff's deputy, and he seemed to be working the rodeo on his day off.

"Please, I have to go check on my friend — the woman who was riding that last bull."

He shook his head. "Only authorized rodeo personnel can be here. I don't see your pass."

"My pass expired yesterday," Rebecca said. "But I still need to check on my friend."

He crossed his arms over his chest and glowered at her. "No can do. Now why don't you go back to your seat and enjoy the rest of the rodeo?"

"But—"

"She's with me, Alvin," Paula interrupted. She had seen Rebecca leave the stands, and knew where she would be heading. "Why don't you let me take it from here?"

Alvin smiled at her. "All right. But keep her out of trouble."

"I sure will." Paula rubbed her hand across his back. "Thanks, hon." She took Rebecca by the arm and led her away from the guard. "In trouble again, are you?"

"No, I've got to see about Shelby." Rebecca rushed away, with Paula barely keeping up. "Did you see what that bull did to her?"

Paula followed for a few steps. "I did. But I also saw her get up on her own and leave the arena."

"I've got to see that she's all right." Rebecca glanced over her shoulder, but Paula stood motionless, her arms crossed. At the pleading look in Rebecca's eyes, she finally conceded and allowed her to pass.

Rebecca found Shelby behind the pens. "Are you all right?" She was out of breath and felt a little light-headed.

"I'm fine. I don't need anybody checking on me."

"Are you sure? I'm only asking because you were down for a long time."

"Yeah, sure was. How would you like being left lying in the dirt by your supposed peers?"

"It was terrible, Shelby! Then I kept trying to get by security, but they wouldn't let me through until Paula told them I was with her."

"Don't worry about it. I'm okay." Her voice was bitter, and the look on her face was even more sour.

Rebecca wanted to brush the dust off the back of Shelby's white shirt, but stopped her hand before she touched her. "I guess this shows that you're not behind all the accidents, if something like that gate hanging up happened to you."

"No, that was just the gate man. He's a friend of Rob's. I figure—wait a minute." She looked Rebecca in the eye. "*You* think I've had something to do with the accidents around here?"

"Well, not exactly. I mean, Paula said—"

Shelby spun on her heel to leave. "And of course that busybody is more dependable than I am, right? After all, I'm just some has-been bull rider who sleeps with a different woman every chance she gets."

Rebecca grabbed Shelby's arm. "Wait. That's not it at all. But since you're being so defensive, *are* you behind any of this?"

"I might as well be, since you and everyone else seems to

think so." Shelby walked away. Even through the anger and bitterness that the bull rider was radiating, Rebecca could tell she was hurt by the accusation.

Now what do I do? The only answer that seemed right to Rebecca would have been wrong to anyone else: she followed Shelby.

HOT TEARS BURNED her eyes as Shelby strode out into the evening, and she wiped at them angrily. She had never been so mad in her entire life. It was bad enough that the people she had known for years had turned against her, but she honestly thought that maybe she and Rebecca were starting to build a foundation for a friendship, at the very least.

Her heart was heavy and her body ached. She unlocked the door to her trailer and went inside, not bothering to close it behind her. After throwing her gear on the floor, she reached into the tiny refrigerator and was disappointed to come up empty. She sat on the bed then lay down and stretched her legs out. A discreet knock on the outside of the trailer caught her attention. "What?"

"Can I come in?" Rebecca's face poked around the corner, and she looked almost as upset as Shelby felt.

"Are you going to blame me for anything else?"

"No."

"Then I guess you can." Shelby didn't bother getting up, but she did move her feet so that Rebecca would have a place to sit.

Rebecca looked around the tiny trailer. It was clean, but there wasn't much room. She couldn't believe a person could actually live in something like this. "I'm sorry if I upset you."

Shelby covered her face with one arm, trying to appear relaxed. "Do you really believe what they're saying about me?"

"I don't want to, Shelby. It's just—"

"It's just what? You chase around, acting like you want to be my friend. Then when things get the least bit rough, you bail on me?" Shelby swung her legs over the side of the bed and rose. She went to a pan in the sink, and poured some water from a gallon jug to wash her face. Once she was done, she didn't even bother to dry it, but let the water drip down her cheeks instead. "If that's the kind of friend you are, then no thanks."

Rebecca shook her head and started to cry. "No, please. I do want to believe you. But, you have to admit, a lot of things point toward you."

"But a friend wouldn't have to ask," Shelby explained quietly.

"I know, and I'm sorry." Rebecca held out her hand. "Truce?" When Shelby didn't take her hand, she let her hand drop and tried to change the subject. "So, is there where you live all the time?"

"Yeah. I know it's kind of small, but it works okay for me." Except that she had to use the showers at truck stops and use public restrooms.

"Small? Well, I guess it is. I think Patches stable is bigger." Rebecca's joke fell flat, as Shelby scowled at her, and her eyes went wide.

Shelby walked to the door. "I'd like for you to leave, please, before I do or say something I shouldn't."

Rebecca stood. "I'm sorry, Shelby. I didn't mean—"

"Sure you did. I bet I'm just one big joke to you, aren't I?"

Without another word, Rebecca slipped out the door. Shelby waited until she was off the steps and on the gravel. "Go back to your own life, Rebecca, and leave me to wallow in my own." She closed the door firmly, hoping to shut the other woman out of her life just as easily.

AFTER BEING KICKED out of Shelby's trailer, Rebecca wandered around the campgrounds. She couldn't believe she kept opening her mouth and saying such horrible things to the woman when all she really wanted to do was be her friend. *Mom would say I wasn't raised to be that way, and she's right.* She bent down and picked up a discarded soda can, then tossed it in the trash. *Now I've just got to figure a way to make up for it.*

She smiled and waved at a few people who recognized her from the rodeo and even signed a few autographs. Rebecca was surprised that anyone would want her signature, but seeing the thrill it gave them outweighed her embarrassment.

"Looks like someone's popular," Fred Tanner scoffed jealously as he walked by a group of barrel racing fans gathered around Rebecca. "It sure didn't take you long."

"I don't know what you're talking about." Rebecca gave her attention to the children swarming around her. "How many of you have ridden a horse before?" she asked, hoping the man would take the hint and go away.

Two or three small hands went up, while others looked on sadly. "If you haven't," Rebecca whispered loudly, "that's okay. I didn't start riding until I was a teenager." The sad faces disappeared and were replaced with hopefulness. Rebecca looked over to where Fred had been standing and was relieved to see he'd left. She answered a couple more questions for the children before they moved on with their parents.

Rebecca hadn't gone very far when Fred stepped up to walk beside her. "I saw you coming out of Fisher's trailer. Do you think that's a very wise choice?"

"What are you talking about?"

"She's trash, girl. It's best you know that now." Fred tipped his hat to a pair of young women who waved to him as he walked with Rebecca. "I've never known her to have more than two nickels to rub together. She's lived in that damned piece of shit trailer her whole life, and I know for a fact she doesn't have much of an education. Not to mention all the women she's been with."

"So? What is it you're really trying to say?" Rebecca wanted to ask him if being a clown that reeked of stale bourbon was any better, but wisely decided to keep quiet.

Fred put his hand on her elbow to appear solicitous, but did it mainly to keep her from getting away from him. "Just stay away from the bitch, that's all I have to say. You'll be much better off for it." He released her arm and hurried off.

"Why couldn't I have taken up a safer hobby, like sky diving?" Rebecca asked herself out loud. The glamour of the rodeo was gone, replaced by too many dramas to keep track of. "This is getting to be just too much."

Chapter Eight

THE NEXT EVENING, with the rodeo officially over, quite a few of the contestants who traveled planned on staying to enjoy the fair. Shelby would normally be out with the rest of them, but all the talking behind her back made her want to stay in her trailer instead.

She was sipping on a warm beer and staring at the ceiling of her trailer when a knock on the door brought her out of her reverie. "What?" The knock came again, this time more insistent. "Damn it, who is it?" On the third knock, Shelby got off the bed and swung the door open.

Rebecca was standing there, holding a single yellow rose. "I was hoping you'd be home." She held out the flower to Shelby, who looked at it as if she'd never seen one before. "I came by to see if you would go to the fair with me."

"Like a date?" Shelby asked, completely surprised. She wasn't expecting to see Rebecca again, especially after the way she treated her the day before.

The question seemed to throw her off guard for a moment, but Rebecca recovered quickly. "Yes. A date." She crooked her arm and held it out to Shelby. "May I?"

"Oh yeah, sure." Shelby started to join her, but looked down at the gray tee shirt she was wearing, which sported a ketchup stain from her hotdog lunch. "Would it be okay if I," she gestured to the shirt.

Rebecca bit off a smile. "I'll just wait out here."

Shelby closed the door and looked around the trailer frantically. "Clean shirt, clean shirt. I've got to have a damned cleaned shirt in this place, somewhere."

Shelby didn't know that outside, Rebecca could hear the entire conversation that she had with herself, and was covering her mouth to keep from laughing.

When the door opened again, Shelby stood in the doorway wearing a navy blue western shirt. She tucked it into her jeans as she hurried down the steps. "Thanks for waiting. I just didn't want to, you know, look like, you know what I mean..." She trailed off, realizing she was babbling like a fool, but couldn't help herself. Since Rebecca showed up bare-headed, Shelby left her cowboy hat inside.

Rebecca handed her the flower. "Do you have something you can put this in? It will last longer if it's in water."

"Oh, yeah." Shelby took the flower and disappeared into the trailer for a minute, then hurried back out. "I poured out what was left of my beer, and filled the bottle with water. It worked perfectly."

"Good idea." Rebecca wanted to laugh, but dared not to. Only Shelby would think of using a beer bottle as a vase, and the thought charmed Rebecca. She linked her arm with Shelby's. "Let's go see what kind of trouble we can get into."

The walk to the fairgrounds wasn't far. Shelby wanted to reach out and take Rebecca's hand, but knew that due to where they were, it probably wouldn't be very wise. That, and she was afraid her attempt would be rebuffed, even though Rebecca had been the one to ask her out. From desperation more than anything, she decided to start the conversation. "So, tell me about *your* family."

"My mom and dad have lived in the same house since they were married twenty-eight years ago, and I have a younger brother, Terry, who's nineteen and thinks he knows everything. He still lives at home while he's going to the community college."

"What about you?"

"What about me?"

Shelby bumped Rebecca with her shoulder. "Where do you live, did you or do you go to school, that sort of thing. I'd like to know everything I can about you."

"Are you writing a book or something?" She looked at Shelby mischievously.

"No, just curious. Where will you go, and what will you do, when the rodeo is over?"

"Okay. Well, I live in a small apartment above some stables, outside the other side of Somerville. I work for the stables part time, to pay for Patches' stall and my apartment. I also work full time at the only western wear store in the county, so I stay pretty busy. I never felt the need to go to college, because to tell you the truth, it just wasn't something I wanted to do with four years of my life."

Hearing about Rebecca's take on college made Shelby feel better about her lack of education. She knew she wasn't stupid, but it was nice to know not everyone wanted to go to college and get a degree. "I dropped out of high school when I was sixteen."

Rebecca shrugged her shoulders. "Did that work for you?"

"At the time, yeah."

"Then don't worry about it. You can always go back and get your diploma, if you want."

The thought of being stuck in a classroom with kids horrified Shelby. "I'm not setting foot back in a school! Those people would laugh me right out onto the street."

"You don't have to do that anymore. There are classes you can take through the mail, or even study for the test online."

"Online?"

"The Internet?" Rebecca queried. "Oh, right. I don't suppose you'd have much use for computers with all the traveling you do. They're also pretty expensive and a bit frivolous. My parents thought I would use it for school. Instead I use it for everything *but* that."

"I've heard of it, just never really gave it much thought. But I could really get my diploma without going to school?"

Rebecca hip-checked her, playing around to keep the conversation light. "That's right. You'd still have to study for the test and maybe take a course or two. But I'd be glad to help."

Shelby almost opened her mouth to accept Rebecca's offer, when she realized where and who she was. "The next rodeo is down around Houston, next month. I won't have time."

"Skip it."

Could she? "I don't know, Rebecca. If I skip that one, I might as well skip San Angelo the month after that." The two rodeos had excellent purses, and Shelby knew she had a good chance of making enough money through one or the other to last her for several months.

Rebecca linked her arm with Shelby's again, not caring who saw. "So? You won a good purse this time. Use it."

"Let me think on it, okay?" This was all moving too quickly for Shelby, who liked to think things through meticulously. She let Rebecca lead her to a ticket booth at the carnival entrance and was set to argue when Rebecca paid for their tickets.

"You can buy dinner."

Shelby acquiesced. She knew she wouldn't win the argument, so she took the loss as gracefully as possible. "And I'll buy the next tickets, too."

"But—"

"No arguments." When Rebecca stuck her tongue out at her, Shelby wanted to lean over and show her just what to do with it. "You're playing with fire, woman."

"So? I've always liked things a little *hot*," Rebecca teased. She ran her tongue around her slightly opened lips. "Just wait. It'll get even hotter before the night is over."

Oh, God, Shelby thought.

SEVERAL TIMES DURING the evening, Rebecca said or did something that set Shelby's libido on fire, then she'd put a slight damper on it. She rubbed up against her, whispered in her ear, and touched her when no one was looking. Poor Shelby felt as if she would combust at any moment.

They walked through one of the nearly-empty exhibit halls where Rebecca relentlessly continued her teasing until Shelby had enough. She grabbed Rebecca by the hand, pulled her behind a partition, and sank into a chair pulling Rebecca down with her.

Rebecca found herself sitting on Shelby's lap, their faces inches apart. The dark eyes so close to hers were sparkling with need, and she lowered her head and covered Shelby's lips with her own.

There was nothing gentle about the kiss, as one had wanted it as badly as the other. Rebecca's tongue demand entry, and Shelby quickly granted it, moaning when Rebecca tangled her fingers in her hair and pulled her face even closer. Shelby cupped Rebecca's rear, bringing her nearer so that their breasts were touching.

Finally breaking her mouth free to breathe, Rebecca put her forehead down on Shelby's shoulder. "Damn, but you're good at that." Now she knew for certain that she wasn't straight. *As if I needed any help in that department.*

Shelby kept rubbing Rebecca's back. "Funny, I was going to say the same thing about you." She looked around to make sure they hadn't been seen. "Would you like to look around some more?"

"I don't know about you, but it's going to take me a minute to be able to walk after that."

"I can wait. Or," Shelby winked playfully, "we can neck."

"Hmm. Now that's a tough choice." Rebecca placed her arms around Shelby's neck and kissed her again, more gently but with just as much need.

"Oh, my God! How utterly disgusting," a woman tsked from nearby. "I think I may faint."

Rebecca hurriedly climbed off Shelby's lap, blushing. She was mortified they got caught, but Shelby seemed to enjoy it.

"Lady, maybe you just need to get laid," Shelby told the

woman as they passed. "I'll be here through Sunday, if you need me." She grinned at the woman, who practically swooned in shock.

OUTSIDE, REBECCA SLAPPED Shelby on the arm. "That was mean."

"It sure was, interrupting us like that." She couldn't tell if Rebecca was upset or embarrassed. "Are you okay with what she saw?"

"To tell you the truth, I'm not sure. This is all pretty new to me."

"We can take it as slow as you need to, Rebecca. There's no hurry."

"Thanks." Rebecca reached out and took Shelby's hand. "That means a lot to me."

Shelby almost floated from the sensation of Rebecca's hand in hers. That and the fact that Rebecca hadn't run off screaming by now was a good sign, at least in her book. "Well, since I've got a diploma to get, I guess I'm not going anywhere for a while. That is, if you're still willing to help me."

Rebecca swung herself into an unsuspecting Shelby's arms. "That's wonderful. I've got the computer back at my apartment, and I'll be glad to help you download what you need."

"Download?"

"Just another weird term. You'll understand them all in no time, believe me."

Shelby wasn't as sure, but she trusted Rebecca. "If you say so." She was glad when Rebecca linked arms with her again. "What's next?"

"How about the carnival midway? I love that whole area." Rebecca could have bitten her tongue as soon as the words left her mouth.

How insensitive can I be? Her mother left to be with a carnival worker. "We don't have to, though, if you don't want to."

"No, that's fine. Maybe we can find another place to scandalize someone." Shelby loved the blush that colored Rebecca's face. "Come on. You look like the type that can win me a teddy bear."

They spent well over an hour walking the small midway, and Rebecca not only won Shelby a teddy bear, but a bull-shaped coin bank as well. In between games, they often sneaked around to the back of a tent and shared short, but searing kisses, making both women weak in the knees.

As they passed one of the tents, Shelby noticed an older

woman who looked vaguely familiar. *No, that would be close to impossible.* But she had memorized that small picture her father had saved of her mother, which he had cut from a discarded rodeo program. The man had been a hopeless romantic. *And a hopeless drunk.* It was one of the many reasons that Shelby herself would only drink beer and limited herself to three at any one time. She refused to turn into her father, no matter what others might think of her. Now she was staring across the midway at a woman who might or might not be her mother.

"What's the matter?" Rebecca asked, when Shelby stopped and stared.

"That woman...she looks like, like..."

Rebecca turned and gazed the direction Shelby was staring. "Do you mean you think that's your—"

"No." Shelby shook her head. "My mother died for me 23 years ago. If that woman *did* give birth to me, she left me behind for a reason." When Rebecca started to argue, Shelby held up her hand. "I don't want her to ruin our night, okay? Let's go get a funnel cake and see how big a mess we can make on each other."

"Sounds like fun to me."

THEY STAYED UNTIL the carnival started to shut down and walked back to Shelby's trailer holding hands. The large parking lot which had been home to so many during the last few weeks had clearly lost some of its tenants. Shelby stopped at the foot of her trailer's stairs. "Thanks for a great time tonight. I can't remember ever having that much fun."

"Well, it might have to do with how much you ate," Rebecca ribbed. "I'm guessing that you have a hollow leg, or something, since you're not much bigger than me, and a heck of a lot skinnier."

"I happen to think you're built perfectly. Don't ever think otherwise."

Rebecca looked at her feet. "I've always felt a little fat, if you want to know the truth."

"You? Damn, woman. You're about the most un-fat person I've ever seen. As a matter of fact, you're beautiful." Shelby put her arms around Rebecca's waist and pulled her close. "Absolutely beautiful." She leaned forward and kissed Rebecca tenderly, trying to instill in actions what her words couldn't.

The tingling sensation of Shelby's kiss wasn't lost on Rebecca, who suddenly knew exactly what she wanted. She broke away and looked into Shelby's eyes. "Let's go inside."

"Are you sure? Because I don't think—"

"I'm very sure." Rebecca kissed Shelby again. "I'm a big girl, Shelby. I know what I want, and what I want is you."

Shelby led her into the trailer and turned on the light. "Is this okay?" For the first time in her life, she was nervous about taking a woman to bed. *Maybe it's because for the first time in your life, this woman means something to you.* She saw the dirty shirt that she had hastily left on the kitchenette counter and picked it up. "Let me just get rid of this," she said, tossing it in the bathroom.

Rebecca sat on the bed and held out her arms. "Come here." She watched with some amusement as a very nervous Shelby made her way across the small trailer. "Kiss me."

"Okay." Shelby sat on the bed and took Rebecca in her arms. The kiss they shared was filled with hope and longing, which grew into need and passion. Shelby felt herself being forced back onto the bed, and her shirt slowly unbuttoned and slid from her body. Once her shirt was off, she felt Rebecca's hands at her belt.

Struggling with the buckle, Rebecca could only growl, "Off, off!" Shelby snickered and helped her unbuckle the belt, and it didn't take long for Rebecca to unsnap and unzip Shelby's jeans. She pulled the denim down slender legs, feeling the muscles for the first time. It was only when she got to the boots that Rebecca knew she was going to need some help, since Shelby's pants were bunched down around them. "Shelby, please!"

"Calm down, baby. We've got plenty of time." Shelby sat up and helped with her boots and jeans, leaving herself in just a sports bra and panties. She looked to Rebecca, who was still fully dressed. "I think you're wearing too many clothes, darlin'."

Rebecca looked down at herself and grinned. "Your turn." She dove onto the bed and held out her arms. "Strip me as you will, expert."

Shelby laughed at her. "All right. You asked for it." She straddled Rebecca's waist and leaned over to kiss her soundly, until Rebecca began to squirm. While she kissed her, she pulled Rebecca's tee shirt out of her jeans and ran her hands up underneath it, raising it from her body. Shelby broke the kiss just long enough to slip the shirt over Rebecca's head, then tossed the garment to the floor. She ran light kisses over the other woman's chest and was electrified when Rebecca's nipples hardened underneath her white silk brassiere.

"Shelby, oh!" The few times Rebecca had been with clumsy men had been uneventful and unfulfilling. Already Rebecca felt more than she had all those times combined.

"Just wait. It gets better." Shelby quickly removed Rebecca's shoes and jeans and was about to slide the straps down on

Rebecca's bra when her hand was covered.

"Can you turn out the light?" No matter what Shelby had told Rebecca, she was still embarrassed about her body. Anyone else would have seen a beautiful woman with curves in all the right places, but Rebecca had spent too many years hearing about "baby fat."

Shelby looked down at her with love in her eyes. "Sure, baby. Hold on." She kissed Rebecca on the tip of the nose and got up to switch off the lamp. The outside lights from the parking lot were more than enough to see by, for which Shelby was grateful. She'd had her share of "dates" that she'd rather have kept the light off, but this certainly wasn't one of them. When she got back into bed, she noticed that Rebecca had crawled under the sheets. "Are you all right? We don't have to—" Her mouth was quickly covered by Rebecca's.

Rebecca couldn't believe how considerate a lover Shelby was being. She wanted, no, she *needed*, to make love with her. Here. Now. Pulling out of the kiss, Rebecca looked up into Shelby's shaded face. "I need you, Shelby. Please."

"Okay." Shelby kissed Rebecca again, and was about to remove the rest of her undergarments when she realized that Rebecca was nude under the sheets. *Guess that answered that question. She is ready.* She ran her hands along Rebecca's sides and placed light kisses on her throat. At Rebecca's moan, she moved her hands to cover her breasts, gently pinching the nipples with her fingers.

Wanting to feel more of Shelby's skin, Rebecca tugged at her bra, then waited patiently as Shelby took the hint and removed the rest of her clothes. Now, both naked, they pressed their bodies together for the first time.

Shelby thought that she might orgasm on the spot just from the feel of Rebecca's skin. Never in her life had sex felt like this. But then she realized, in that moment, that what the two of them were doing together was more than sex. It was making love. That thought should have scared Shelby, but she was too busy enjoying the moment to be bothered.

For Rebecca, she couldn't believe how soft Shelby was. Her skin was so smooth, and Rebecca couldn't wait to touch it everywhere. She used both hands to caress Shelby's back, mapping it out in wide, sweeping motions. When her hands found a firm ass to squeeze, she did just that.

"God, Rebecca." The sensations that Rebecca's roaming hands caused were almost Shelby's undoing. She ground her hips into Rebecca's, who moaned in appreciation. Wanting to give pleasure to her lover, she brought one of Rebecca's nipples into her mouth to suck on it gently.

Rebecca almost cried out at the exquisite feeling. She used one hand to hold Shelby's head to her breast, while she used the other to feel between them. Shelby was practically kneeling between her legs, so it was easy for Rebecca to place her hand between Shelby's legs, feeling a slick warmth.

The shock of Rebecca's hand almost caused Shelby to jerk away. Catching herself, she followed suit and sought out Rebecca's moistness, until both women were gasping in pleasure.

The heavy orgasm that rocked Rebecca's body soon after was like nothing she'd ever experienced before. She cried out, and seconds later heard Shelby call out as well. They both collapsed, clutching at one another, and lay twisted in the sheets, spent.

HOURS LATER, JUST as dawn was breaking, Shelby awakened to shouts. She rolled over enough so that she could see through the window, and was shocked at what she saw. Heavy smoke was coming from the main barn, and the sounds of animals crying and men yelling drove her into action. She hurried out of bed and was almost fully dressed before Rebecca even stirred.

"What's going on?"

"It looks like there's a fire over at the barns. I'm going to run over and see if I can help."

Rebecca sat up. "Give me a minute, and I'll go with you." But her eyes were half slits, and she looked as if she would fall back to sleep any minute.

"Why don't you go find a phone, and make sure the authorities have been notified? I'll see you over there, okay?" Shelby knew better than to try and keep Rebecca away from the action.

"Okay." Rebecca knew the ruse for what it was, but she also knew it was a good idea. "Be careful?"

"Sure." Shelby leaned down and gave Rebecca a quick kiss. "You be careful, too." She hurried from the trailer before Rebecca had even gotten one foot out of bed.

The fire was in full force, flames going high in the morning sky, and some of the men stood around. The sounds of frightened animals were heard, and Shelby spied a handful of ropes from a nearby pile of discards. "What are you idiots doing? They could be dying in there!"

"They're just stupid animals," one man yelled.

"No, the stupid ones are out here," she yelled back. Shelby scooped up some coils of rope and ran into the blazing barn. She heard sirens in the distance.

HAVING FINALLY MADE the call at a nearby payphone, Rebecca wished she hadn't left her cell phone in her purse, which was locked up in her car. She showed up at the scene and asked the men where Shelby went. They all pointed at the barn, and Rebecca rounded on them. "How could you let her do that?"

"Do you think that you could stop her?" one of the men asked.

"Probably not. But I sure as hell wouldn't have let her go in alone." Rebecca started for the barn, but two of the men held her up.

"You can't go in there."

She struggled, but couldn't break free from their grips. "But you let Shelby."

"She'll get what she deserves."

"Damn it, you fools. She's not guilty of setting the fire, or any of the other things that have been happening around here. She was with me last night."

Henry jogged up. "What the hell is going on here?" He jumped to one side when a horse came flying out of the barn. "Raymond, run up and watch the main gate. Let the emergency vehicles in, but keep the animals from running off."

"Right."

Rebecca looked at the other men just standing around. "Is anyone going to help her?" More animals raced outside, some on fire. Men grabbed what they could to put out the fires and help the animals.

"Help who?" Henry asked.

"Shelby. She's in there letting the animals out."

A fireman showed up then. "You have someone inside? That's extremely dangerous."

"No shit," Rebecca snapped. "But I'm sure she wasn't about to stand by and let helpless animals die while other people sat out here chatting. I should be in there—*we* should be in there helping her."

The firemen had rolled out their hoses and were spraying the barn as animals continued to race out. Finally, a frantic horse burst from the flames with a rider astride, riding until they were far enough away from the fire. Shelby slid from the animal's back and fell to the gravel. She coughed heavily through the shirt she had tied around her face. It had left her in her sports bra, but Rebecca could see that she was too tired to care. The fire captain was standing over her in an instant. "Miss, that was an exceedingly stupid thing to do."

"Shut up." Rebecca dropped to her knees beside Shelby and held her in her arms. "It's going to be okay, sweetheart. There's an ambulance on the way." She held on to the soot-covered woman, who had slipped into unconsciousness, rocking her gently. Unfortunately, when the medics arrived, they refused to allow Rebecca to ride with Shelby to the hospital.

The men who had stood around as the fire raged continued to stand around to watch the ambulance leave the fairgrounds. One commented, "You have to admit, that took more guts than sense."

Someone else said, "Yeah, you're right. Although she could have done it just to throw the blame off herself."

"You're all full of shit," Rebecca yelled. "Not to mention a bunch of cowards, letting a woman go in to save the animals, while you all stood out here and watched."

A heavyset man stepped forward. "That doesn't make us cowards, girl. Just makes us smarter than her. No one in their right mind would have gone into that blaze unless they had a real good reason. Maybe she needed to cover up something."

Rebecca threw up her hands. "But she was with me all night. There's no way she could have started the fire."

The heavyset man wasn't convinced. "Are you sure? Did she leave your sight for any length of time? It wouldn't take long to toss a cigarette or something in a bale of hay."

Before opening her mouth again, Rebecca thought back. Shelby *had* already been dressed when she woke up. Had she just come back, or was she truly innocent? *No. The woman who made love to me so gently could not have started that fire.* "She's innocent."

"If you say so." The heavyset man moved by Rebecca. "We might as well go back to our own business, though. There's nothing left for us to do here."

Rebecca couldn't have agreed more. She hurried over to the parking lot and got into her car, worried about Shelby. She hoped to be at the hospital shortly after the ambulance arrived. The bull rider had remained unconscious while they loaded her in the back of the vehicle, apparently overcome by too much smoke.

REBECCA HATED HOSPITALS. She wasn't sure if it was the smell, the morbidity of it all, or if she just had a repressed memory. All she knew for sure was that no matter how much she hated being here, she wouldn't leave until she could take Shelby with her.

Shelby was on oxygen, but breathing without a ventilator. The few minor burns on her upper back, shoulders, hands and arms had been treated. The shirt around her face had helped block out some of the smoke, but not enough, and they still wanted to keep her at least overnight to make sure her lungs were not damaged. She was asleep at the moment.

Rebecca, standing over the bed, spoke softly, even though she knew Shelby probably couldn't hear her. "You scared me to death." Rebecca watched Shelby's chest rise and fall, and looked at the oxygen meter. "You've gone up three more points in the last hour. That's good news." The doctor had told her that as soon as Shelby's oxygen levels had risen enough, they'd let Rebecca take her home.

Shelby's eyes opened at the sound of her lover's voice. She looked around the room, confused at first, then panicky.

"You're okay. It's just that you sucked up a lot of smoke, and your throat and lungs are not real happy with you right now."

Shelby pointed to Rebecca.

"Actually, I'm rather proud of you. And you proved to those jerks that you weren't the type to *cause* harm, but to protect from it."

Again, Shelby pointed to Rebecca.

"Sweetheart, I knew it *before* I ever asked it. I was just being an idiot."

Rebecca saw the muscles of Shelby's face move under the oxygen mast, smiling at the term of endearment. "Now what's that silly grin for?" Rebecca sat on the edge of the bed. You can't be happy about being in here."

Shelby slipped the mask away from her face. "Swee—" she croaked. She allowed Rebecca to help her with sucking on a few ice chips from a nearby cup.

"Oh, I get it. You liked me calling you sweetheart?" At Shelby's nod, Rebecca smiled too. "Good. Because I like it, too." Rebecca brushed the hair away from Shelby's face. She had tried to use a damp towel to get her lover clean, until a kind nurse took pity and loaned her a bar of soap and a sponge.

A knock at the door disturbed them, and Shelby looked to Rebecca, who shrugged. She walked over and opened the door, where a man in a dark suit stood. "May I help you?"

"I'm Deputy Jeremy Trotter, with the Brownyerd County Sheriff's Department. Is this the room of Miss Shelby Fisher? I have a few questions I need to ask her."

"As you can see, she's recuperating from inhaling most of the smoke at that barn. Can't this wait?" Rebecca crossed her arms over her chest and stood between him and the bed where Shelby lay.

Deputy Trotter stepped to one side of Rebecca. "I'm sorry, Miss—?"

"Starrett. But as you can see, she can't even talk yet. So if you'll just leave us your card, Shelby will call you back as soon as she can." Rebecca moved to get between him and her lover again.

"Miss Starrett, if you don't move, I'll arrest you for obstructing justice. Now if you'll behave, I'll let you stay."

A croak from the bed made Rebecca race over to where Shelby lay. "What is it?"

"Tough stuff," Shelby rasped. She tried to keep from laughing, but failed.

"Hush. You're going to hurt yourself."

The deputy came over to the bed. "I'm sorry to bother you, ma'am, but I have a few questions, then I'll leave, okay?"

Shelby nodded.

"Do you, or did you know, a Rob Sanger?"

Shelby nodded again.

"Did he have any reason to carry a grudge against you?"

Shelby shrugged, then nodded. She pointed to Rebecca, who filled in the blanks. "She means, other than the fact the sun came up? The man's a weasel. What's he claiming she's done to him, now?" Rebecca was tired of the stupid questions already, and they hadn't even started yet.

"Nothing. We found him in one corner of the barn, with a can of gasoline. We believe that he died of smoke inhalation, but only an autopsy will tell for sure. It seems like he wasn't a very good arsonist. Or someone wanted to make it look that way."

"He's dead?" Rebecca didn't like the man, but she hadn't wished death on him. "How horrible. You can't be suggesting that Shelby had something do to with him being in the barn?"

Trotter looked up from his notes. "I'm not suggesting anything, Miss Starrett. But you have to admit that since they were the only two in the barn, it does look suspicious."

The door opened, and a nurse poked her head inside the room. "That's all for today, deputy. You'll have to come back tomorrow. Doctor's orders."

Rebecca felt relieved, and Shelby looked tired. "I don't know when she's being released, but give me your card, and I promise she'll contact you when she can."

"All right. Thanks." He handed Rebecca a card and started to leave, but was almost knocked into the doorframe by Jessica.

"Shelby, darling! I came as soon as I heard." Wearing her rodeo finery, Jessica plopped down on the bed, causing Shelby to wince. "You really must stop doing such brave things, it's just not safe." She spied Rebecca, who was exchanging glances with the plainclothes deputy. "Who are these people?"

"I'm sure you remember me. I'm the one who beat your time at barrels," Rebecca explained just as sweetly. "And if you were smart, you'd get away from *my* girlfriend."

Jessica stood up, shocked. "Girlfriend? Since when?" She grabbed Shelby's hospital gown and started to shake her. "For God's sake, you fucking bitch. We're still dating!"

Shelby tried to fight off the crazy woman. "Never was," she forced out. "You wish."

Deputy Trotter hurried back into the room and grabbed Jessica. "Calm down, lady. You can't go around beating up on convalescing people."

"Let go of me, dammit!" Jessica screamed. "First Rob, now her. I can't keep anyone." Her screams dwindled to sobs. "He'd do anything for me, you know. Natalie's saddle so I could become queen, Andrea's gear, just a few of the things he did for me. He hated you so much."

Using his cuffs, Trotter quickly subdued Jessica. He began to quietly Mirandize her, but she continued to speak over his voice.

"Why couldn't you like me? I thought I was your type," she asked Shelby, who couldn't, or wouldn't answer her. "I loved you."

Shelby shook her head.

As the deputy led her away, Jessica began to cry again. "Don't hate me. I couldn't stand it if you hated me."

Rebecca watched them leave, then went over to Shelby. Her oxygen level had dropped almost ten points in the last few minutes. "Please be quiet for a while, okay? Let the good air do its work?"

Shelby sighed. There was so much she wanted to tell Rebecca, explain to her how she had changed. How she hated the old Shelby, and wanted to be someone that Rebecca can be proud of.

Rebecca kissed Shelby's forehead. "I think you're beginning to grow on me."

Those words meant more to Shelby than anything else she'd ever heard. She pointed to her own chest, then held up two fingers.

"You too, huh?"

Another happy nod.

"I think I like you quiet. Easier to keep you in line." Rebecca kissed Shelby again, then stroked her cheek. "Sleep. I'll be here when you wake up."

SHELBY WOKE AGAIN, and the lighting of the room had changed. It appeared to be dark outside, so she was pretty sure she'd slept the entire day away. Rebecca was curled up in a chair, covered with a hospital blanket. Shelby looked over at the oxygen monitor and was glad to see it was close to one hundred percent. Her throat still felt as if it was on fire, and she could swear that someone was standing on her chest. But seeing the woman in the chair next to her bed made everything better. *Life is good.*

She thought about what happened earlier in the day. Hearing Jessica admit to being behind all the problems and of using Rob to do her dirty work had made Shelby feel sick inside. *I used her like I used so many, and it came back and bit me on the ass. I need to tell Rebecca about her.*

"You're thinking pretty hard about something," Rebecca's voice drifted through the room. "I hope it's a good thing, and it's me."

Shelby looked at the lovely face she had dreamed about. *We'll talk, but not right now. She looks so tired.* "I dreamed about you."

"Good dreams, or nightmares?"

"Good."

Rebecca smiled. "Then that's all that matters, right?"

Shelby grinned. Before she could say anything else, a nurse walked into the room. "Look who's awake. Let me go notify the doctor, and she'll be right in to check on you." She checked Shelby's vitals then patted her shoulder.

Rebecca sat on the edge of Shelby's bed and held her hand. "Is there anything I can get you?"

"Out?"

"Not yet. Try again."

The door opened again, and a petite, dark-haired woman stepped into the room. "Hi, I'm Dr. Wong. My nurse seems to think you're doing better, Ms. Fisher."

"Shelby."

"My, that's a lovely croak you have there, Shelby. Mind if I have a look inside?" The doctor took out her light and shined it down Shelby's throat, then up her nose. "Ouch. You're going to be sounding a bit hoarse for a few days, and I want to run one more set of blood tests. But barring anything major, I think we'll let you leave our fine establishment tomorrow."

"Great."

Rebecca stood and held out her hand. "Thank you for taking such good care of her, Dr. Wong."

"I think I should be saying that to you." The doctor left the room.

"Cute blush," Shelby croaked, teasing her lover. "Need a picture."

Rebecca shook her head. "Oh, no you don't." She covered her face with her hands.

"Beautiful," Shelby uttered, this time totally serious.

"What kind of drugs do they have you on?"

Shelby shook her head. "You."

The blush deepened, and Rebecca moved to sit next to Shelby again. "You are a sweet talker, Shelby Fisher. I can see I'm going to have to keep my eye on you."

Chapter Nine

THE NEXT MORNING, Rebecca came into the room waving the local newspaper around. "I found this in the cafeteria," she announced. "You are officially a hero."

"What?" Shelby glared at her, but couldn't keep the interest from her features.

"'Champion Bull Rider Saves Animals,'" Rebecca read out loud.

"Bullshit."

"No, it says it right here." When Shelby shook her head again, Rebecca had to disagree. "I'm sorry, but it's right. You *are* a hero." There was an old publicity picture of Shelby in the paper, showing her accepting congratulations from some older man.

"No. And I'm no champion, either." The ice chips helped, so Shelby continued to suck on them as they spoke.

"Maybe not this time, but I bet you were once, right?" Rebecca refused to let it go.

Shelby sighed. "Ten years ago, maybe. I think I still have the buckle somewhere. But it didn't last. Told you I wasn't any good."

Rebecca got an evil smirk on her face. "I beg to differ with you, my dear. You're *very* good. And not just at riding bulls."

Now it was Shelby's turn to blush. Before she could reply, a timid knock on the door interrupted them.

"Come in," Rebecca answered.

The door opened, and an older woman came into the room. "Shelby? Is that really you?" Her light brown hair was liberally streaked with gray, and she looked much older than she was. Her teeth and fingers were stained with nicotine, and her voice was rough and raspy from too many years of alcohol abuse. Weary eyes were red-rimmed, and her whole demeanor was of someone who had been beaten down for too many years.

Shelby studied her, and realized it was the same woman

from the carnival the night before the fire. "Vivian?"

"I'm your mother, couldn't you call me that?" Vivian stepped further into the room. "It's been so many years, baby. God, how I wish I could go back in time and change a lot of things." Her voice cracked.

"Don't," Raising her voice caused Shelby's throat to burn, so she chewed some ice for a moment. "You left me."

Vivian looked over at Rebecca, who rose as if to leave. "Maybe I should—"

"Stay," Shelby begged, holding out her hand to her lover. "Please?"

Rebecca gave Vivian an apologetic look, but took Shelby's hand and sat beside her on the bed.

"Why did you run off?" Shelby asked Vivian.

Vivian looked around the room as she took a seat in the only chair in the room. "I had to. Your father was a mean drunk. Sooner or later, one or both of us would have ended up dead, and where would that have left you?"

"The same as it already did. With one parent." Shelby coughed, then took a few more ice chips into her mouth.

"I've tried to follow you all these years, you know. I've rarely missed a rodeo. You're a lot better than your father ever was." She raised a hand to her hair, and Shelby saw it was shaking. "It's not been easy, but I've watched you."

Shelby shook her head. "But why didn't you take me with you?"

Vivian looked down at the floor. "I was afraid of failing you. At least your father could ride for a living, but I had no skills. My family disowned me when I married your father. And I sold off my horse and tack when we got married."

"What about when he died?"

"You went to live with your aunt. I didn't want to change that. She was much better for you than I could have been. At least she had a real home to give to you."

"I was fucking twelve," Shelby yelled, then instantly regretted it. She grabbed her throat in agony, and coughed uncontrollably.

Rebecca soothed Shelby, then told Vivian, "I think you need to leave."

Vivian looked at her, with an irritated look on her face. "Who are you?"

"Her girlfriend."

"I don't think so." Vivian glared at Rebecca, then looked at her daughter. "My daughter is not like *that*. And you have no right to tell me what to do."

"She is." Shelby whispered. "And I am. Now get out, and don't come back. My mother died when I was six." She rolled over, turning her back on Vivian and effectively ending the conversation.

"IT'S JUST FOR a few days," Rebecca pleaded. "I've already talked to my boss." It was already after noon that same day, and they had been arguing with Shelby for over an hour.

"Not to mention it's the only way I'm letting you out of here," Dr. Wong added. "Although the blood tests came back clear, I want you to have someone around in case your lungs fill with fluid."

Shelby rolled her eyes. She *did* feel better, but silently agreed that she'd do whatever it took to get out of the hospital. "Okay."

"Stubborn woman," Rebecca whispered in her ear. "I promise not to smother you."

She was so close, that Shelby was tempted to steal a kiss. But she wasn't sure how the doctor would react, and the woman had treated them both with respect and kindness. "I know," she whispered instead.

"Now, if you're through throwing your fit, I'll sign your release papers." Dr. Wong filled out the necessary forms and handed copies to Rebecca. "Make sure she stays in bed for a few days."

"I sure will," Rebecca answered, then blushed when Shelby laughed. "I mean, I'll take good care of her."

Shelby laughed again, and was slapped on the leg for her trouble. "Not my fault."

The doctor started to leave the room. "Just don't overdo it," she ordered, just as the door closed behind her.

Both women blushed.

"I HOPE YOU don't mind, Shelby, but my boss drove your truck and trailer out to the stables. They were closing down the fairgrounds, and it had to be moved. The biggest I've ever pulled is a two-horse trailer, and I didn't want anything to go wrong." Rebecca chatted nervously, still not knowing why she volunteered to take care of a woman she had just met a couple of weeks previously. *And already slept with*, a little voice inside her head reminded her. Rebecca didn't know what had come over her. She never did anything rashly, but that's all she seemed to do around Shelby.

Shelby watched the passing scenery go by. "I'm sure it's fine." She looked at Rebecca. "Thanks again for springing me from the hospital. But you don't have to babysit. I won't tell if you won't."

"Sorry, I gave my word to Dr. Wong, so that means you're stuck with me."

"I feel just fine. No sense in going to all this trouble for nothing." Shelby cleared her throat. "I sure could use a cigarette about now, though."

Rebecca glanced at her passenger. "Nope. Doctor's orders there, too. You'll just have to do without for a while."

"Is that all I have to do without?"

"Shelby." Rebecca blushed again. "Is that all you think about?"

"Around you, it's pretty close." Shelby settled back against the seat and quieted. Rebecca drove her car through an open gate. When the graveled road forked, she took the left but pointed to the right. "The main house is up that way about half a mile. I like having the privacy of the barns, if you want to know the truth." In another minute of so, they could see Shelby's truck and trailer parked beside a two-story barn. "Mr. Lockneer just ran an extension cable out from the barn to your trailer, I hope that's okay."

"That's more than I have sometimes," Shelby said. "There've been plenty of times when I've had to make do with an ice chest for perishables and bottled water to drink. Is there someplace I can take the trailer to empty out the tank, like a campground?"

"Mr. Lockneer took care of it on his way out here. He didn't think you'd be up to doing it for yourself for a while."

"Wow. I don't know what to say. He didn't have to do that."

"It wasn't a problem. I think he was impressed with the newspaper accounts of your heroism in the stable fire." Rebecca parked her car next to Shelby's trailer. "If you'd like to get cleaned up, you're more than welcome to use my bathroom. I've got a shower/tub combo, so you can do whatever your heart desires."

"Taking you into my trailer and having my way with you is what I desire. But I don't think either one of us is up to that right now."

Rebecca reached over and caressed Shelby's face. "I think you're right, although it sounds really good. How about you come upstairs with me, get cleaned up, and then you can get some rest?"

"Okay." Shelby got out of the car on her own and followed Rebecca into the barn, to the entrance of her apartment. They climbed a set of stairs until Rebecca opened a heavy wooden door.

Turning on the light, Rebecca hoped that she had picked up everything before she left. Looking around, she was glad to see the apartment was in decent shape, although it could use a quick dusting and sweeping. "Disregard the dust rabbits. The bunnies grew."

Shelby laughed. "At least your place is big enough for them. Mine fight for space under the bed."

Rebecca looked around the apartment as Shelby was surveying it. It would probably be small by other standards, but it looked huge to her after seeing Shelby's tiny trailer. The living room, dining room and kitchen were all in the same main room. Worn but well-taken care of furniture complemented the room, which was made bright by two sets of windows along one wall. A small desk sat in the corner, on which a dark monitor sat. Two doors, both currently closed, led to the bedroom and bathroom.

Shelby said, "This is really nice."

"Thanks. The price is right, and I get to be around horses all the time, which is another plus." Rebecca opened one door. "Here's the bathroom, so feel free to borrow it at any time. Just bring it back when you're done."

"Funny." Shelby crossed the room as if to check out the bath. She took Rebecca in her arms and held her close. "Thanks for all that you're doing for me. I don't know what I did to deserve it, but I appreciate it."

Rebecca melted into the embrace. "You're welcome." She stepped back. "Come to bed with me. Your trailer is safe downstairs, and I'll make sure you're safe up here."

Shelby couldn't argue the point. She wordlessly followed Rebecca into the darkened bedroom and allowed her lover to strip and help her into bed. She barely felt Rebecca's nude form next to hers before she was sound asleep.

Chapter Ten

THREE DAYS LATER Shelby perched on a bale of hay and watched Rebecca feed the Lockneer horses. "Are you sure I can't help you with that?"

"I'm used to it. But, if you want to go upstairs and start breakfast, I wouldn't mind."

Shelby laughed. "Sure, what do you want? Fruit Loops or Frosted Flakes?"

Rebecca patted Patches, her last horse to feed, and stepped out of the stall. "Don't tell me you can't cook."

"You've seen my kitchen. Just how much cooking do you think I'm able to do in there? I have to go outside to use the can opener."

"Fair enough. Let me get cleaned up, and I'll show you some basics around the kitchen."

Shelby followed Rebecca back upstairs, and watched as she made them a breakfast of scrambled eggs, sausage and toast. "That's all there is to it? I thought it would be harder than that." They took their places at the two person kitchen table.

"Nope. Well, it can be more difficult if you try harder recipes, but I've got pretty simple tastes." Rebecca took a forkful of food into her mouth and chewed.

"You must, since you took me in," Shelby teased. Seeing the look on Rebecca's face, she tried to backpedal. "I was teasing."

Rebecca put her fork down. "That's not funny. You're not simple at all. What do you plan on doing while I'm at work today?"

Relieved that she hadn't ruined their breakfast, Shelby swallowed her food before speaking. "I thought I'd study that stuff you printed for me last night." Now that Rebecca had talked her into going for her diploma, Shelby was determined to make her proud.

"That's a good idea. Is there anything you'd like for me to bring home for you today?"

"Just you," Shelby replied, leaning over and kissing Rebecca. She soon had her hands all over Rebecca's body and pulled her shirt free from her pants.

Rebecca scooted her chair around so she could reach Shelby better and ended up practically in her lover's lap. When she broke away from the kiss, she gasped, "If we keep this up, I'll never make it to work on time."

"How much time do you have?"

"I should have left five minutes ago." Rebecca stood up on shaky legs and adjusted her clothes. "Remind me to get up earlier to take care of the horses, and we can have a little bit more time together in the mornings."

Shelby stood and cleared away the dishes from the table. "Or, you can let me help and we can be done in half the time."

"That's an even better idea," Rebecca agreed. She picked up her purse and kissed Shelby lightly on the lips. "I'll be home around six-thirty. If you want, set out some steaks, and I'll cook them up when I get home."

"Do you have a grill? Because that's one thing I *can* cook on."

Rebecca reached up and brushed Shelby's jaw with the back of her knuckles. "It's nice to see you look happy. The grill is in the storage room of the barn. There should still be some charcoal left over from the last time I cooked on it. I'll even bring you some beer to go with it."

"You don't have to."

"I know, but I want to. Besides, beer is good with steak." Rebecca kissed Shelby again, this time a little longer. "I've really got to go."

Shelby watched her leave, then spent some time washing the dishes. Then she went out to the barn, found the grill, and wheeled it out by her trailer to clean it up. She was scrubbing vigorously with a wire brush when a Lincoln Town car drove up and parked nearby. The man who climbed out was in his late fifties and had a friendly smile on his face. "If you're looking for Rebecca, I'm afraid she's gone to work," Shelby told him.

"Actually, I came here to talk to you."

"Me? I don't understand."

The man put his hands in the front pockets of his pressed khaki slacks. "I'm Walter Lockneer."

Oh. Shelby wiped her hand on her pants and edged around the grill to hold out her hand. "It appears I owe you a thank you, Mr. Lockneer. Rebecca told me you brought my trailer out here for me. I appreciate it."

"No thanks are necessary, Miss Fisher." He shook her hand

and looked around. "But I may have a proposition for you."

I should have known. No one wants to give anything away for free. "Call me Shelby. What is it I can do for you, Mr. Lockneer?"

"You can wipe the wary look off your face. It's nothing like what you're thinking, I'm sure. My proposition has to do with what's going on here."

"Which is?"

"Well, if you're anything like me, you don't like to just sit around doing nothing. Am I right?"

Shelby nodded.

"I'm building another barn just behind this one and will be buying about a dozen more horses. Are you as good with animals as Rebecca says you are?"

"I don't know, since I'm not sure what she's said. But, I like them, if that helps."

He jingled the change in his pocket. "That helps a lot, Shelby. I thought you might want to work here, for a while. I'm offering you a job. What do you think? The pay won't be that great, but you'll get free use of the electricity, and I'll have another apartment built over the new barn."

The prospect of having a steady job almost scared Shelby. Getting up every day and doing the same thing, at the same place? She didn't know if she had it in her. "Can I think about it, Mr. Lockneer?"

"Certainly." He pulled a card from his wallet. "Just give me a call and let me know. You can use Rebecca's phone, I'm sure."

"Thanks." Shelby watched him leave, then sat back and thought hard about her future.

ON THE FOLLOWING day, since she was feeling better, Shelby decided she needed to go into town and talk about the fire to the Brownyerd County law enforcement personnel. She called and made an appointment with Deputy Trotter. Rebecca insisted on driving her, partly because she wanted to make certain Shelby didn't end up in jail for something she didn't do. The ride into Somerville was a quiet one, both women thinking about what the day's revelations could bring.

Once they were parked in front of the building that housed the sheriff's department, Shelby was stopped from getting out of the car by Rebecca's hand on her arm. "Let me come in with you."

"Why? I'm sure it's just routine questions. It's not like I'm guilty of anything."

"We both know that, but I don't think they're too sure about it."

Shelby shrugged. "Well, okay. But we'll probably get in there, and he'll just want me to sign some papers or something. I just wanted to save you the trouble."

Once they were inside, a woman directed them to a couple of chairs at the deputy's desk. A clerk and dispatcher sat toward the other end of the room along with another deputy who seemed to be typing a report on the computer. Deputy Trotter was nowhere to be seen, but she assured them she'd let him know they were there.

The deputy arrived a few minutes later. Unlike the visit at the hospital when he was in plainclothes, this time he wore a uniform. "Sorry I wasn't here when you arrived." He looked at Rebecca, perplexed, then to Shelby. "She's not your lawyer, right?"

"No, just a friend."

"That's what I gathered at the hospital, but I thought I better be certain."

Shelby leaned back in her chair. "Do I *need* a lawyer?"

"Of course not. With the confession I already have, there are just a few more questions I need to ask you before I close this case out." He looked to Rebecca. "If you want, there's a nice break room just down the hall. I'm sure all of this will bore you."

Rebecca smiled sweetly at him. "That's all right. I'm perfectly comfortable here. Besides, I was outside the barn that night, you know, and I can answer any questions you might have from that point of view."

"Fine." Shuffling through some papers, Trotter looked up at Shelby. "Ms. Fisher, the fire report says that you were in the barn for several minutes during the fire, is that correct?"

"Yes. I was trying to get as many animals out as possible. Luckily, the fire was set away from the pens, and I was able to reach a lot of them."

"Did you see the deceased while you were in there?"

Shelby shrugged her shoulders. "No, the smoke was so thick, I was lucky to find and release the animals."

The deputy scribbled something down, then looked up. "Witnesses say you had more than enough time to disable Mr. Sanger before leaving the barn."

Rebecca gasped. "Now wait just a damned minute! She released almost every animal in there, at risk to her own life, and you're trying to blame her for that asshole's death?"

"Rebecca, please. Calm down," Shelby whispered, feeling the eyes of the other occupants of the room upon them. "It's okay."

"No, it's not. I've read the newspapers and seen the news

reports. *Deputy Trotter*, did you notice that the pens were on the *opposite* side of the barn from where they said the fire had started? How could she have been two places at once? Especially with the heavy smoke?"

He looked uncomfortable. "We're not trying to place any type of blame on Ms. Fisher, ma'am. I just need to get her account of the incident for my report."

Shelby examined his face, looking for signs of guile. She wasn't sure what to think. He seemed on the up-and-up . . . and yet, she still had a warning bell going off.

The deputy looked back and forth between Shelby and Rebecca, then let out a sigh. "Why don't I just get a few more timeline details, and I'll just have your statement typed up so you can leave?"

Rebecca sat back, pleased. "That sounds great. Right, Shelby?"

Shelby could only fight back a grin.

DAYS AFTER LOCKNEER'S proposal, Shelby still hadn't decided whether she was going to accept the job offer or not. She walked around the barn, wondering if she would feel comfortable staying in one place. The thought unsettled her.

"Penny for your thoughts," Rebecca's voice called.

Shelby turned and gave her lover a small smile. "Not much to pay for, to tell you the truth. I was just looking around." She wanted to go out and do something alone, but wasn't sure how she was supposed to tell Rebecca. "Do you think your boss would mind if I rode one of the horses? I'd kind of like to get out for a bit."

"I know of something we can do that doesn't require going anywhere." Rebecca moved closer and ran her hands up and down Shelby's arms. "Would you like to come upstairs?"

For the first time in as long as she could remember, Shelby wasn't in the mood. Now she had to come up with a way to break it to Rebecca, who seemed *always* to be in the mood. "Honestly, darlin', I just need a little time to myself. Is that okay?"

Just as Shelby feared, Rebecca looked hurt. She snapped back, "Sure. I'll just be upstairs, waiting for you if you decide you need some play time. That's all I am to you, aren't I?"

"Do you really think that? Because if you do, there's something seriously wrong." Shelby started to walk away but Rebecca grabbed her arm.

"Don't you walk away when I'm talking to you."

Shelby frowned. "What's your problem? I just need a little fresh air."

"Dammit, Shelby. I can feel you drifting away from me. What have I done wrong?"

"I'm not drifting. But I'm beginning to wonder why you're acting this way. Have I said or done anything to make you this clingy? This is a new side of you I don't think I like very well."

Rebecca released the grip on Shelby's arm and backed away. "I knew you'd get tired of me, I just didn't think it would be this soon."

"Baby, no." Shelby moved forward and pulled Rebecca into her arms.

"Then why won't you move into the apartment? I hate that you live in that little trailer."

"Because the trailer has been my home for a lot of years. I just want to take this slow, okay? But don't think I'm going to go running off just because I won't move in with you."

Rebecca cupped Shelby's face in her hands and kissed her. "Take Patches. She could use the exercise." She kissed her again, then turned and went upstairs to the apartment, leaving Shelby wondering.

AFTER THE ARGUMENT in the barn, both women tried to be more considerate of the other's feelings. Some nights they slept together in the apartment, others they snuggled up together in the trailer. Shelby told Rebecca it wasn't necessary, but her lover was determined to make Shelby comfortable, whether it be in the apartment, or Shelby's trailer.

It was on one such occasion they were awakened by a heavy knocking on the trailer. Confused, Shelby wrapped the top blanket around herself and opened the door. A man who appeared to be in his late teens or early twenties stood in front of her. "What do you want?"

"Do you know Rebecca Starrett?"

You have no idea how well I know her, buddy. "Why do you want to know?"

"I'm Terry Starrett, and she's my sister."

Now that he mentioned it, Shelby could see the resemblance in their features, although his hair was dark brown instead of red. "Uh, well—"

He studied the apartment windows. "She was supposed to meet me for breakfast, but didn't show. I tried calling her apartment, but she didn't answer."

"Who's at the door, honey?" Rebecca called from the bed.

Terry climbed the two steps to the trailer and glanced behind Shelby. "What are you doing here?" He turned and squinted at Shelby, wrapped in the sheet and still standing at the door. "And with her?"

Rebecca was mortified. This was not how she wanted to tell her brother about her sexuality. "Terry, wait. You've got to understand."

"I don't have to understand shit," he yelled. "I can't believe you're a queer."

Shelby grabbed his arm and practically tossed him from the trailer. "She'll be out in a minute," she told him, then closed the door. Turning back to her lover, Shelby moved to sit on the bed. "Are you all right?"

Still in shock, Rebecca shook her head. *This is such a mess.* She got out of bed and got dressed quickly, without so much as a glance Shelby's way. *I don't know what I'm going to do about this. What if he tells our parents? They don't even know I'm gay. I didn't realize it until a few weeks ago. Oh, damn.* She brushed by Shelby and closed the trailer door behind her.

Outside, Terry leaned against his car with his arms crossed over his chest. He looked as if he'd been crying. "So how long has this been going on?"

Rebecca looked down at the ground. "A few weeks." Even though she was older, Terry had always been able to push her around.

"And so you're gay now?"

"I think so."

Terry walked up to his sister and grabbed her arms. "You *think* so? Dammit, Becca, you'd better be sure before you tell mom and dad. This is going to kill them." His voice had continued to rise until he was yelling again.

"Why do I have to say anything to them for a while? I'm still getting used to the idea." Rebecca finally looked up into her brother's face and saw the pain and disgust in his eyes. "And quit yelling at me."

"I can yell if I want to. At least I'm not some sort of fag. Did she trick you into going to bed with her? Because if she did, I can take care of her."

"No, it was nothing like that." Rebecca looked at the trailer and saw one of the curtains move. "Let's go upstairs to finish this, okay? I'll make you breakfast."

He saw where she was looking, then acquiesced. "Sure. But this isn't over. Not by a long shot."

From her vantage point in the trailer, Shelby watched the two walk up to the apartment. She had heard the entire argument and wondered just where she fit in to Rebecca's plans, since she hadn't even been acknowledged after Terry showed up. Hurt, angry, and confused, Shelby lay down on the bed and cried.

FROM WHERE HE sat at the table, Terry watched his sister putter around her kitchen. He could see that she was on the verge of tears, but he was so upset at the moment he didn't care. "I still don't see how you can be," he found the words hard to say, "like that."

"I think I've always known, deep down inside," Rebecca tried to explain.

"But you've dated men. I've met some of them."

She stopped what she was doing and joined him at the table. "And I was confused. But I think for the first time in my life, something feels right."

Terry shook his head, still not willing to accept what she was saying. "You keep saying you think. Is it that hard to know for sure?"

Rebecca stood up and paced, trying to get the words in her head to come in the right order. "Like you, I've been programmed all my life to believe that anyone who wasn't the same as everyone else is wrong. So you'll have to forgive me if I'm still trying to get myself in the right frame of mind. I care for Shelby a lot, and she's been very patient with me."

"So she *did* seduce you?" Terry stood up to face his sister. "Get over it, Becca. It's just a phase, right?"

"No, it's not. And for the record, I chased her."

"That's sick." Terry grabbed Rebecca's arms and shook her. "You can't be a fucking dyke!"

Rebecca broke free and slapped him. She was surprised when he slapped her back. "Get out, Terry. I think we've said all we can on the subject."

"I'm sorry," he started, reaching out for her, only to see Rebecca pull away. With tears in his eyes, Terry went to the door. "I'm sorry," he apologized again, before leaving.

With her hand covering the cheek that had been slapped, Rebecca waited until the door closed before she began to cry in earnest.

THE SOUND OF Terry's car leaving brought Shelby out of her self-pity. She cleaned up the best she could at her kitchen sink, then got dressed. She waited for Rebecca to return to the trailer, hoping that her lover could offer some explanation for her actions.

When Rebecca didn't show, Shelby decided to go to the apartment to make sure she was okay. She climbed the stairs slowly, not certain what she would find. Shelby knocked on the door but didn't get an answer, so she opened it slowly.

Rebecca was curled up on the sofa, her muffled sobs still loud enough to be heard by Shelby. She was wrapped around a pillow, and her face bore a red handprint.

Shelby saw the handprint and growled. "I'll kill that son of a bitch," she vowed. "I don't care if he is your brother." She dropped to her knees beside the couch. "Shhh. Don't cry, baby. I'll take care of you." Shelby brushed the hair away from Rebecca's face, but was shocked when her lover moved away from her touch.

"Don't."

"Don't what? I just want to make you feel better."

Rebecca sat up and wiped her eyes with the back of her hands. "I need some time alone, Shelby."

Fear and hurt warred within Shelby. "How much time? Today? A week? Or would you rather I just leave altogether?"

"No. I just need to get my thoughts together. Just give me until tonight."

"Okay, then. How about I take you out to dinner? We can go into town and find a nice place to wind down."

Rebecca almost answered yes, until she thought about being seen in Somerville with Shelby. The woman wasn't overly butch, but with her short hair, style of dress, and mannerisms, it wouldn't take much imagination to know she was a lesbian. "I have a better idea. Let me cook for you, to make up for all of this."

"You don't have to."

"I know I don't, but I want to."

Shelby stood and put her hands in her back pockets. She wasn't stupid, and had a pretty good idea what was going on in Rebecca's head. "Sure. Then I guess I'll be going. Is it okay if Patches and I go for a ride? I think we've started to bond."

"Sure. She's probably enjoying all the extra attention."

"All right then." She went to the door. "I'll be in my trailer later, if you need me."

"Thanks. But I think I just need the quiet time to think." Rebecca hated being the one to put that look on Shelby's face, but her need for self-preservation was strong. She needed to come to terms with what her brother had said and done, and think about what her lifestyle change would do to her family.

THE EVENING'S DINNER was subdued. Very few words were spoken, although Shelby did her best to cover her hurt at being left out of Rebecca's life. "Patches showed me some interesting trails today. Seems she's been just about everywhere around here."

"What can I say? I like to ride." Rebecca went back to her meal, barely looking at Shelby.

"I didn't mean it was a bad thing, just—"

Rebecca cut her off. "I know. I'm sorry." She looked up into the hurt eyes of her lover. "I really suck at making small talk tonight, don't I?"

Waiting until she swallowed, Shelby shrugged. "Don't worry about it. You've had a rough day."

"It's still no excuse to snap at your every word."

Rebecca looked exhausted. It was apparent that Terry's actions earlier in the day had upset her terribly.

"That's okay." Shelby finished her meal and carried her plate over to the sink. She started to run water in one side of the sink when Rebecca called out to her.

"Don't worry about the dishes. I'll do them later."

I guess that's a nice way of saying, don't let the door hit you on the ass on your way out, Shelby. "Okay." Shelby faced Rebecca. "I take it you want to spend the night alone, too?" Although they hadn't made love every night, Shelby had gotten used to having someone to hold each night since she had come to the stables. This would be a first in their budding relationship.

"If you don't mind. I'm really sorry."

"Don't apologize. You have the right to sleep alone if you want to." *Well, you wanted some space, remember? It goes both ways, hypocrite.*

Rebecca got up from the table and crossed to where Shelby stood. "Thanks for understanding." She held the other woman's hands and kissed her, almost chastely. "I just need to get some things straight in my head."

"That's okay." Shelby understood all too well, since she had heard the same line from countless women over the years. "Just let me know when you need me, and I'll be here." She kissed Rebecca on the cheek and left the apartment, her heart breaking.

THE NEXT DAY, Rebecca was in the barn feeding the horses when Shelby walked in. She kept her back to Shelby while she did her chores, unable or unwilling to meet Shelby's gaze.

"Good morning," Shelby greeted, trying to sound cheerful. She didn't know why Rebecca continued to avoid her, but she was determined to find out. They couldn't go on the way they were for much longer.

"Morning." Rebecca didn't stop, but in fact made it a point to continue her work, edging by Shelby.

Shelby leaned against one of the stalls and crossed her arms over her chest. "Doesn't that tire you out?"

"What?"

"Going out of your way to ignore me," Shelby accused.

Rebecca stopped what she was doing for a moment and finally met her eyes. "I'm not. It's just that I've got a lot of things I need to get finished around here before I go to work, and I'm running behind."

Checking her watch, Shelby knew the lie for what it was. Normally Rebecca didn't have to leave for another fifteen minutes or so, and she hadn't seemed to have been in any hurry before Shelby walked into the barn. "What's going on with you, Rebecca?"

"Nothing." Rebecca stood in front of Patches stall and rubbed the pony's nose, purposely not looking in Shelby's direction.

"Bullshit." Shelby pushed off where she had been standing, and marched over to Rebecca. She grasped her by the shoulders. "What have I done to deserve this kind of treatment from you? I thought we lo—" she paused, taking a deep breath. "I thought we were getting along pretty well." Shelby's heart beat frantically in her chest over her near declaration of love.

"We are." Slipping from the other woman's hold, Rebecca ducked underneath Shelby's arms and stepped away. "I've got to go."

Shelby watched her leave, feeling a heavy weight in her chest.

REBECCA KNEW HER aloofness was hurting Shelby, but she was so troubled by her own problems that she couldn't see past them. She was busy tagging merchandise at the store when a voice behind her made her jump.

"Do you give discounts to obnoxious little brothers?" Terry stood with his hands in the front pockets of his pressed khaki slacks, looking very remorseful.

Rebecca wanted to stay mad at him, but it was almost impossible. "Are you going to yell at me some more? Because if you are, I'll have you thrown out."

"No." He went over to the rack of clothes and flipped through them, although he'd never worn anything remotely western in his life. "I came to apologize." When he didn't hear anything from Rebecca, Terry turned around to face her.

She hoped that the hug she gave him answered all his unasked questions.

"I take it I'm forgiven, then?" He met her eyes and waited.

"Not completely. But we'll work on it." She touched his cheek. "I'm sorry for slapping you. I never thought I'd hear you say something so hateful to me, and I was shocked."

Terry looked down at the floor. "So was I. I'm sorry for slapping you back. That was way out of line. But on the bright side, it took us nineteen years to hit each other. That's got to be a record for siblings, right?" They had always been extremely close, so their prior argument tore at both of them.

"Something like that. But let's try to break that record next time, okay?" Rebecca hugged him again.

"Okay."

She opened her mouth to speak, then hesitated, but he must have seen the unasked question on her face. Terry said, "I didn't tell Mom and Dad anything, just so you know."

"Thanks. But why not? I figured you'd run home and tell them all about Shelby and me."

"I had time to think on the drive home, and I realized that you were old enough to do what you wanted. But I think you should tell them before they find out about it like I did."

Now wouldn't that be entertaining? The idea of her parents seeing her *in flagrante delicto* with Shelby brought a heated blush to her face. "I know. But I honestly don't know how to bring it up. What if they disown me, or something? I can't lose that."

Terry shook his head. "Our parents have always been open-minded and understanding, and I've never heard either one of them utter one derogatory phrase about anyone or anything. What makes you think that would change?"

"Because they've never had to face it in their own house." She had heard and read stories about how other people's families dumped them after they came out. "I don't know if I can survive losing my family over this."

"Well, you won't lose me," Terry assured her. "I'm not much, but I'll always be here for you."

Rebecca embraced him again. "Thanks, little brother. I love you."

Embarrassed with the attention, Terry wiggled out of her embrace. "Uh, yeah. Me, too. I've got to go, okay? Just think about what I said." He left Rebecca standing in the store, a more relaxed look on her face.

ANOTHER DAY WENT by, and Rebecca still avoided Shelby. As much as she cared for the other woman, she worried about how her parents would take their relationship. She went into the barn to brush Patches where she literally ran into Shelby. "Oh. I'm sorry."

"Sorry that you almost knocked me down, or sorry that you've seen me?"

"Shelby, please. Is that really fair?"

"Fair? You're talking about what's fair? That's rich, coming from you." She watched as Rebecca took a brush and used it on the paint pony. "You've given that animal more attention in the last few days than you have me."

"I've had a lot on my mind," Rebecca retorted. "You could at least not jump to conclusions and give me a little credit here." She was going to say something else when the honking of a car horn interrupted them. "That's got to be Terry. He's taking me out to dinner tonight. Will you be okay out here?"

"Please. I'm a grown woman and have taken care of myself just about my entire life. I can handle one night alone." Shelby held out her hand for the brush. "I'll finish up for you."

"Thanks." Rebecca kissed her lightly on the lips and waved in the direction of Terry's car before she hurried upstairs to wash up.

The engine silenced before Terry got out of the vehicle. He strolled into the barn and watched as Shelby brushed Patches. Not saying anything, he continued to glare at her while she worked quietly.

"What's your problem?" Shelby asked, tired of being stared at.

He crossed his arms over the top rail of the stall and propped his chin on them. "You."

"Me? We've never even been introduced." This was another sore spot for Shelby. She thought that if she were sleeping with Rebecca, she should at least know her brother.

"That's just it. Before, Becca's always introduced whoever she's dated. But I don't know a thing about you."

Shelby wanted to knock the smirk off Terry's face with the brush she still held. "That makes two of us. She never talks about *you* to me, either."

Terry didn't rise to the bait. "What's in it for you? I think you're just using Becca."

"What would I be using her for? Great sex?" Shelby was glad that her words embarrassed the young man. "Well, there is that. Not that it's any of your business."

"I think my sister *is* my business." He examined the old

jeans she wore. "And you're never going to be good enough for her."

Shelby opened the door to the stall and closed it behind her, then went to brush another horse. She figured if she kept her hands busy, they wouldn't end up around Terry's throat. "That's not up to you."

Terry followed her and stood outside the stall. "Do you love her?"

The question caught Shelby off guard. She found herself thinking about it, but was unable to answer since she hadn't been able to voice her thoughts to Rebecca yet. She remained quiet, concentrating on brushing the dark coat in front of her.

"Maybe Becca will come to her senses soon. She always liked to experiment, and that could be what you are to her. That's why she didn't go to college, because there were just too many options, and she couldn't decide."

"Or maybe, unlike some people, she just didn't want to waste her parents money," Shelby snapped. His words had stung her, but she refused to let it show. "Besides, I know all about women who experiment. And I probably have a lot more experience than you do, or ever will."

"I'm ready to go," Rebecca's voice broke in. She was far enough away that Shelby was sure she couldn't have heard the conversation she was having with Terry. *And thank God for that. I was about to climb over the stall and kick little brother's ass.* Shelby gave Terry an insincere smile. "Have fun."

He mouthed the word *bitch* and went to meet his sister at the foot of the stairs. "I thought I was going to have to go up and bring you down."

Rebecca waved to Shelby from a distance. She didn't feel like getting into another argument about her relationship, and was afraid that anything she said or did would be misconstrued by her brother. She saw Shelby's half-hearted wave, and instantly regretted her actions, but her brother was already starting the car. As they backed away, she felt more and more despondent about the way she had treated her lover.

Chapter Eleven

SHELBY GREW TIRED of Rebecca's distance. They could be in the same room, yet Rebecca was far away. Rebecca treated her more like an acquaintance than someone she had been intimate with. They hadn't made love since the night before Rebecca's brother showed up, and, as much as she hated to admit it, she felt uncared for and thoroughly neglected. One day, as she sat in her trailer studying for her high school diploma, she got mad and threw the papers across the small space. "Fuck it!" Rebecca was at work, and Shelby decided to drive into Somerville and confront her. She was tired of all the games.

It felt good to be back behind the wheel of her old pickup truck. With the window down and the wind blowing in her face, Shelby felt alive and free for the first time in weeks. Even though she cared for Rebecca, she knew some things were going to have to change if their relationship was to work.

Since it was after the time that Rebecca usually took lunch, Shelby decided to look around the quaint little town, then just wait until Rebecca got off from work. She wasn't too sure where the western wear store was, but since Rebecca had said it was the only one, she didn't think there would be any problem in finding it. A small neon sign caught her eye proclaiming the building before her to be *Ron's Catfish Hut and Bar*. Lunch and a beer sounded good to her, so she pulled into the half empty parking lot.

Once inside, Shelby was led to a booth near the salad bar, and after the waitress took her drink order, Shelby looked around. The décor was cheap and the carpet threadbare where it existed, and she couldn't be happier. *Cheap and tacky suits me fine.* The smells coming from the kitchen made Shelby's mouth water, and she smiled at the waitress when she brought her beer. "Thanks."

"No problem," the blonde replied. Shelby glanced at the nametag on the woman's right breast. Sherry. She was young and cute, and gave Shelby the eye more than once during the course of the afternoon, and was even bold enough to sit at Shelby's table when she was writing up the tab. "I get off in an hour," Sherry said, after Shelby finished her meal. "The bar isn't really open yet, but since I work here, we can go in and have a drink if you like."

Flattered, Shelby was sorely tempted. She had a pretty good idea what the woman sitting across from her would let her do to her in the cab of her pickup, or even in the ladies' room, with nothing more than the price of a drink or two. Her thoughts flashed back to Rebecca, and she frowned. "Thanks for the offer, darlin', but I've really got some place to be."

"That's a shame," Sherry pouted. She took one of her tickets and wrote a number on it. "My name is Sherry, and you can almost always reach me either here, or at this number."

Shelby took the paper and casually put it in her pocket. She knew she'd end up tossing it in her trash can when she got home. From past experience, women who were that easy were never faithful. And no matter what else could be said about Shelby, she was always faithful to whoever she was sleeping with at the time. She looked at her watch, and decided that she had enough time to get back to the stables before Rebecca got off work. Suddenly, she didn't feel like confronting her lover any longer.

REBECCA WAS CURLED up in bed, an unread book by her side. She missed Shelby's presence beside her, but didn't know how to bring her lover back into her life, much less her bed. She was about to get up when her phone rang. "Hello?"

"Becca, hi. I hope I didn't wake you," her mother said.

"No, not at all. I was just reading."

Kathy sighed in relief. "Good. What are you doing this Sunday?"

Rebecca tried to think of something, anything, to answer to her mother. "Umm—"

"We'd love to have you over for lunch. You *do* remember where the house is, don't you? It's been weeks since you've been over. I've resorted to looking at the pictures on the walls to remember your face."

"Mom."

"Okay, so maybe it hasn't been *that* long, but it seems like it."

Unable to make up an excuse, Rebecca sighed. "I'll be there." She talked with her mother for a few more minutes, then hung up the phone. "Wonderful. Just when I thought things couldn't be going any worse."

SUNDAY MORNING, SHELBY was in her trailer sorting her laundry. She was thankful that Rebecca didn't mind sharing the washer and dryer which was located in a separate room in the barn, as it kept Shelby from having to go into Somerville to find a laundromat. She was just about to take a load in when there was a knock on her door. "Come in."

Rebecca opened the door and peered inside. Shelby had her arms full of clothes so she held the door open for her. "Let me grab a handful for you."

"Thanks." Shelby took her armful of clothes and headed for the barn.

"You're welcome." Rebecca followed, uncertain. Once they were in the laundry room she watched as Shelby stuffed her clothes in the washer. Rebecca piled the jeans she had carried on top of the dryer, and, as her usual habit, checked the pockets. In the last pair, she found a wadded piece of paper. "What's this?"

"What?" Busy adding soap to the washer, Shelby didn't bother to turn around.

Seeing the phone number and name on the paper, Rebecca felt as if she had been kicked in the stomach. "Who's Sherry?"

"Who?" Shelby closed the lid to the washer and turned around. "What are you talking about?"

"This." Rebecca moved forward and thrust the paper in Shelby's face. "Just what have you been doing while I'm at work?"

Shelby took the paper and looked at it. *Shit. That damned waitress.* "It's not what you think."

"Are you bored with me already? I know we never said anything about being exclusive, but—"

"Dammit, Rebecca, listen to me! I had lunch in town, and this waitress gave me her number. I never asked for it, honest." Shelby hated the begging tone in her voice. *I don't know why I'm acting guilty. I didn't do anything wrong.* "I think you're overreacting. I haven't called her, and I wasn't planning to." She reached for Rebecca, who yanked her shoulder away.

"Don't touch me." She didn't want Shelby to have the benefit of seeing her cry, so Rebecca turned her back on Shelby. "I guess all the stories I heard about you were true, after all." She fled the small room and raced up the stairs to her apartment.

"Rebecca, wait!" Shelby started to follow, but stopped. *I don't need this shit.* She gathered up the pile of jeans and went back to her trailer.

UPSTAIRS, REBECCA LAY across her bed with her face buried in a pillow to muffle her sobs. Even though she had been half expecting Shelby to break things off with her, she didn't expect it to be like this, or so soon. *Or so painful.* It took her a while to get her emotions back under control, and when she did, she realized she was late for her lunch with her family. *Great. Just what I need.*

She slipped from the bed and padded into the bathroom to wash her face. Looking into the mirror over the sink, Rebecca frowned at her reflection. *Did I overreact? Shelby hasn't given me any reason before now to doubt her word. I just don't know. From what I heard at the rodeo, she's always been a player. I can't possibly think that she's satisfied with just me.*

When Rebecca left the apartment, Shelby was no where to be found. Her truck and trailer were where they normally parked, but something seemed wrong. Knowing her mother would give her the third degree if she were too late, Rebecca decided to let it pass.

Half an hour later, Rebecca parked in front of her parent's house and turned off the car engine. She would normally be excited about spending time with them, but with everything that had happened in her life lately, she didn't know where she stood.

The meal was strained since Rebecca wasn't her usually chatty self. Her mother had noticed her mood as soon as she walked through the door, but didn't call her on it until they were alone in the kitchen, putting the dishes away after lunch. "Is there something the matter, Becca? You've been so quiet."

"It's nothing you could help with, Mom. I'm sorry."

"Don't apologize. I'm just concerned about you. We all are."

When Kathy mentioned 'we,' Rebecca immediately froze. *Did Terry let something slip about me and Shelby? He promised he wouldn't.* "What do you mean?" She followed her mother out of the kitchen and into the living room where her father and Terry sat watching television.

Kathy sat next to her husband on the sofa, leaving Rebecca to sit alone on the loveseat, since her brother had claimed the comfortable recliner for himself. "We just want to make sure that you're happy, living out there by yourself. It must get lonely at times."

"Lonely?" Rebecca looked over at Terry, who shrugged.

"Honey, all your mother is saying is maybe you'd like to come back and live here, until you can find someplace here in town. We just don't like you to be alone. To be honest, I've been concerned about you ever since the dinner after the rodeo. You seemed a little — I don't know — like someone who'd just lost their horse, not rode it to a rodeo ribbon."

"I'm perfectly fine with where I am. I've just got some issues that I need to resolve." Rebecca glared at Terry, who had almost started to say something. "Believe me, once I'm ready, I'll tell you all about it."

Kathy took Greg's hand. "That sounds more than fair to me, Becca. But just remember, if you need us, we're here."

"I will, and thanks." Rebecca relaxed for the first time that day, glad that the inquisition was over.

AT THE STABLES, Shelby thought about how Rebecca had jumped to the wrong conclusion, without even allowing her to state her case. The thought upset her, and she decided that maybe it was time to be moving on. "I've lived all these years without a damned diploma, and it hasn't hurt me yet." She tossed fresh hay into a stall. "Besides, pitchforks and shovels don't seem to care one way or another."

If she left now, she might be able to salvage her heart. Much more time around Rebecca, and she'd be totally lost. And when Rebecca broke up with her, like they all did, she knew it would hurt. But she couldn't help but believing that it would hurt less now than later. *She'll probably be ready for me to leave when she gets back, anyway.*

Shelby finished her work and cleaned up, then decided to hook up her trailer to the truck. She had already gathered up all her things from Rebecca's apartment, except for the shirt that she had loaned to Rebecca the night she had been attacked. She left that behind in hopes that it would provide a few fond memories of her for Rebecca.

It wasn't long before Rebecca pulled up to the stables and saw Shelby hooking her trailer to the truck. She came blasting out of her vehicle. "Where are you going?"

"I think it's time that I move on." Shelby disconnected the extension cord and wound it up. "You obviously don't trust me, and if I drive all night, I still have time to enter the rodeo outside of Houston."

Rebecca stood close by, her arms crossed over her chest. "Were you just going to leave without saying goodbye?" She followed Shelby into the barn as she took the cord into the barn.

"I'm haven't left yet, have I?" Shelby stowed the cord. "Look. We've had some good times, but I'm not the type of person to stay in one place forever. You'd have gotten tired of me sooner or later, anyway."

"Where did you get that idea?" Rebecca moved closer. "I care for you a lot, Shelby. More than I thought possible. Please don't leave."

Shelby wanted to reach out to her, but stopped. "It's not easy for me either. But I really don't think that mucking out stalls is what I want to do with the rest of my life."

"But being tossed around on one-ton animals is? Do you have any idea how ridiculous that sounds?"

"At least it's my choice." Shelby was quickly losing her resolve. "I need to get going." Her heart ached at the look on Rebecca's face, but she knew a quick break was best for them both. "I'm sorry."

Rebecca closed the distance between them and pulled Shelby to her, locking lips with her. Her tongue demanded entrance into Shelby's mouth, and she kissed her, hard. After a minute, she pulled away. "Tell me you didn't feel anything."

"I," Shelby stammered, then tried to look away, "I can't."

"You can't tell me, or you can't leave?" Rebecca raised her hands to caress Shelby's face. "There's something between us that you can't deny. Give me just a little more time."

Shelby saw the lust smoldering in Rebecca's eyes. She pushed her into an empty stall. "I can feel how much you want me," she whispered. Her fingers made quick work of the buttons on Rebecca's shirt, and it was soon joined on the hay-strewn ground by the rest of their clothes. Dropping to her knees, Shelby brought Rebecca's body closer, and kissed a path down her stomach and through the red thatch of hair.

Shelby put her mouth on her and felt Rebecca almost collapse. Rebecca barely held herself up by keeping her hands on Shelby's shoulders. She cried out repeatedly, and Shelby relished the exquisite torture that her tongue wrought. Shelby pushed two fingers inside her lover, and it wasn't long before Rebecca screamed her name and fell limp.

Shelby sank to the ground and sat in the corner of the stall. She watched Rebecca, who still trembled with the aftershocks of her powerful orgasm, and kissed Rebecca's hair and rocked her. *I hope you'll be able to forgive me someday for what I have to do.*

Chapter Twelve

THE NEXT MORNING, Rebecca rolled over in her bed only to find the other side cold and empty. "Shelby?" Not getting an answer, she flipped the covers back and strode nude into the living room, which was also vacant. "Are you here?" She was heading to the bathroom when she noticed a piece of paper next to her coffee maker. Rebecca crossed the room and took the paper in her hand, then shook her head in disbelief. "No. Please, Shelby."

Rebecca,

It's been great, but it would have never worked out for us in the long run. You're right not to trust me. I'd probably ruin it sooner or later. In order for me to get to the next rodeo, I had to leave early this morning. You were sleeping too good for me to wake you, and goodbyes are always uncomfortable. I hope that you can find someone that deserves your love.

Shelby

Not even feeling her legs collapse, Rebecca sank to the floor, holding the paper to her bare chest. Tears ran down her face as she looked unseeingly across the room. She didn't know how long she sat there. She was jarred back to the present by the sound of the phone ringing.

Getting to her feet, Rebecca hurried into the bedroom and picked up the receiver, hoping it was Shelby calling to say she was on her way home. "Hello?" Her voice came out weakly. She sat on the bed, exhausted from the emotional output.

"Becca? Are you all right?" Kathy always went directly into concerned mother mode whenever Rebecca sounded anything less than fully perky. "What's going on?"

"I'm fine, Mom. Just allergies."

"Right. And I'm the Queen Mother," Kathy said. "You can't fool me, you know. But if you don't want to talk about it right now, I can respect that."

"Thank you."

"That doesn't mean I won't ask about it later, though."

Rebecca rolled her eyes. *I know. And sooner or later, she'll get it out of me. She always does.*

Kathy cleared her throat. "Anyway, the reason I was calling, was to tell you that your Uncle Roger is in town, and he brought your grandmother with him to the house. I thought you might want to come over and see them before they leave tomorrow."

Rebecca thought about it for a moment. Roger was her father's older brother, and he took the responsibility of taking care of their mother very seriously. Although frail, the old woman's mind was still sharp as a tack at eighty five years old. Feeling she had nothing better to do, Rebecca was determined not to sit around the apartment and feel sorry for herself. "Sure. Just let me get cleaned up, and I'll be there."

HAVING SPENT MOST of the night thinking about her decision to leave, Shelby struggled to stay awake as she drove. It didn't help that the two-lane highway was practically deserted.

All of her thoughts were of Rebecca, and of how they spent the previous evening. Rebecca was like a woman possessed in the way she kept touching Shelby, not that Shelby minded. She smiled slightly in remembrance. "It's a wonder I can even walk today."

Her smile faded as the sun rose. "Guess it won't be long before she's up." Knowing it was the coward's way out by leaving before dawn, Shelby decided to stop somewhere for breakfast, and maybe a quick shower. "If I drive straight through, I can be there in plenty of time to sign in."

Luckily for her, the next exit held exactly what she was looking for. *Now if I can just get my mind off her, everything will be okay.* But she knew it would take more than distance to break the spell of Rebecca's hold on her heart.

She pulled her vehicle into the truck stop and parked, gathered up a clean set of clothes, and felt the cold air rush over her as she hurried inside the establishment.

REBECCA WAS HALFWAY into Somerville when the tears welled up in her eyes. Again. "Damn her!" She angrily wiped at her face. "This is ridiculous. I'm not going to let her get away with this." Rebecca exited the freeway as soon as she could and took the next turn around to cut back the other direction.

She frowned at her reflection in the rear view mirror. *What am I going to tell my parents?* Rebecca took a deep breath. "The truth. That I've fallen head over heels in love with a woman, and I'll do anything it takes to keep her in my life." She pressed harder on the gas pedal, determined more than ever to catch up with Shelby.

The sun was shining brightly off the blacktop when Rebecca's cellular phone vibrated on her belt. Not bothering to see who it was, she greeted the caller.

"Becca?"

Damn. "Hi, Mom." She had completely forgotten about her prior engagement. "I'm sorry about not making it over to the house, but something came up at work."

"That's funny. I thought the store was closed today. What in the world's going on?"

I guess it's time for a little truth. "I have to make an emergency drive to Houston." Rebecca mentally braced herself for the explosion, which, oddly, didn't come.

Kathy's voice was calm. "This has to do with why you've been so out of sorts lately, doesn't it?"

"Yeah. Sort of." Rebecca paused for a moment, then swallowed hard. "Tell Uncle Roger and Grandma I said hello, and I promise to get up to visit them, soon. Okay?"

"Sounds good, honey. Drive carefully, and if you need anything, just call us."

Rebecca felt tears filling her eyes, again. "I will. I love you, Mom."

"Love you too, Becca."

AFTER A LONG, hot shower, Shelby made her way into the twenty-four-hour restaurant inside the truck stop. She settled heavily on the barstool nearest to the cash register and studied the upside-down coffee mug in front of her.

"What can I get for you, hon?"

Shelby looked up, stirred from her musings. "Hmm?"

The waitress, whose dark brown hair was definitely *not* natural, appeared to be in her late fifties or early sixties. She wore an old blue uniform top, which had two deep pockets in the lower front. "What would you like? I imagine you want something to eat or drink, since you're in here, right?"

Attempting a smile, Shelby nodded. "Black coffee. To go, please."

"That's it?" The woman, whose nametag read Emily, leaned forward and studied her customer. "If you don't mind me saying so, hon, you look like you could use a good meal."

"I'm not hungry. Just the coffee, please." Shelby's appetite had disappeared about the time she left Rebecca.

"All right. Whatever you say." Emily went to get the coffee, shaking her head.

AS SHE GOT closer to the Houston area, Rebecca started to take every exit, in hope of either finding Shelby or at least coming in contact with someone who had seen her. At the latest exit, the truck stop looked like just the place Shelby would stop, so she parked her car and went into the restaurant.

"Just take a seat anywhere, hon. The menu is on the table. I'll be right with you," an older woman called to Rebecca. She held a glass coffee pot in one hand, and a dish towel in the other.

Rebecca sat near the door, and gazed around the room. People from many walks of life were scattered about the room. There were the truck drivers, most of them intent on the food in front of them, and usually reading a newspaper. Also, she could see a few early morning drivers deeply inhaling their coffee, as they tried to get ready for the day. There were even a couple of families partaking of breakfast, the parents trying their best to control the excitement of their children, as they awakened ready for the day.

The waitress stopped at Rebecca's table. "Sorry it took me so long. Do you know what you want?"

Rebecca rubbed her eyes and sighed. I guess I'll take a cup of coffee to go, please."

"Is there a sign somewhere along the highway that advertises our coffee?" Emily was confused by the sudden popularity of the swill she had to serve every day. People usually came in for a rest, and a good breakfast.

"Um, no. Why do you ask?"

"It's just you're the second person to come in this morning and order the same thing. I kept telling that slip of a thing she needed to put some food in her belly, but all she'd take was the coffee."

Rebecca leaned forward. She felt her heartbeat speed up at the possibility that the waitress had come in contact with Shelby. "Did she have short brown hair and deep brown eyes? How long ago was she in here?"

Emily stepped away from the table. "I don't know if I should tell you anything. The woman I saw looked pretty upset."

"We're very close friends, and had an argument. I'm trying to track her down so that I can apologize, and get her to come home." Rebecca just hoped that she didn't sound as needy as she felt. If Shelby was on the road ahead of her, this woman was just slowing her down.

The waitress studied Rebecca's face carefully. "That sure could explain a lot. It's only been about half an hour. She looked like she had lost her best friend."

"She almost did, and so did I," Rebecca said. She stood up quickly, tossing a five dollar bill on the table. "Thank you. Did she mention how much farther she had to go?"

"Nope. Just took her coffee and ran." Emily picked up the five and looked at it. "Wait. Don't you want your coffee?"

Rebecca was almost out the door before she turned around and smiled. "No thanks. Maybe some other time."

Emily was left staring at the closing door. "You run into all kinds in this business." She shrugged her shoulders and went back to checking on her tables.

THE FAMILIAR SOUND of gravel beneath her tires soothed Shelby's frazzled nerves. She could still picture the mistrust on Rebecca's face, and she continued to think about it right up to when she found the rodeo grounds and drove down the long entrance lane. After she parked, Shelby ran her fingers through her hair to rid herself of the memory. "Get over it. I was nothing more than a fling to her, anyway."

Shelby got out of the truck and slammed the door. She decided to set her trailer up later and went in search of the rodeo coordinator. As she stepped into the tin covered building, it took a moment for her eyes to adjust to the dim light. She was halfway past the stables when a hand grabbed her arm.

"Shelby, baby. It's been a while. I couldn't believe my eyes when I saw you come in. What's it been, two years?" The sultry voice belonged to a beautiful blonde woman, who was busy running her hands all over Shelby's upper body.

"I, uh," Shelby blinked her eyes as she stared at the woman. She had no recollection of her face at all. "Two years? I guess it's been somewhere around there." She tried to control her breathing as the woman took a handful of her breast and squeezed it. "Oh, boy." Shelby tried to step away from the determined lady, until she found her back against an open stable gate. "Shit." She was about to push the woman away until her lips were suddenly covered, and she relaxed into the kiss.

Shelby felt her nipples harden as the kiss continued. To push her advantage, the other woman maneuvered them into a stall and pulled the gate closed with her foot. She had Shelby's belt unbuckled and was on the verge of opening her pants when Shelby stopped her. Something didn't feel right. Shelby felt her body respond to the physical stimulation, but her heart was screaming at her to stop. She grabbed the woman's hand and pulled it out of the front of her jeans. "I'm sorry, I can't."

"You can't? What the hell's the matter with you? You were always ready for a little romp in the hay." The blonde stepped closer. "It was hard sometimes to explain to my husband where the extra hay in my clothes came from, as a matter of fact."

"Husband?"

The woman rolled her eyes. "Don't try to act all innocent with me. We *both* laughed about how incredibly stupid he was, considering he's the rodeo coordinator." She fluffed her hair. "You think he would have figured it out by now."

Lurlene. That's her name. Though Lurlene looked older and wore her hair differently, Shelby remembered now. She frowned at how this woman spoke of her husband and felt bad about her own part in their past deception. She couldn't believe how she used to act, not caring for anyone's feelings but her own. "I need to go register. I'm sorry I couldn't—" She wasn't able to finish her sentence. Lurlene reared back and slapped her with all her strength. Shelby stumbled against the wall of the stable, automatically reaching for the side of her face. "I guess I deserved that." She struggled to stop the ringing in her ears, waiting to see if she would be able to move away from the wall without falling down.

"Fuck you, Shelby. I don't know what's gotten into you, but you used to be a lot of fun." Lurlene left the stable in a huff.

What's gotten into me? I think a certain little redhead. Damn her control over me! Shelby pushed herself away from the wall and went back outside, not seeing the shadow that followed her.

REBECCA CONTINUED HER trend of taking every exit and asking if anyone knew about a nearby rodeo. Rejection after rejection began to cause her to lose faith in her plan. She looked down at her gas gauge and noticed she'd have to make a stop for fuel. When she went inside to pay for her purchase, she did her best to not take out her frustration on the teenage boy behind the counter.

"Do you want some peanuts and cola? We're having a sale on them this week."

"No, thank you." Rebecca searched through her purse for

enough money to cover the gasoline bill.

"It's a really good deal, and it's not as expensive as the food is at the rodeo."

Rebecca dropped her purse to the floor in surprise. "Did you say rodeo? Is there one around here today?" She ignored the milling customers behind her, who were probably all anxious to get their own items paid for.

"Yeah. Same one they put on every year." The young clerk studied her carefully. "You're not from this area, are you?"

"No, I'm not. But I am interested in the rodeo. Could you give me directions?"

One of the men behind her cleared his throat. "If you'll give me a minute to check out, I'll be glad to show you the way, Miss." He was dressed in faded denim jeans and a tan work shirt. The baseball cap on his head had seen a lot of years, and advertised what had to be the local farm equipment store. His handful of snacks looked like he was on his way to somewhere as the clerk described.

Finally gathering her wits about her, Rebecca picked up her purse from the floor. "That would be great. I'd really appreciate any help I could get at this point."

HER ANGER SHUT out any other sounds, so Shelby didn't realize someone was right behind her until she felt a hand on her shoulder. She spun around, instantly regretting the move due to her aching head and face. "Oh. It's you."

"Looks like someone got in a lucky shot," Henry said. He fished most of the cubes of ice out of his drink, then wrapped them up in a wrinkled handkerchief. "Don't worry, it's clean." He handed the makeshift icepack to Shelby and tossed the cup in a nearby garbage can.

"Thanks." Shelby grudgingly placed the offering on her cheek and winced as the cold began to draw out the pain. "I didn't know you were going to be here."

He hooked his thumbs on his belt buckle and looked around. "Well, it's going to be too cool soon for my old bones to be out and about, so I thought I take in this one as well as the one in San Angelo. After seeing you hauled off after the last one, I sure didn't expect to see you here."

Shelby looked down at her dusty boots. "Things change, Henry. I think being at these competitions is the only thing left for me to do. I sure can't do anything else."

"I don't know about that, kid. You can do anything you put your mind to."

The sentiment reminded Shelby of Rebecca's faith in her before their last argument, and it caused her to choke back a sob. "Yeah, well. We all know how much good that does me. Thanks for the ice." She turned and started back toward her trailer.

GRATEFUL FOR THE help of strangers, Rebecca parked her car not too far from where she found Shelby's trailer. She knocked on the door, and when it wasn't answered, decided to check out the main building. She was just in time to spy Henry giving Shelby an ice pack, so she ducked back outside so they wouldn't see her. Rebecca wanted to talk to Shelby alone so she decided to wait by the trailer.

When she heard the familiar footsteps on the gravel, Rebecca stepped out from beside the trailer and took in Shelby's appearance. "What happened to your face?"

Shelby stopped in her tracks, but quickly covered her surprise. "I met up with someone who disagreed with me on something. What are you doing here?"

"I couldn't let things end between us like that." Rebecca moved closer, until Shelby held up her hands to ward her off. "Please, come home with me."

"And do what? Hide away in the barn somewhere while you play the perfect little girl to your family? I can't do that, Rebecca."

Rebecca shook her head. "It won't be like that, I promise. I want to introduce you to my family, and tell them how I feel about you." The prospect scared her, but she was willing to say, or do, anything to bring Shelby back with her.

Hope flared in Shelby's heart, but only for a moment. She'd heard that line too many times before, and was tired of getting dumped on by every woman she thought she had feelings for. "I'm sorry, but it's over. Go home, darlin'. You're asking for more than I can give."

Rebecca grabbed Shelby's arm before she could turn away. "Don't you dare walk away from me."

"Excuse me?" It was the second time Rebecca grabbed her, and Shelby was really getting tired of the woman's theatrics. She looked at the hand that gripped her arm, then up at Rebecca. "Let go of me," Shelby whispered, anger coloring her face red. "I think you need to grow up, and learn that the world doesn't revolve around you." Shelby pulled away and climbed into her trailer. She closed the door, leaving Rebecca staring after her.

Before she could knock on the door to get Shelby's attention again, Rebecca heard someone chuckle behind her. She moved away from the door and saw a beautiful blonde woman, dressed in the usual rodeo garb. "Who are you?"

"My name's Lurlene. My husband is the rodeo director, and let's just say I saw enough of what just happened to know you and I are kindred spirits."

"Oh, um, hi. I'm Rebecca. So you know Shelby?" Rebecca asked. She followed the other woman to the barns where it was cooler.

Lurlene smiled. "You could say that. She seemed pretty angry with you."

"We had a misunderstanding, and I was trying to get her to come home. I don't think it did much good, though." Rebecca sat on a nearby bale of hay and sighed.

"Home?"

"She's been staying with me for the past month. I thought we had something really special."

Lurlene laughed. "You're kidding me, right? Shelby would never hook up permanently, especially with a little rodeo princess like you. You're no better than anyone else she's fucked, kid."

"That's not true. We love each other."

"Oh yeah? Then why is she here alone instead of with you?" Before Rebecca could answer, Lurlene waved her away. "Don't even try to pretend you love her. I saw Shelby when she got here. I could tell by looking at her that you haven't treated her any differently than anyone else has." She patted Rebecca on the shoulder. "Just leave her be, kid. She's better off alone."

Rebecca watched Lurlene leave and thought about what she said. Could it be possible that she had just used Shelby? Or that Shelby had used her? She didn't think so. But Shelby obviously didn't want her here, and she didn't have any reason to stay. Rebecca stood and dusted off her jeans. She wiped the tears from her eyes and walked back out into the sunlight, wishing it could melt the ice she felt forming around her heart.

Chapter Thirteen

REBECCA WAS SURPRISED to see Terry waiting in his car when she got back to her apartment. She had cried most of the way home and wiped hastily at her face to try to make herself presentable. When her car door opened, she felt herself practically pulled from the vehicle and enveloped in a massive hug. After a moment, she stepped back and looked into Terry's eyes. "Not that I'm complaining, but what brought that on?"

"I've been worried sick about you, Becca. When you didn't show up at the house, and I couldn't find you here, I thought something bad happened to you. And then there was the cryptic call to Mom. Did your pet leave?"

"Can we not talk about her right now? I want to go upstairs and get cleaned up." She headed for the barn.

Terry was right on her heels. "I know what happened. You got tired of playing 'lesbian' and sent her packing, right?"

"I wasn't *playing* lesbian, Terry. It's who I am." Rebecca tossed her keys on the table. *At least the trip back was good for something. I was able to clear a lot of things out of my head.* "Are you going to still be here when I get out of the shower?"

He shrugged. "If you don't mind. I can take you to dinner, if you'd like. Or we could go back home. I'm sure Mom has something left over in the fridge."

Rebecca returned from her bedroom, carrying clean clothes over one arm. "Whatever. I'll be out in a bit." She went into the bathroom and closed the door behind her.

Terry sat in the living area, looking around uncomfortably. *How could she suddenly be a homosexual?* The thought still disturbed him. He looked at the sofa he was sitting on. *Oh my God. What if they – no. Not out here. That's just too much to wrap my brain around.* The sound of the bathroom door opening caused Terry to jump from his seat. "That didn't take long."

"I didn't plan on being in there all night," Rebecca snapped. She brushed her hands back over her wet hair. "If you don't mind, I think I'll skip dinner. I'm not that hungry."

"Sure." He waited until she got comfortable in the chair opposite him. "So, what really happened to your *friend*? Did you run her off by changing your mind?"

Rebecca jumped to her feet. "I haven't changed my mind. I love her, Terry." She paced around the room. "I followed her, and she wouldn't listen. There's got to be something I can do to make Shelby realize that she can have a home here with me."

"A home? Are you listening to yourself? You haven't even come out to our parents, and here you are talking about setting up house with someone you haven't known for very long. Have you completely lost your mind?"

"Maybe I have. I don't know." Rebecca dropped gracelessly into the chair again.

Years of watching his sister get her way finally came boiling to the top for Terry. He leaned forward so that he had her full attention. "You know I didn't like her. It wasn't only the fact that she was a woman, but I think you can do better." He held up a hand to forestall any argument from her. "But I have to admit, I admire the fact that she didn't stick around to kowtow to the princess."

"A princess? What's that supposed to mean?"

"Think about it, sis. All your life our parents have given you everything you want. They've spoiled you. You wanted a horse, you got it. You wanted to learn to be a barrel racer, Dad hired someone to teach you. When you wanted a car, it was parked in the driveway for your twenty-fifth birthday. You've been handed everything you ever wanted on a silver platter, and the first time someone tells you no, you don't know what to do."

Rebecca slowly stood. Her eyes were blazing, but her voice was calm and quiet. "Get out."

"I didn't mean to upset you, Becca, but I think it was time you heard the truth." Terry stood and made his way to the door. With his hand on the knob, he turned and looked over his shoulder. "I know I'm the younger one, but I think it's time for you to grow up." Terry left and closed the door quietly behind him.

A FEW HOURS after she had last seen Rebecca, Shelby was scheduled to ride her first bull for the contest. Usually she could feel the adrenaline rush through her, but all she felt was dead inside. She ambled toward the gates, not really caring how she fared on her ride.

"Shelby, wait!" Lurlene yelled, jogging to catch up. "I saw

the first bull you drew. He looks like he'll give you a good score."

"I suppose." Shelby continued to walk, just wanting to be left alone.

Lurlene moved closer. "How about I give you a nice rubdown after the first event? I think I remember how you like them."

"I don't think so. But thanks, anyway." Shelby brushed Lurlene's hand off her shoulder. "I'm not in the mood."

"Now there's something I thought I'd never hear. Shelby Fisher not in the mood. Let me call the local papers. This is a bulletin."

Shelby glared at the heavily made-up woman. "Fuck off. I know there are plenty of people to keep you busy around here." She moved by Lurlene, feeling very tired.

Once she was in the chute and settled, Shelby began to wonder why she was there. There wasn't a part of her body that didn't ache, and here she was, about to do it all over again. The gate opened. Shelby hung on for dear life, her natural reactions to the twisting motion of the bull keeping her in place. Once the buzzer sounded, Shelby dropped to the churned dirt floor and picked up her hat, which had fallen off during the ride. She was not only surprised that she had stayed on the required time, but worried that she didn't remember one instant of the ride. She knew that it only took a momentarily loss of concentration to get her killed, so she counted herself lucky. *I'm getting too old for this shit.*

The long trek back to her trailer was quiet and lonely, and once again Shelby wondered at her decision to leave Rebecca. *I'm sure she's already on to her next game by now.* She stepped into her trailer and closed the door, the weariness weighing heavily upon her.

"HOW DARE HE!" Rebecca had paced around her apartment for well over an hour. "I am not a princess. I can't help it if my parents love me and want to show it." She went into her bedroom and fell onto the unmade bed. Rebecca reached across and grabbed the pillow that Shelby had rested her head upon. She wrapped her arms around it and buried her face, inhaling deeply. The slight, earthy scent of her lover caused Rebecca's tears to come once again.

Rebecca took a shaky breath and sat up, which allowed the pillow to fall beside her. Thinking back to the conversation with Terry, she couldn't help but sigh. "He and Shelby both told me to grow up." She looked around the room. "I'm twenty-six years old and living on my own. How much more grown up can I get?"

Rebecca was deeply upset by Shelby's rejection. But what distressed her the most? Shelby saying no, or the idea that Shelby might not return her love? *No, that just isn't possible. If I know anything, I know that Shelby feels something for me.* "I need someone to talk to." Rebecca stood. "I just hope she won't be too freaked out to listen."

THE HOUSE WHERE she grew up loomed from the angle on the street where Rebecca sat in her car. Most of the lights were on downstairs, so she knew it wasn't too late to call. She got out and left her purse in the locked vehicle, before walking up the steps. The heavy wooden door opened before she reached it, and she was suddenly face-to-face with her father whose concerned look was almost her undoing.

"Hello, sweetheart. How's my girl this evening?" He was surprised at the response he got, when Rebecca wrapped him in a bear hug. "What a surprise. Let's go inside and sit down, and you can let us know what's bothering you."

Rebecca followed her father into the living room, where her mother and brother sat watching television. When they looked up at her, Rebecca released a shaky breath. "Hey there."

Terry stood and met her eyes. He looked away with a guilty expression. "If everyone will excuse me," he said, "I have some studying to do."

"I'm so glad to see you, Becca." Her mother patted the spot next to her on the sofa. "Come sit over here." Once everyone was seated, she put her hand on Rebecca's leg. "Now tell us what's the matter. You haven't been acting yourself lately."

Her father leaned forward from where he sat on a nearby chair. "Your mother's right." His face went totally serious, and his voice dropped. "Are you pregnant? Or is it drugs?"

If the situation hadn't been so grim, Rebecca would have laughed. "No, it's not drugs. You know I'd never do anything like that. And I know for a fact I'm not pregnant." She looked down at her lap, where her shaky hands were fighting for dominance over one another. "I," her throat tightened, causing the next words to be barely audible, "I'm gay."

"Did you just say you're gay?" Greg waited until Rebecca nodded. He fell back against his chair looking sick to his stomach. "At least you're not pregnant." He exchanged looks with Kathy, who also appeared pale.

She removed her hand from Rebecca's leg, and instead

wrapped her arm around her daughter's stooped shoulders in support. "Isn't this somewhat sudden? How do you know you're gay, Becca?"

Rebecca faced her. "It's really not that sudden, Mom. I've been this way my entire life, but I've just refused to face it until now." Since her parents hadn't tossed her out of the house or started ranting, she felt much stronger.

"But you had a boyfriend in high school," her father protested. "And you don't look like a, uh. . ." He was unable to continue.

"Lesbian, Dad. And there isn't any particular way we look."

Kathy tried to keep her daughter calm. "We know, honey. It's just that this is a bit of a shock to us, that's all. How did you come to realize that you are, ah, gay?"

"I met someone." Rebecca raised her head so that she could look each one of her parents in the eye. "Her name is Shelby, and I think I'm in love with her."

Greg stood up. "I'm going to leave you girls alone to talk."

Rebecca watched her father leave, her stomach churning. "Do you think he's disappointed in me?"

"Of course not. He loves you, just as I do. But you know how guys are when you talk about mushy stuff like love." Kathy hugged Rebecca close. "This is going to take us some getting used to. I hear about it all the time, but you never think about it hitting your own house."

Rebecca laughed. "Mom, it's not the plague, or something. I promise it's not contagious."

"I suppose you're right. Now, tell me about this Shelby of yours. How did you two meet?"

"At the rodeo. She's a bull rider."

Kathy tried to remember the other women from the rodeo. Hidden beneath hats, very few of them stood out. Except some of the ones Rebecca competed with. "If she's not a barrel racer, then I don't know who she is." She stood and held a hand out to Rebecca. "Why don't we go into the kitchen and see what kind of goodies we can find? I always listen better on a full stomach."

THE PARKING LOT lights shone through her windows, painting the inside of the old trailer in a familiar glow. With her body stretched across the bed and her hands interlocked behind her head, Shelby's eyes focused on one point in the wall. She couldn't stop thinking about Rebecca—her touch, her taste, her smell. She remembered their last night of passion, when Rebecca had seemed insatiable.

Thoughts of their lovemaking quickly faded into her memory when Shelby tried to remember other things about her lover. What were her parents' names? Where did she grow up? Did she have any pets? All she knew was Rebecca's brother's name. And that was more by accident than anything else. Things had moved so fast between the two of them, they knew next to nothing about each other. It would certainly explain what Shelby was afraid of, that Rebecca used her just to see if she liked women. That revelation hurt.

Something floated up into Shelby's conscious thought. She couldn't believe that Rebecca would drive all this way if she wasn't serious. *Benefit of the doubt and a little bit of trust. That's what I asked of her, but didn't return it when she asked for it.* Shelby drew to a sitting position and ran her hands through her hair. "I need to talk to her."

THE EVENING WENT better than Rebecca had hoped with her mother asking good questions and Rebecca doing her best to answer them honestly. She explained how she met Shelby, and the way she'd chased the surly woman to befriend her. That certainly raised Kathy's eyebrows. Rebecca left out the sexual part of their relationship, deciding that it really wasn't her mom's business, and it was a little too embarrassing to talk about.

Rebecca sat on the bed in her childhood room and looked around. It was late, and her mother had asked her to stay so she wouldn't worry about her. Rebecca had agreed, especially since she felt she didn't have anything—or anyone—to go home to. She would go home early in the morning to tend to the horses.

Everything was how she had left it, old posters on the walls and bookshelves covered with remnants of her youth. Awards from school mixed with small items she had collected over the years, either as gifts or as things she'd found. Rocks that she once thought of as special took their place along side of music boxes, and a collection of sea shells sat next to an exquisite wooden carving of a rearing horse.

She tried to take it all in as others would see it. Yes, it was a nice room. She sighed. The few friends she had from school were either married with children or off to the larger cities with nice careers. Was it so wrong of her to want to work in the western wear store and live a simple life? Not immediately getting any answers from her tired mind, she stood to go downstairs. "Maybe a nice cup of hot chocolate will help me sleep."

SHELBY SLAMMED THE receiver down on the payphone. It was past three in the morning, yet she couldn't reach Rebecca. Her fears that something happened to her lover outweighed her anger. "Where is she?"

"Right here," a sultry voice called from behind Shelby. Lurlene ran her hands up and down Shelby's back. Having just finished some *business* in the office, she had seen Shelby come into the barns to use the phone and couldn't resist. A cowboy had slipped from the same room only seconds prior. "Are you here to take me up on my earlier offer?" She didn't even hear the cowboy leave the office behind her.

With the contact of the manicured fingers tracing patterns over her tee shirt, Shelby closed her eyes. She fought the strong undercurrent of desire the touch brought, and refused to turn around. "No." Her voice sounded weak, even to her ears. "Leave me alone."

"But you're trembling. I know you want it, sugar." She slid her hands around until they were at Shelby's waist. The belt buckle loosened easily, and Lurlene had no problem lowering the zipper then sliding one hand inside the waistband of Shelby's underwear. "We don't have to go anywhere, you know. There's no one else here at this time of night." She had almost reached her desired target when Shelby spoke out again.

"Stop. I can't." Shelby removed Lurlene's hand, then shakily zipped up her jeans. She couldn't, or wouldn't, allow anyone near her until things were cleared up with Rebecca, one way or another. Shelby turned and met Lurlene's gaze. "I'm leaving, and I don't think I'll be back in time for the rest of the competition. Let your husband know." She pushed by the other woman and headed for her trailer, deciding to take some action of her own.

THE KITCHEN DOOR swung open and startled Rebecca, who was almost finished with her mug of hot chocolate. She looked up to see Greg, who shuffled into the room. "Hi, Dad. What are you doing up so late?"

"I could ask the same of you." He walked over to the stove and lifted the hot water kettle. "Are you going to want more of this?"

"No, I think one's my limit."

Rebecca waited until her father had fixed his drink and joined her at the table. "I assume Mom filled you in?"

He mustered up a smile. "Yes, she did. It sounds like the rodeo was quite an experience for you."

She blushed as she examined his face for the animosity she had at first seen in her brother's face, but she saw no anger, no attempt to mask his feelings.

"So, when will we get to meet your girlfriend?"

At the word girlfriend, Rebecca's eyes filled with tears. "I don't know. I think I screwed it up before we got started."

"What do you mean?"

Rebecca recounted how she brought Shelby back to her place after the fire and that Shelby had stayed in her own trailer. She also gave him a little bit of background on Shelby, and of how she grew up practically alone. "It started out so well, and Dad, I was so happy. But then I got a little freaked out—freaked about what you would think and what would happen with Mom. Then Terry and I got into it, and I—well, I have to admit, I didn't handle it very well. I was afraid of what you and Mom would think. I treated her badly. I was a jerk. It's all my fault. Early this morning, she left. I went after her, but she told me to grow up." Rebecca looked up into her father's eyes. "Grow up. That's the same thing Terry said to me yesterday. Why is everyone telling me this? I support myself and live on my own." She leaned forward until she was in her father's embrace. "Why does Terry hate me so? He called me a spoiled princess."

"Your brother doesn't hate you. I think he's trying to help you the only way he knows how. Maybe that's my fault."

Rebecca leaned back so that she could see her dad's face. "How can this be your fault? You didn't know anything about this until tonight."

"I could never tell you no. Whenever you expressed an interest in something, I did my best to give it to you. I should have made you work more for the things that you wanted." He grasped her hands in his. "From what little I've been told about Shelby, she hasn't been given very many breaks in life. Have you ever considered what your relationship meant to her?"

"I'm not at all sure what it meant. She turned me away today. She was like a different person. But I know that's not the real Shelby. I think she's hurting like I am."

Greg watched Rebecca's face carefully as he spoke. "You told us tonight that you love her. Do you really?"

Rebecca began to cry in earnest. "More than anything."

"Even more than always getting your way?" He wiped the tears from her face with his fingertips. "No one has really demanded anything from you before, Becca. Cleaning up around the house, doing schoolwork, working for a paycheck—all that is pretty easy. But love demands a lot. Anyone who's been in love can tell you that." Greg took a deep breath to calm himself. He knew his daughter's feelings ran deep, but they always did when she focused on something, until she lost interest. "I'm willing to bet that Shelby left because you demanded too much from her, without giving anything in return. What did she ask for?"

Rebecca had to think about that for a moment. It was painful to admit the truth to herself, much less to her father. "My trust. She has a history, and I guess I kept thinking of that, instead of believing what she told me." Rebecca blew her nose on the paper towel that her father handed her. "What can I do to get her back?"

He looked at her sympathetically and started to speak, then paused. He bit his lip and seemed to make a decision. "I honestly don't know. But if you really do love this woman, then you'd better be willing to compromise on more than a few things to get her back." Greg stood and kissed the top of her head. "It's late. Why don't you sleep on it, and maybe things will look better in the morning."

Rebecca watched the door swing behind him. "I hope so," she murmured in the quiet kitchen.

Chapter Fourteen

IT WAS STILL dark when Shelby pulled up to the familiar sight of the Lockneer barn. She could see that Rebecca's car wasn't there, but she parked her truck and trailer in the place she had vacated just the morning before. Once that was done, she climbed out of the cab of her vehicle and took a quick look in the barn. Nothing seemed out of place, although the horses nickered their greetings.

"Do you know where she is?" Shelby asked Patches, rubbing the gentle horse's nose. She was butted in the chest and glanced down to see that the water bucket was nearly empty. "Looks like she hasn't been here for a bit, has she, girl?"

Shelby fed and watered each horse. By the time she finished, the sun was peeking over the horizon. She washed up in the laundry room sink and went back to her trailer for a clean shirt. The white tee shirt clung to her damp body, but she didn't feel the chill in the air. So as to not miss Rebecca when she returned home, Shelby decided to sit on the stairs to the apartment. It wasn't long before she leaned back and fell asleep, exhausted from not only the long drive, but the emotional toll the last day had brought upon her.

NOT ABLE TO sleep, Rebecca was up before anyone else stirred in her family's house. She looked around the kitchen, and realized that the house no longer seemed like home to her, but her parent's home. She wrote a quick note explaining why she'd left so early and placed it on the memo board on the refrigerator.

As she made her way through the house, Rebecca took it in with new eyes. The living room furniture changed every three years or so, as did the paint on the walls. Her mother was forever decorating one part of the house or another, yet left Rebecca's room alone. *I think I understand what everyone has been telling me. Even though I've been out on my own, my family has always made it very easy for me to come home. That's it. No more running back when things get a little rough. I'm going to stand on my own two feet from here on out, if it kills me.*

Feeling stronger than she had ever felt before, Rebecca took a deep breath and silently slipped through the front door, closing it gently behind her. As she did, she felt the door to her youth closing as well. It wasn't a bad feeling, after all.

The drive passed quickly and she headed back to her apartment to take care of the horses and for a long, hot shower. Her car made the last bend in the road, and the sight before her almost caused Rebecca to run off the gravel and into the trees.

There, next to the barn, sat Shelby's truck and trailer, as if it had never left. Upon closer examination, though, she saw that the truck and trailer were still connected. Rebecca gathered her wits about her and parked in her usual space. She climbed out of the car and headed for the open trailer. "Shelby?" When there was no answer, she stuck her head inside only to find the trailer empty. *Now where could she be?* Quietly, Rebecca stepped into the barn. She held one hand across her mouth to smother her gasp of surprise.

Shelby was stretched across the stairs leading up to Rebecca's apartment, sound asleep. Her head leaned unnaturally against a post that held up the banister, and her legs draped down the steps. Her arms were crossed over her chest, as if to keep her warm while she waited. Rebecca wondered just how long the poor woman had been in what looked like a very uncomfortable condition. She moved closer and kept her voice low, so as to not frighten her. "Shelby?"

"Mmm." Shelby sighed quietly and twisted, as if to get into a more comfortable position. Her head slipped from its perch against the post. Shelby jerked awake and tried to correct her balance before she fell through the horizontal slats of the banister. She sat up, which caused her to slam her head against the top rail. "Ow."

Rebecca quickly sat next to Shelby. "Are you all right?" She wanted to reach over and check her head for any damage, but pulled back. "I didn't expect to see you here."

"I didn't expect to be here, either." Shelby rubbed the top of her head for a moment, then faced Rebecca. "I realized that I didn't give you much of a chance to talk yesterday, and I wanted to apologize for that." She stood and held out a hand. "Do you think we could go upstairs and talk about it? I already took care of the horses."

"You did? Just how long have you been here, anyway?"

"A couple of hours, I think. I kept trying to call you, but your cell phone just rang and rang. Where have you been all night?"

"Why would you care? It seems to me that you dumped me, so I can't see that it's any of your business where I spend my time."

"I told you I'm sorry for that." Shelby dropped her hand back to her side. "I think if we talk about it, we can maybe work something out. That is, if you still want to." She moved as if to walk away, across the barn, and out of Rebecca's life once more, but she paused. "I know I'm no great prize, but I can tell you this, I've never stopped caring for you, Rebecca."

The thought that Shelby would leave again caused Rebecca to jump to her feet. "Wait." Rebecca held out her hand. "I think you're right. Let's go upstairs so we can try to work this out."

Shelby took Rebecca's hand and did not resist being led up to the apartment. She closed the door behind them.

Rebecca paced around the room, suddenly feeling awkward. "Um, would you like something to eat, or drink? I think I have the makings for a decent omelet, if you'd like."

"Sure. An omelet would be great, if it's not too much trouble." Shelby started to sit at the table, then stopped. "Is there anything I can do to help?"

"No, I think I've got it. Go ahead and sit down and relax." Rebecca gathered the ingredients she wanted for breakfast, and placed them all on the counter. "I can't believe you drove here in the middle of the night."

Now that she was close to Rebecca, Shelby felt all her inhibitions fade away. Her idea to let things go slow suddenly fell by the wayside. She stood, walked over to the counter, and wrapped her arms around her lover. "You're worth it. I'm just sorry I left without talking to you." She placed soft kisses on Rebecca's neck.

Rebecca stopped what she was doing and turned around so she could meet Shelby eye to eye. "I'm sorry, too. I should have trusted you and listened to you when you tried to explain things." She searched Shelby's face, seeing nothing but sincerity in her dark eyes. "Where do we go from here?"

Shelby leaned forward and kissed Rebecca tenderly. "How about after breakfast, we get some sleep? I think we could both use it."

"Sounds like a great idea." Rebecca stole another kiss, before pushing Shelby toward the table. "Have a seat. It shouldn't take me long."

After breakfast, and while Shelby took a shower, Rebecca decided to call her Mom and let her know of the latest developments. She waited impatiently as she waited for someone to pick up the phone at her parent's house.

"Hello, Becca? What a nice surprise. Is everything all right?"

"It's more than all right, Mom. When I got home, Shelby was here waiting for me. Isn't that wonderful?"

Kathy took a calming breath, so she wouldn't say the first thing that popped into her head. "I'm sure it was. Did you two work out your differences?"

"We talked all through breakfast. I think we share the blame as to what happened, and we're going to work hard on not letting the lack of communication split us apart again." Rebecca was giddy with relief, and was thrilled to have someone to share it with.

"That's great, dear. We'll have to get together soon and meet this friend of yours. How about dinner sometime?"

"Thanks, Mom. Give us a few days to get resettled, and I'll let you know, okay?"

"I'll call and we can make plans. Have a good day, honey."

Rebecca put the phone away, just as the door to the bathroom opened. She couldn't keep the smile off her face as Shelby strode into the bedroom, with a small towel draped over her shoulders, and another one wrapped around her hips. "Come here, baby. You're wearing too much just to be getting into bed."

Shelby dropped the towels and grinned. "Now that's the best offer I've had all day." She pounced on Rebecca, who squealed with delight.

WHEN SHE AWOKE, Shelby noticed heavy rain beating against the windows. She decided there was no reason to get out of bed, so she was content to run her fingers through Rebecca's hair.

"This feels good," Rebecca sighed, her head pillowed on Shelby's stomach. "I love touching your skin and feeling it against my face."

"It feels pretty damned good to me, too." Shelby riffled her fingers through Rebecca's hair, fascinated at the different colors of red. "I don't think I've ever met a redhead that hasn't got freckles somewhere," she marveled. And she had looked *everywhere* for them on Rebecca's body.

Rebecca turned her head so that she could look at Shelby. "I think it's because my hair is so dark red. Sometimes people actually think it's dark brown unless I get out in the light."

"I think it's beautiful," Shelby whispered, kissing the hair in question.

"You're biased."

Shelby laughed. "But honest."

Rebecca took a deep breath, hoping she wasn't about to ruin their afternoon. "I want you to do something for me."

"What's that?"

"Meet my family." She could hear Shelby's heart speed up, but the look on her face didn't change.

"Are you sure about that? I've already had a couple of run-ins with your brother, and he's less than fond of me."

Rebecca sat up so that she could see Shelby better. "He hasn't gotten to know you, and that's my fault." She brushed her fingertips across her lover's cheek. "I should have introduced you properly, instead of falling apart like that."

Shelby leaned into the touch, craving it as she would air. "I do have to admire him, sticking up for you like that."

"He was out of line. I'm a grown woman who is more than capable of taking care of herself. Besides, I'm seven years older than him. Who's supposed to be protecting whom?"

"You know how pigheaded guys can be. Just look at how they almost railroaded me at the rodeo."

"I know, and I was one of them. I don't think I can ever apologize enough for that, Shelby."

"Darlin', you have nothing to apologize for. You didn't even know me then." Shelby pulled Rebecca closer. "That's all in the past, so let's just forget it and move on, okay?"

Rebecca sighed. "Okay." But she knew that her guilt wouldn't go away just because Shelby forgave her. *That* would take some time.

THE CALL FROM her mother a week later was welcome. Rebecca had been feeling the angst of her family's distance the entire time, and not even spending every night in Shelby's arms could erase the pain. She was lying across Shelby's body when the phone rang in the early evening. With a sigh, she rolled over and picked up the receiver. "Hello?"

"Becca? I hope I didn't interrupt anything."

"No, not at all. What's up, Mom? Is everything all right?"

"Everything's fine. We were just hoping that you and your," Kathy paused, not knowing what exactly to call Shelby, "friend, could come to dinner on Saturday."

Rebecca mouthed the word *Saturday* to Shelby, who nodded. "Sure Mom, I don't see why not. Is there anything we can bring?"

"No, no. Just yourselves. We'll be having spaghetti, if that's okay with you."

"You know that's one of my favorites." Rebecca didn't know what was wrong with her mother, who had never sounded so filled with trepidation before. "Are you sure you're okay?"

Kathy sighed. "I'll admit I don't know how to act, or what to say. I suppose I'm just afraid I'll offend your friend."

Rebecca studied Shelby in the low light of the bedroom. "Just be yourself, and we'll all be just fine."

"All right. Then we'll see you both Saturday evening."

Shelby waited until Rebecca placed the phone back on its cradle before speaking. "I take it we're invited to your folk's on Saturday?"

"Yes." Rebecca lay down beside her lover and was glad for the comforting embrace Shelby offered. "Can I apologize now for Saturday? I have a feeling it's going to be less than fun."

"Your parents love you, Rebecca. That's a good thing. If they give me a hard time, just remember that."

WHEN THEY ARRIVED at the house on Saturday, Shelby and Rebecca were greeted by Terry. "Mom's been a wreck all day," he warned them, "and Dad's been really quiet."

"Thanks for the warning." Rebecca led Shelby into the old two-story home that her parents had lived in since they were married. It had belonged to her father's family, and upon their death was passed down to him when he was a sophomore in college.

They were almost to the living area when Rebecca's father met them. Shelby recognized the tall, thin man from the day she'd seen him at the rodeo.

"I didn't even hear you come in," he commented, taking his daughter into his arms for an embrace. When they broke apart, he warily eyed Shelby. She was dressed in creased jeans and a dark blue long-sleeved cotton shirt. With a rather obvious swallow, he held out his hand. "I'm Greg, Rebecca's dad."

"Shelby Fisher," she answered, shaking his hand. "This is a beautiful home you have here, Greg."

"Thank you." He led the way into the living room, where Rebecca's mom had risen from where she'd been sitting on the sofa. He said, "Rebecca and Shelby are here, honey."

Kathy crossed the room and wrapped her arms around her daughter. "I'm so glad you came," she whispered in her ear. She backed away and looked Shelby over. "Hello, I'm Kathy."

Shelby extended her hand, hoping it wasn't moist with nervous perspiration. "Pleased to meet you, I'm Shelby." Of all the people she wanted to impress, Rebecca's mother was top on her list. She had heard all the stories from her lover about how close the two were, and she didn't want to do anything to destroy that bond.

For her part, Kathy was impressed at how Shelby looked her in the eye, yet also seemed to never keep her eyes from Rebecca. There was a glow about her that spoke her true feelings for Rebecca, even if the two of them were careful not to touch too much around the house. "Dinner is ready, if you'd like to have a seat at the table. Becca, why don't you help me in the kitchen?"

With an apologetic glance over her shoulder, Rebecca followed her mother through a swinging door, leaving Shelby in the living room with Greg and a hostile Terry.

"I was surprised you showed up," Terry hissed, showing Shelby the way to the dining area. He directed her to the single chair on the opposite side of the table and took the space across the table, next to where Shelby assumed Rebecca would sit. "Can't find any rodeos to ride in?"

"Oh, the rodeo. That's right," Greg added, joining them in the dining room. He lowered himself into a chair at one end of the table. "I read about you in the paper, Shelby, saving all those animals from the fire at the barns. Tell me about what you do at the rodeo."

"Remember? I told you she rides bulls," Rebecca interjected, carrying a large bowl of pasta to the table and setting it down. She waited until her mother brought the salad before she went back for the bread.

Kathy took her place at the table, just listening to the conversation. She wanted to hear more from Shelby.

"That's right, bulls." Greg looked impressed. "That would scare me to death."

Shelby looked across the table at Terry. "They're just like anything else. You have to give them respect, then they're pretty easy to handle."

"Why would anyone want to respect something that is obviously not as smart as they are?" Terry asked. Rebecca came back with bread wrapped in hot tinfoil, and Shelby saw how Terry gave his sister an engaging smile when she quite obviously noticed the seating arrangement. Shelby bit back a smile when Rebecca picked up her plate and utensils and moved across to sit next to Shelby. Everyone helped themselves from the serving dishes and filled their plates.

Realizing Terry was talking about more than bulls, Shelby thought for a moment before saying anything. "Sometimes if you think you're smarter than a bull, you can end up in a world of hurt. I've seen it happen too many times."

Terry took a mouthful of food and hastily swallowed. "Maybe." He waited to see if his parents would say anything, and when they didn't, decided to continue his questioning. "Are you planning on going back on the road anytime soon? I'm thinking there aren't a lot of jobs around here for out-of-work bull riders."

"I haven't decided yet." Shelby looked at Rebecca, who was watching the whole discourse with slight dismay. "Actually, Mr. Lockneer came over a couple of weeks ago to offer me a job at the stables."

"He did?" Rebecca asked. "Why didn't you say anything about it sooner?"

Shelby shrugged. "There was some other stuff going on, and I truly forgot about it until just now."

Kathy dabbed at her mouth with a napkin before speaking. "Would you be happy in a job like that? Or is there something else you'd like to do?"

"I'm afraid I don't have enough of an education to do much else. But I plan to work on that."

The table settled down to small talk while they finished their meal. Once everyone had their fill, Greg and Kathy rose to collect the dirty dishes to take them back to the kitchen when Shelby volunteered to help. She stood up with her plate. "That was a wonderful meal, Kathy. The least you can do is let me help clean up."

"Well, okay. But you don't have to."

"I have to find a way to work off part of this great food. I see Rebecca got her talents in the kitchen from you."

Kathy blushed, but accepted the compliment. "Thank you, Shelby. And I can see you're just as full of it as my husband can be." But her voice was teasing, and her eyes sparkled with mirth.

"I'll help, Mom. Why don't you and Dad go relax," Rebecca offered. "The two of us will have it done in no time." She gathered what was left of the food and took it into the kitchen.

"I don't like her," Terry sneered softly, but loud enough for his parents to hear. "She's trash."

Greg glared at his son. "She seems nice enough to me, honest and straightforward, and she put up with an awful lot of intrusive questions. What's your problem with her?"

"They're sleeping together!" Terry yelled, pointing into the kitchen. "Doesn't that bother you?"

Hearing her brother's voice, Rebecca went back out into the dining area.

"Terence, lower your voice," Kathy demanded. "We have a guest."

"She's a dirty, two-bit whore who's lured my sister into her bed!"

Rebecca wanted to slap her brother again. "Terry, what is wrong with you? I thought we worked this all out."

"Not really. I just figured that once Mom and Dad met her, they'd make you come to your senses and quit sleeping with her. But now I find out that everyone seems to think she's Little Miss Perfect."

"No, son, we don't," Greg said. "But your sister is old enough to decide who to have in her life. I'm not sure I like the fact that she rides in rodeos, but only because I'm afraid she'll tire of the sedentary life, move on, and break your sister's heart." Greg looked at his daughter. "But we love Becca and only want her to be happy."

"I *am* happy," Rebecca said. "More so than I ever thought I could be."

"But she's a woman!" Terry yelled again.

"Who loves your sister with everything that she is," Shelby spoke up from the kitchen doorway. She blushed when she realized what she said, and where she was when she said it. *Not the most romantic place in the world, but it got my point across.*

Everyone quieted and stared at Shelby, who turned beet red. Greg, obviously feeling sorry for her, waved his hand. "Come on, Shelby. Let's go out on the front porch for a little chat." The two of them exited, leaving the others behind.

Inside, Rebecca stared after the closed door in shock. *She loves me? But I was going to tell her that, first.* She heard her mother say something. "What?"

"I was asking if you knew she was going to say that. But, from the look on your face, I'd have to say no."

"It's wrong," Terry reiterated, interrupting them. "I've had enough of this mess." He hurried upstairs to his room.

Rebecca watched her brother leave, then glanced at her mother. "What about you? How do you feel about all this?"

"Are you happy?"

"Very."

"Then that's all I can ask for," Kathy assured her. Seeing the tears well up in her daughter's eyes, she pulled Rebecca close.

GREG WAITED UNTIL Shelby was seated on the porch swing, then he leaned up against the railing so that they could look each other in the face. "So, Shelby. What are your intentions toward my daughter?"

"Intentions?" Shelby squeaked, feeling fear for the first

time. *He's not talking about marriage or something like that, is he? We just made it through our first fight. Not to mention we just started sleeping together.*

Greg grinned. "I'm sorry, Shelby. I was just teasing you."

"Thank God. I thought I'd have to run out and buy a ring tonight."

"No, you can wait until Monday."

"What?"

"I got you again," he joked. "There's something you're going to have to get used to if you stay around us for long, Shelby. We love to tease each other."

Shelby returned his smile. "I think I can handle that."

"Seriously, Shelby, I really do want my daughter to be happy. And this is a really big adjustment of all of us. Please allow me to apologize for Terry's outburst. That was uncalled for, and he'll be beaten within an inch of his life after you leave."

Shelby's eyes widened, then she saw the twinkle in Greg's eyes and relaxed. "To be honest, he's already let me know he doesn't approve."

"He's young, so please be patient with him. I hope he comes around."

"Yeah, me too." But she'd dealt with worse bigots before than a big-mouthed nineteen year old kid, and she figured she could handle Terry.

They sat out on the front porch enjoying a cool breeze and making small talk. She found out that Rebecca's father was an accountant, and his wife had her own home decorating business. After a while, she followed Greg back into the house, but came up short when she saw an upset Rebecca in her mother's arms. Kathy let go of her daughter, and Greg motioned to his wife to join him in the next room leaving a tearful Rebecca facing Shelby.

"What's with all the tears? Am I that bad a find?" Shelby asked. She rushed over to take Rebecca in her embrace.

"I'm just overwhelmed. Terry just threw a fit, and my mother—well, she's being really good about this. I just feel so emotional, and—and—and," Rebecca hiccupped, "I was going to be the one to tell you I loved you, first."

Touched that Rebecca felt the same way about her, Shelby raised Rebecca's face so that they were eye to eye. "As long as we both feel the same, does it matter?"

"No, I guess not."

"Good." Shelby kissed Rebecca tenderly.

Chapter Fifteen

SUNDAY AFTERNOON KEPT both women busy. Shelby shoveled out the stalls, while Rebecca rinsed them and then added clean hay. Both were hot and sweaty in no time, but Rebecca decided that Shelby had never looked sexier. The tank top that she wore with her boots and jeans clung to her body. Rebecca tossed a sprinkling of hay at Shelby, who spun around with an unreadable gleam in her eye.

"What did you do that for?"

"You looked hot," Rebecca explained.

"And this helps me, how?"

"Well, we brush down horses with hay when they get hot."

"Now you're comparing me to a horse?" Shelby began to stalk Rebecca, who backed up slowly.

"No, not exactly." Rebecca grinned evilly. "Although I could say that you're beginning to smell like one." She yelped when Shelby tackled her, but quickly gained the upper hand by rolling over and straddling her lover. "Ah ha! I have you right where I want you." She pulled the tank top out of Shelby's pants and was working on the buckle of her belt when someone cleared his throat behind them. She whipped around and saw the owner of the property, glaring at the two of them. She leapt to her feet. "Mr. Lockneer, what brings you out today?"

"I was on my way home from church, and I thought I'd see how you were doing." The disgust on his face told her what he thought of the sight before him. "Rebecca, you've been here for over two years, and in all that time, I never knew you were one of *those* kinds of people. I can't tolerate that."

Rebecca reached a hand down and helped Shelby to her feet. "It's not, I mean, we were just—"

"What she's trying to say, sir, is that I'm to blame for this. I'll leave immediately." Shelby started to walk by her lover, but Rebecca grabbed her belt from behind and stopped her.

"No. She's not to blame for anything," Rebecca said.

Lockneer sneered. "I want you *both* gone. And Rebecca, you have exactly one week to get yourself and your horse out of my stables." He turned on his heel and left, climbed into his silver Lincoln, and sped away from the stables.

Rebecca watched the car leave, but didn't say anything. Her mind raced with a combination of fear and shame and anger — and nothing made any sense for a moment, but in a surprisingly short time, it all coalesced into one clear thing.

"I'm sorry, baby." Shelby stood beside Rebecca as she stared at the car disappearing into the distance. "I feel horrible about this."

"I don't."

"Why not? You just lost your home."

Rebecca let out a big sigh, realizing that a lot of facts had just come together. "Because I have you, Shelby, and because I just realized I don't want to grow old living above some damned stables owned by a small-minded, mean-spirited asshole anyway." Rebecca tugged on Shelby's hand. "Let's go upstairs and get cleaned up, then we can look in the paper for a new place to live."

"AS YOU CAN see, this apartment has a lot of charm," the realtor explained to Rebecca. "I know it doesn't seem like much, but for someone who doesn't mind using a little elbow grease for the deposit, I think it's a great find."

Rebecca looked around the squalid kitchen, fighting back a shiver when she saw an army of roaches race each other across the cracked linoleum countertop. "I don't think this is what I had in mind when I gave you my price range."

The woman looked at Rebecca. "Honey, you're not going to get much better, I'm afraid. There's not a lot out there for what you're offering to pay." She hefted her purse higher on her shoulder. "But since you're not interested in this lovely," she looked around, "hovel, let's get out of here before we catch something."

The next three apartments were almost as bad, and even the realtor began to lose her positive attitude. "Let's go back to my office to regroup and see what else I can come up with."

Rebecca resigned herself to her fate. "No, I think I've wasted enough of your time, Mrs. Skimmerly. I think, at least for the time being, I'll just make do with what I have."

"All right." The realtor took a card from her purse. "But please give me a call if you change your mind. I really hope I can come up with something you can live with, and in."

"I will, thank you." Rebecca hoped that Shelby was faring better with her task.

SHELBY'S TASK WAS bringing her only frustration. She'd had no luck with newspaper ads for stables, so she walked into the feed store to look around. She wanted to see if it had a bulletin board, and if so, if there were any places listed that could house Patches. Horse liniment, feed, and dust all combined into an unfamiliar but not unpleasant smell that Shelby inhaled as she walked to the back of the building.

Three old men sat at a small card table. "I tell you what, those kids are getting less and less respectful every day," one man grumbled. "He practically ran me down in the store, and not one word of apology."

The other two nodded, and as the speaker spit in a tin can beside his chair, one said, "Tell me about it, Claude. My own grandkids never say anything to me unless it's to ask for money."

Shelby could hear the pain in their voices as each recounted a similar experience. She quietly made her way over and studied the array of paper tacked haphazardly to the bulletin board.

One of the men noticed her and cleared his throat. "You looking for anything in particular, young lady?"

Turning around, Shelby put her hands in the back pocket of her jeans and gave the group a smile. "Yes, sir. As a matter of fact, maybe you gentlemen can help me."

"We'll certainly try," Claude assured her. He pointed to an empty seat, which she took. "I'm Claude, and these two old reprobates are Jesse and Ted."

Nodding to the other two, Shelby leaned forward in her chair and made direct eye contact with each of them in turn. "The reason I'm here is simple. When I was a kid, my granddad told me that if you ever need any real answers, go to the men that hang around the feed store. They always know what's what and won't steer you wrong." Since she hadn't even *known* her grandfather, she hoped this little white lie wouldn't hurt anyone.

"Finally, a youngster who knows the truth," Ted exclaimed. He was quickly shushed by Jesse, who studied the young woman carefully through narrowed eyes.

"And just what real answer are you looking for?"

"I've got a six-year old paint pony that needs stabling, and I don't have a lot of money to do it with." She waited patiently, keeping her gazed locked with Jesse's. "Do you have any ideas, or should I just go back to that old board over there? I think there are some ads up there from before I was born."

Claude patted her knee. "Don't let Jesse upset you any, young'un. He's a bit more serious than we are, but he means no harm." He looked at the other two men, and the three of them came to a silent understanding. "I think we may have just the place for you. An old friend of ours lives just outside of town, and he has a small barn on his place that's not being used."

Half an hour later, Shelby drove up to a run-down old farm and got out. The barn, offset from the house, looked as if it would collapse at any moment.

What few boards it had still in place were bleached by the sun, and even from the distance, she could see the knot holes and splits in the slats.

Shelby turned her attention to the house. She could see that someone had once taken great pride in its appearance, but the overgrown garden in front attested to the owner's recent apathy.

The weathered wood had lost most of its paint, and the steps that led to the front porch were completely broken apart. The porch itself was missing many of its planks, and the window in the front door appeared to have been boarded up for years.

There was too much dirt accumulated on the windows that were left to see inside, but Shelby wasn't there for the house, anyway. A wizened old man appeared on the rickety front porch.

"What do you want?" he yelled, shielding his eyes with one hand. "If you're from the bank, I'll just go back in and get my shotgun." His clothes hung from his thin frame, and he looked to be in the same disrepair as his home.

Holding her hands out to her sides, Shelby tried to keep the smile from her face. "No sir, I'm not from the bank. Fact is, they probably wouldn't like me much. Are you Mr. Groves?"

"Yep. Come on up here. Anyone who's not a friend of those snakes is welcome." He waited until Shelby got to the porch and looked her over. "You're a gal."

"So I've noticed," she retorted. "Some of the guys down at the feed store sent me, figured we might be able to help each other out."

Groves motioned for her to precede him inside. "All right."

Once inside, Shelby waited for her eyes to adjust to the dim light. The interior of the living area wasn't in much better shape than the exterior, and there were stacks of newspapers and magazines everywhere.

"Before you say anything, I like to read." He walked to one of the doorways. "I'm going to get some coffee. How do you like yours?"

"Black and strong, if possible."

"No other way," the old man chortled, leaving Shelby alone in the dark and musty room. She could barely make out a few old picture frames on the walls. A pile of empty pork-and-beans and chili cans lay next to a torn recliner. Before she could investigate any further, he came back into the room and handed her a mug.

Peering down into the thick liquid, Shelby wondered how old the coffee was. She took a cautious sip and almost gagged. *At least as old as I am. This stuff tastes like dirty socks.* She quickly looked at his feet, relieved to see the footwear peeking out from beneath his pants. "My name's Shelby Fisher, and I have a horse that I'm looking to board. I figure I could pay you about fifteen dollars a week cash, plus I'll do any work out here that you need to have done."

"That's a pretty generous offer, Miss Fisher, especially when I've got twenty years of work needing doing out here. Why are you so desperate?" Sitting down in the recliner, he propped his coffee cup on one arm of the chair. The material was worn down so much that it was shiny, and she could see the stuffing beneath.

"Because I can't find any place that'll take less than sixty a week, and I don't have that kind of money lying around."

"Well, at least you're honest." Groves leaned forward in his chair. "So I'll be the same. The bank has been after me for months because they think they can sell this old dump for more than I'm paying now. I don't have the money to move anywhere else, so I stay. And I'm too old to fix it up enough to sell."

Shelby discreetly placed her cup on a nearby table. "Then maybe we can help each other out, Mr. Groves."

REBECCA SAT AT the kitchen table at her parent's house, drinking ice tea with her mother. "I didn't think it would be this hard to find another apartment. But they're all so nasty or overpriced."

"I was afraid of that, when you told me you would be looking for something else," Kathy said. "And there was no way you could talk Mr. Lockneer into changing his mind? That was such a good deal for you."

"I know. But he's a narrow-minded bigot, although I never knew that about him." Rebecca expelled a heavy breath. "And we were just playing around in the barn—not even doing anything bad, Mom." *Not yet, anyway. Another five minutes, and he would have really gotten an eyeful.* "He was rude and disrespectful, and I want nothing more to do with him."

"If it's that much of a problem, why don't you just take your old room here? I hadn't moved that much of my sewing things in there yet, and we can get your bed out of the storage area above the garage."

"No way, Mom. You just now got it set up for your arts and crafts. That's that you should be using it for. I'm an adult now. I don't want that space." She grinned. "I just want you to listen to me whine."

"Honey, it's your home, too. You're welcome back anytime."

"It's so nice to know that, but I hope it won't come to that. Even if we did have to stay here for a bit, though, I promise we won't take up much room or be a bother."

Her mother looked thunderstruck. "I assumed Shelby would find her own place, Becca. I don't know if your father would go for having you both sleeping in your room. Besides, she and your brother would be at odds the entire time. I don't think it would be good for the family."

"Are you saying that Shelby isn't welcome here?"

"No, not at all. She's welcome to *visit* any time. Just not to live, I'm afraid."

Rebecca stood up from the table so quickly her chair fell over. "Wow. I didn't expect *that*. Then I guess I'd better quit whining and keep looking." Upset, she left the room.

SHELBY RETURNED TO the apartment to find Rebecca boxing up the last of her books and knick-knacks. "Did you find a place?" She hoped the packing meant Rebecca was successful in her pursuit.

"No." Still angry at from the conversation with her mother, Rebecca slammed a book on top of an already full box.

Crossing the room, Shelby grabbed Rebecca's hands, afraid of the damage her lover would inflict on the inanimate objects. "What's wrong? Don't worry. We'll find a place."

"It's not that. I had an argument with my mother."

"Anything I can help with?" Shelby asked. She led Rebecca over to the sofa and sat.

Rebecca looked everywhere except at Shelby. "No. I think it's something I'm going to have to handle myself, but thanks." She gazed around the room. "You know, when I pack this stuff up, I realize I have damn little to show for my life so far."

"Things don't show whether your life is worthy or not."

"I guess I'll just have to stay in the trailer with you."

Shit. I didn't want to tell her about it this way. "I'm afraid you can't."

"Why not? I mean, I know it's small, but I'll be at work for a lot of the day, so I won't be in your way."

"It's nothing like that. You could never be in my way, darlin'. It's just that I don't have the trailer any more. I sold it."

Rebecca faced Shelby, and almost slid from the sofa. "You what? Why would you go and do a thing like that? Where are we going to live?"

Shelby stood and started to pace the room, almost afraid to look Rebecca in the eye. "I spent the whole day trying to find a stable for Patches, and most of the places were so expensive, I was running out of hope." She stopped when she reached the kitchen table and placed her hands on the back of a chair, gripping the wood tightly. "I ended up at the feed store and talked to some old guys sitting around in the back."

"I know who you mean. They're retired, and they meet there every day so they don't have to stay at home with their wives," Rebecca related with a smile.

"Right. Anyway, I figured I didn't have much to lose, so I asked them if they knew of any place I could board a horse for a low price." Shelby released her grip on the chair and started to pace again. "They sent me out to an old farm, not that far from where we are now."

Rebecca frowned as she tried to think of the place Shelby was talking about. There was only one farm nearby that might fit the bill. "The old Groves place?"

"Yeah. He's something else, isn't he?"

"You could say that again. I rode too close to his property once, and he threatened to shoot me." Rebecca's eyes widened. "Are you trying to tell me that's where we're going to leave poor Patches? Not there! And why did you have to sell your trailer?"

"I'm getting to that." Shelby sat next to Rebecca again in an attempt to calm her. "He's really not a bad guy once you get to know him. Just lonely, I think."

Rebecca shook her head. "Lonely or not, I don't know if I want my horse around that crazy old man."

"But that's where selling my trailer comes in." Shelby looked very proud of herself. "You're looking at the new owner of the Groves farm."

"What?" If Rebecca hadn't been sitting down, she would have fallen to the floor. "You bought the place?"

Taking Rebecca's hands in her own, Shelby felt inordinately proud at that moment. "I did. Or at least, I used some of the money I got for the trailer as a down payment. It was the best solution for all of us, really."

Rebecca realized what Shelby had given up. "But that had

been your home your entire life."

"And nothing in it worked, and there's no way either one of us could have lived in it without paying a lot of money to fix it up. Don't you see? Patches will have her own stable, and poor Mr. Groves can move into a retirement center like he wants to. We'll make monthly payments on a contract for deed, and once I get the stables fixed up like I want them, we can start taking in horses to board." Shelby brought Rebecca close. "You should see that place. I don't think he's thrown anything away since before we were born, and a lot of the stuff is fixable—a regular treasure trove of junk."

Rebecca snuggled into Shelby's arms but she looked worried about what she was hearing. "It sounds like a lot of work."

"It will be a lot of work, but I think the end result will be worth it."

"You're really something else, did you know that?" Rebecca asked, leaning forward and kissing Shelby. "Why do I think that you did this as much for him as you did for Patches?"

Shelby returned the kiss. "Land is always a good investment, Rebecca. And I'm not getting any younger."

"Uh huh. My tough bull rider has turned into a softie." Rebecca giggled when Shelby tickled her ribs.

"I'll show you who's tough," Shelby promised, stretching out on the sofa and taking Rebecca with her.

"WHAT HAVE YOU gotten yourself into?" Rebecca asked Shelby, as they stood inside the old house. Mr. Groves had happily left them everything except his bed and a few personal belongings. "This place would have to go up on the scale to even be considered a dump."

"You don't think it has a certain 'rustic charm'?" Shelby asked. "Seriously, this is why I thought you might be more comfortable staying with your family, at least until I can get part of the house fixed up."

Rebecca sighed. "I pretty much already burned that bridge," she said. "Besides, who's going to save you in case you get a snake or spider bite or fall through this rickety old floor?"

Shelby looked around the living area at the stacks of newspapers and magazines that covered the dusty furniture. "It's not that bad. A few trips to the dump will take care of these."

"And what about the bedroom?" They had found out, much too late, that the bedroom of the small house had a hole in the roof and ceiling, about the size of someone's foot. "It's a wonder that old man survived out here," Rebecca said. "And let's not forget the plumbing in the bathroom." Where the toilet used to be was just a hole, and the sink was propped up by a board from underneath. Rebecca was afraid of what was probably growing in the old claw-foot tub.

"I told you it was a fixer-upper."

"Shelby, the kitchen doesn't have a sink."

"Sure it does. It's just out back," Shelby assured her. "Once I get Patches' stall fixed, I'll start on the house."

Rebecca shook her head. "My horse is *not* staying in that lean-to. That barn could fall over at any minute. And I don't want you inside when it does."

"It's not that bad."

Walking over to Shelby and tapping her on the forehead, Rebecca spat out, "Hello? Is this thing on? Did you even look around before making an offer on this place?"

Shelby felt some of her earlier elation deflate. "I had someone come out and inspect the house. They said that other from the obvious problems, it was sound. I figure I'm strong enough to do the work, and when I'm done, we'll have a decent place to lay our heads. What's so wrong with that?"

Rebecca suddenly felt very ashamed of her behavior. She realized that maybe it was Shelby's dream to own property, just as she had her own dreams. "I'm sorry."

"No, you're right." Shelby looked around the room in defeat. "I'm probably just fooling myself. I've bitten off a whole lot more than I can chew."

"Not if you have help."

"I can't ask you to do that."

Rebecca stepped closer to Shelby and put her arms around her. "You're not asking, I'm offering." She turned slightly so that they were side by side, but still touching. "It'll take a lot of work, but I think we can do it."

"You do, huh?"

"Yep." Rebecca knew she had said the right thing when she felt Shelby's arm around her tighten and squeeze.

SHELBY'S FIRST CONCERN was the barn, since without it, Patches had no protection against the elements. Although one wall of the structure *did* need serious work, the majority of the barn was in good shape. She spent a full day on tearing apart and rebuilding the wall until she was satisfied with the result. From the outside, she could already see a difference as the barn was now square and standing upright.

It was almost dusk when Rebecca stepped out of the house, and she was shocked at what she saw. With most of the boards now in place, the barn was no longer a complete eyesore. She walked down to the barn and looked inside to find Shelby putting the finishing touches on Patches' stall. "I can't believe you got all this done in one day."

Shelby looked up from her work and smiled. She was covered with dirt and grime, and her once-white tee shirt was liberally streaked with brown and gray, and a few other colors that were hard to distinguish in the fading light. "It wasn't that hard, really. Just a few nails."

"Right. Like I believe that." Rebecca was tired from working inside the house, but Shelby looked positively exhausted. "Why don't we go into town and stay in a motel for the evening? The bathroom still needs work, and I think we could both use a nice hot shower."

Although a part of her wanted to stay in her new house the first night, exhaustion and good sense won out over Shelby's pride. "That's the best idea I've heard all day." She tossed the old hammer she had been using into a wooden crate that doubled as a tool box. Mr. Groves had left all his tools behind, citing that he wouldn't need them to chase the widow women around in the retirement home. She smiled when she thought about how he had been just as excited about the prospect of leaving as Shelby was about moving in. She brushed her hands down her thighs to remove at least the first layer of dirt. "I'll even buy you dinner."

Rebecca laughed. "Hopefully you're talking about a drive-thru somewhere. In this condition, I don't believe either one of us will be welcomed anywhere else." Her own work in the house left her just as filthy. It had taken Rebecca all day to gather up all the empty food cans and newspapers, and now they were bundled up in the bed of Shelby's truck. She planned on dumping them off at a recycling dumpster on their way to the motel. Both took a clean change of clothes with them as they left the farm in the truck.

SHELBY STEPPED OUT of the bathroom, one towel wrapped around her body, while she used another to dry her hair. She could see that Rebecca hadn't bothered to put on clothes after her shower, either. The other woman was in one of the motel chairs, also clad in a towel.

"Feel better?" Rebecca asked. Her hair was damp, and the dark red strands fell to her shoulders. She pointed to the table she was sitting next to. "I hope you don't mind that I started without you."

"That's fine." Shelby took the other chair, barely getting seated before attacking her hamburger and french fries. "Mmm," she groaned, "I didn't realize how hungry I was." She practically inhaled the food, slowing down only to take sips from her drink.

Rebecca ate almost as quickly. She finished before Shelby, and tossed her empty wrapper into the nearby trash can. "Two points," she cheered.

"Lucky shot."

"Nope. I'm actually a fairly decent basketball player." Rebecca wadded up more paper and threw it toward the trash can. "See? Two for two. Did you think that the only thing I did was ride horses all the time?"

Shelby wasn't too sure how she was supposed to answer that question. "To tell you the truth, I never really thought about it." She popped the final bite of burger into her mouth and chewed, then swallowed before continuing. "So you're not only a damned good barrel racer, but you play basketball. What else should I know about you?"

"Oh, I don't know. Why don't you ask some questions, and I'll answer them?"

"That sounds fair." Shelby wiped her mouth with a paper napkin, then wadded it up in her empty wrapper. She turned and tossed it at the trash bin, but missed. "Shit."

Rebecca tried to keep from laughing. "And you were closer, too."

"Shut up."

"You could have practically dropped it in from where you are sitting," Rebecca continued to tease. "Thank goodness you're a good bull rider."

Shelby stood and went over to where the paper lay on the floor. She bent to pick it up, and a loud whistle came from behind her. Spinning around, she saw a grinning Rebecca. "Liked what you saw, did you?"

"I do."

Rebecca stood, but before she could move, Shelby charged her and they both ended up on the bed, Rebecca on bottom. Shelby grinned down at her lover. "That'll teach you to whistle at me."

"Are you kidding? I've got you right where I want you."

"You always say that."

"Because it's always true." Rebecca wrapped her arms around Shelby's shoulders and pulled her closer. Their lips met softly at first, then with more urgency. She felt her towel fall away and didn't even realize she was nude with the lights on until she saw the look of affection on Shelby's face.

"Has anyone told you how absolutely beautiful you are, Rebecca?" Shelby put all her weight on one hand, while she traced a light pattern down Rebecca's neck and chest. "Absolutely perfect." Her attention caused both of her lover's nipples to tighten, and she gently took one in her mouth.

Rebecca moaned and tangled her hands in Shelby's hair, trying to pull her closer. Shelby sucked harder and Rebecca said, "Oh, God, I swear I could melt on the spot. God, Shelby. Please," she begged.

Shelby continued to suck on Rebecca's breasts, while her free hand made a path down her soft belly. When she found how wet Rebecca was, she moaned also. While using her fingers to stroke her lover, Shelby's lips persisted with their attention to Rebecca's nipple. Feeling that Rebecca was close, she sucked hard, and was rewarded by hearing her named gasped out loud. She rolled over to one side and pulled Rebecca into her arms and held her close. "I've got you," she whispered to the trembling woman. "It's okay, baby. I'm here." She looked down at Rebecca, who was already falling asleep. *I've fallen hard for you, Rebecca Starrett. And that scares me more than riding any bull ever could.*

REBECCA WOKE THE next morning to an empty bed. She looked around the motel room for any sign of Shelby, but found she was alone. Taking her time, she showered then dressed. She was just tying her sneakers when the motel room door opened, and in walked her lover carrying a bag. "Good morning, Shelby."

"Good morning to you, too, darlin'." Shelby put the bag on the small table. "How'd you sleep?"

"Very well, thanks to you. What's in the bag?"

"Breakfast. I don't know about you, but I was starving when I woke up." She started pulling things from the bag. By the time she was done, they both had coffee, and egg and bacon or sausage sandwiches. "I wasn't sure what you preferred, so I got both bacon and sausage."

Rebecca took one of the wrapped sandwiches and opened it. "I like both, thanks."

The two women quieted while they ate. Shelby was the first to finish, and she tossed her wrapper at the trash can, happily surprised when it went in. "Ta-da!" She waved her hands in the air. "Thank you, thank you," she said to her imaginary audience, while Rebecca looked on and shook her head.

"Lucky shot." Rebecca couldn't help but throw Shelby's words back at her.

"Nope. That was total skill." Shelby glanced down at her watch. "I guess we'd better finish this up, so you can get to work. Do you want me to just drop you off, and then pick you up this afternoon? I don't know if we have time to go get your car, or not."

"If you're sure it's not too much trouble, I'd love a ride." When Shelby grinned at her, Rebecca blushed at what she had said. "Stop that."

"What? You're the one who said it."

Rebecca rubbed her face with one hand. "Did you say something about taking me to work? I think we'd better leave, now." *Before I forget I have a job, and throw you down on that bed and have my way with you.*

They gathered up their dirty clothes from the night before and placed them in a plastic bag. "I'll wash these, and any others, if you want," Shelby volunteered. "I have to do my laundry, anyway." She had spied a laundromat while she was getting breakfast and decided that housekeeping chores would have to take precedence over working on the new property.

"You don't have to do my clothes. I can just take them over to my parents' and do them over there." But Rebecca thought it was incredibly sweet of Shelby to offer.

"It's no trouble. I usually don't have enough clothes for full loads. Besides, I thought you were on the outs with your parents. Let me take care of this."

Rebecca moved closer until she was inches away from Shelby. "Do you know how wonderful you are?" she asked, encircling the other woman's waist with her arms. "You're going to spoil me if you're not careful."

Shelby looked into Rebecca's eyes and saw the depth of her emotion. "You deserve to be spoiled. I just wish there was more I could do for you."

"You do plenty." Rebecca leaned forward and kissed Shelby. They broke apart slowly, both breathing heavily. "I wish we had more time this morning."

"Me too, But I don't want you to lose your job." Shelby kissed Rebecca again, this time more slowly. They both swayed for a moment until Shelby was finally able to step back. There was so much she wanted to say, yet she didn't know how. "Rebecca, I—" The light touch of Rebecca's fingers on her lips silenced her.

"I know." Afraid of her own feelings, Rebecca didn't want to hear what Shelby was about to say. They had already proclaimed their love for one another, but it was quickly moving past those feelings. *We haven't known each other long enough for that. I can't be this in love with her this soon.* She looked deep into the brown eyes close to hers. *But God help me, I am.*

Chapter Sixteen

REBECCA WAS BUSY marking down a rack of western shirts when her assistant manager Regina tapped her on the shoulder.

"You have a phone call on line three. I think it's your mother."

"Thanks." Rebecca hurried over to a nearby phone and picked up the receiver. "This is Rebecca."

"Becca? Honey, I'm sorry to bother you at work, but I need to talk to you. Can we meet for lunch?" Her mother didn't sound panicked or anything, but she did seem upset about something.

Rebecca looked at her watch. She was due for her lunch break in twenty minutes. "Sure. The usual place? Around twelve-thirty?"

Kathy expelled a heavy breath. "That's perfect. Thank you, sweetheart."

"No problem, Mom. Is there anything you can talk to me about now? I'm not that busy."

"I really don't want to get into it over the phone. Twelve-thirty is soon enough. I'll see you then."

Rebecca looked at the dead receiver in her hand and sighed.

Regina, who was lurking nearby, stepped forward. "Is everything all right? Do you need to leave early today?"

Thinking about what she could do if she left early, Rebecca still had to shake her head. "No, I don't think it's serious. Just my mom being melodramatic."

"Isn't that what moms are good at?"

"Mine sure is," Rebecca agreed. "We're talking gold medal holder, at the very least."

Regina laughed. "Guess that gives mine the silver." She took an extra marker out of her pocket. "Why don't I help you get this rack done? Then we can finish putting out the latest shipment of jeans."

"Sounds good to me." Rebecca liked having someone else

help her with the tedious work. It made it go by faster, and she enjoyed the company. *And it will make the time fly until I get to see Shelby again.*

SHELBY FINISHED HER laundry in record time, and was now back at the farm to work on the house. There were a few things she wanted to have done before Rebecca got off work, and she knew she'd need the entire afternoon to accomplish the jobs.

She had found the toilet behind the house, covered in what she hoped was mud. Unable to pick it up easily, Shelby went to her truck and grabbed a length of rope, then wrapped it around the porcelain. It was much easier to drag the item than to carry it, although the back steps stopped her cold. "Now what?" She looked around the yard and was happy to see a stack of old boards by a tree.

After making a ramp, Shelby dragged the toilet up on a board, cursing when the old wood broke on the middle step. She kicked at it, then cursed again when that hurt her foot. "Dammit all to hell! Stupid piece of shit!" Without thinking, she bent down and picked the whole thing up, and placed it on the porch without any problem.

"Well, hell." Surprised at her own strength, Shelby looked down at the offending item and scratched her head. She grabbed the rope once again, and pulled the toilet into the house and down the short hallway to the bathroom.

Realizing her plumbing skills were practically non-existent, Shelby decided she'd better go into Somerville and get a book on the subject. "Maybe two," she said out loud, remembering all she had to do in the kitchen.

THE RESTAURANT WASN'T overly crowded, even for lunch time, and Rebecca easily saw the table her mother sat at. She walked over and after kissing the older woman on the cheek plopped down into the chair across from her. "Hi, Mom."

"Hello, Becca. I'm so glad you could make it." Kathy nervously fiddled with her water glass, and looked relieved when the waiter came over immediately to take their order. "I'll have the number four special."

He looked at Rebecca. "And for you, Miss?"

"Bring me the number two, and hold the onions, please. And a glass of iced tea." Rebecca handed him her menu, which she barely looked at. She waited until the waiter left before speaking. "What's the big mystery, Mom? Is everything okay at home?"

Kathy looked down at the table. "Things are a bit strained at home. It's your brother."

"Terry? What's wrong with him?"

"He's suddenly turned very angry, Becca. I know he's almost grown at nineteen, but your father and I are both terribly worried about him. His grades have already dropped drastically, and he's been coming home drunk at night. We thought that maybe you might be able to help."

Rebecca had a fairly good idea what Terry's problem was, and she knew that she would only make it worse. "I don't think—"

"He worships you. He always has. Maybe if you could just come over and talk to him, everything would be okay." Kathy didn't look at Rebecca, seeming more focused on watching a bead of condensation work its way down her water glass. "He and your father got into a really nasty argument last night, and I was afraid they'd hit each other."

"What was the fight about?"

Kathy mumbled something unintelligible as the waiter set down Rebecca's drink.

"What?"

"You." Kathy looked up with tears in her eyes. "They were fighting about you."

Rebecca almost choked on the drink of tea she had taken. "Me?"

"I know, it's ridiculous. But your brother thinks that Shelby has led you astray, his words, not mine. Your father told him it was none of our business, and we should just be glad that you're happy. Terry didn't see it that way."

"And you think that by me talking to Terry, he'll change his mind? I don't know, Mom. I think it might just make things worse."

Kathy sighed. "I just don't know what else to do. Your father threatened to kick Terry out of the house if he didn't straighten up."

Rebecca felt the weight of her family's problems hit squarely on her shoulders. She knew that her brother wouldn't be acting this way if he hadn't caught her and Shelby together. *Maybe if I had just talked to him first, before he found out, things would have turned out differently.* Then again, since when did he get to use her relationship and her happiness as an excuse to act like a jerk? "No promises, but I'll see what I can do, okay?"

"Thank you, Becca. I knew I could count on you." Kathy smiled at the server placing a plate in front of her. "Gosh, I'm suddenly quite hungry."

Looking at her plate, Rebecca felt just the opposite. She just hoped she could get through the meal without throwing up.

THE HOME IMPROVEMENT store was new, and therefore very popular. Shelby had to drive around the lot three times before she found a parking space, and even then it wasn't very close to the front doors. She looked down at her grubby clothes, and hoped that the people inside wouldn't be too offended.

She had just left the feed store, and the old guys there had recommended it. They weren't put off by her appearance, so Shelby assumed that she'd be okay. They had all gotten a good laugh at her story of moving of the commode, and Claude had made a bawdy joke at her expense, which she enjoyed. She thanked the men and now here she was, parked outside the store.

Stepping inside, she waited for a moment while her eyes adjusted to the difference in the light. It was a huge warehouse, with everything from light bulbs to lumber. Shelby strolled over to the help desk where two women were talking, both wearing aprons with the store's logo on front. "Excuse me. Do you have any books on plumbing?"

The younger of the two women gave Shelby a quick once-over and wrinkled her nose. "We have five or six self-help books over there to the right, and I believe they all have chapters on plumbing."

"Thanks." Shelby ignored the fact the woman was so rude and walked over to the shelves where the books were. She saw over half a dozen books for working around the house and wondered which one would be best. She didn't have to think long because the older woman, whose nametag read Marge, came around the counter and picked up one of the books.

"This one covers just about everything there is to know about plumbing, as well as other household chores. Are you remodeling your house?"

Shelby looked into the Marge's eyes. "Yes, ma'am. I just bought a place that's a real fixer upper." She hefted the big book, which she estimated weighed a good three pounds. "Thanks for the advice. I want to try and do as much of the work as I can myself."

Marge smiled. "That's admirable." She pulled a card from her apron pocket. "But if you get stuck, give my husband a call. He's a professional handyman, and just tell him Marge recommended you."

"Thanks, Marge. I really appreciate that." Shelby tucked the card into her jeans pocket and went to check out, wanting to return to the house and get back to work as soon as possible.

IT WAS LATE afternoon, and Rebecca stood outside the closed western wear store, wondering where her ride was. Before she could worry any more, Shelby's truck tore into the parking lot and skidded to a stop in front of her. Shelby was apologizing through the open window before the vehicle even came to a full stop. "I'm sorry I was late. I wanted to get a shower before I picked you up." Shelby's hair was still wet. She leaned over and opened the door for Rebecca, who climbed into the truck with a bemused look on her face.

"You weren't that late. I'd only been standing there for a couple of minutes at the most." Rebecca fastened her seat belt. "And I really appreciate you taking the extra time," she teased.

"Yeah, well, it was either that, or you'd probably want to ride in the back. And I'd rather have you up here with me." Shelby grimaced at how she sounded. *Pathetic.* She looked over at Rebecca, who wore a huge smile on her face. *But then again, maybe it was the right thing to say.* "How was your day?"

Now it was Rebecca's turn to grimace. "Work went okay, but I had lunch with my Mom."

"Is she giving you a hard time about us?" Putting the truck in gear, Shelby drove more carefully out of the parking lot.

"No, it's not that."

Shelby continued to drive in silence, deciding that Rebecca would tell her if she wanted her to know. She took in the scenery of the small town while she drove, thinking to herself that it wouldn't be a bad place to put down roots, if she was so inclined. Her first thought when she bought the Groves place was to fix it up and let someone rent it. Now that she and Rebecca were on stable ground again, she wanted the two of them to work on the house together, and make it their home. Her thoughts were interrupted by Rebecca.

"It's Terry. He's been acting really out of character since he found out about us. Mom wants me to talk to him." Rebecca looked out her window and stared at the passing scenery. She hated being put in the middle. Her brother, being the youngest, was even more spoiled as a child, she realized, than she had been. *And he called me a princess. Ha!*

"Are you going to?"

"I don't want to, because I think it's going to just make things worse. But I told her that I'd try." Rebecca felt close to tears, and all she wanted to do was curl up somewhere and have a good cry.

Shelby could feel Rebecca's distress, and she looked around for a place to park the truck. Finally seeing an empty church parking lot, she wheeled the vehicle in and turned off the engine. She unclipped her seat belt and held out her arms. "Come here, sweetheart."

Not having to be asked twice, Rebecca slid across the long bench seat and snuggled up against her lover's chest. Finally feeling safe and secure, she let her tears fall.

After Rebecca cried a bit, she got herself under control, and the two of them went to dinner. Once they both had finished, Rebecca decided she'd try to talk to her brother right away, so they headed back to the farm for Rebecca to pick up her car.

"Are you sure you don't want me to go with you?" Shelby asked. She had already been turned down twice before, but didn't want Rebecca to be alone when she faced her brother. *Especially if the little toad's been drinking.* She knew all too well what alcohol could do to a person.

"I'm sure." Rebecca reached over and squeezed Shelby's arm. "This is something I really have to handle on my own. "But I won't mind meeting up with you afterward."

"Of course. I'll work at the farm for a while, then later on tonight I'll check back in at the same motel, hopefully the same room. Will that work?"

"That will be perfect."

They finished the trip in silence, and it wasn't long before Shelby parked the truck beside Rebecca's little car. They got out and met by the driver's door. Shelby held out her arms and Rebecca immediately rushed into them. "Now you remember," Shelby murmured, "that I'm close by."

"I will." Rebecca squeezed Shelby harder. "I don't want to do this."

"Then don't." Shelby stepped back just far enough so that she could look into Rebecca's eyes. "He's a grown man acting like a child. Maybe he should get a dose of tough love from your folks."

"Are you saying that you think he should be kicked out of the house? I don't think he'd be able to work a full time job and go to school full time, too."

"I just think it's time he stood on his own two feet. He's obviously had everything hand fed to him. It's actually crueler to keep babying him."

Feeling a little sick, Rebecca backed farther away from Shelby. "You want my parents to kick him out of the house and just sit back and watch him fall flat on his face? Just how is that good for him?"

Shelby noticed the distance Rebecca put between the two of them, and it made her heart hurt. "All I'm saying is that maybe it's time for Terry to act his age. And I think it's time for your parents to take that responsibility, instead of placing it all on your shoulders."

"Oh? So suddenly you're the expert where families are concerned?" Rebecca saw the hurt look cross Shelby's face, before it was hidden by stoic indifference. "Oh, Shelby. I didn't mean—"

"No, you're right. I have no room to talk." Shelby turned and walked toward the old farmhouse, fighting the urge to run. She ignored Rebecca's calls, and only when she was in the house and heard Rebecca's car drive away did she allow her tears to fall.

REBECCA DROVE WITH tears streaking her face. She hated herself for what she had said to Shelby, who she knew had only been trying to help. She had thought about following the other woman into the house, but was afraid of the confrontation. So, she did what she usually did—she ran. Rebecca still wasn't sure if she was going to talk to Terry or not, or if she was going to follow Shelby's advice. "She did have a point. He does need to quit being such a baby about everything. Maybe I'll get lucky and he won't be home."

When she pulled up to her parent's house, she was dismayed to see her brother's car parked in the driveway. "I guess there goes that excuse." Rebecca got out of her car and climbed the steps to the front door. Hearing loud voices, she hurriedly opened the door and went inside.

"As long as you live under this roof, you will obey our rules," her father was yelling, his face red. "Your coming and going at all hours disrupts the entire household, and it will stop."

Terry was standing barely a foot away, his hands clenched at his sides. "I'm a grown man, and you can't tell me when I can come home."

"There's no reason for you to be out after midnight. That curfew has always been fine for you and your sister—"

"Don't bring that dyke's name into it, Dad. She's not—" Terry paused when he caught sight of Rebecca. "Speak of the devil."

Greg took a breath and turned. "Becca? Hi, honey." He walked over and enveloped her in a hug. "I'm so glad to see you."

"He's the only one," Terry commented with a sneer.

"Terry, watch your mouth," Greg warned. He kept one arm around Rebecca. "To what do we owe this unexpected visit?" he asked his daughter.

Mom didn't tell him? Oh, boy. This really ought to be fun. "I thought that I'd come over and talk with Terry. It seems like we haven't had enough time together lately."

Terry flopped down on the sofa then crossed his arms over his chest. "That's probably because you've spent all your time with your little *girlfriend*."

Before Greg could speak, Rebecca moved to sit on the coffee table across from Terry. "Okay, I think I've had just about enough of your shitty attitude. What is it? Is it the fact that I'm gay that bothers you? Or do you not like Shelby? What has your underwear in a knot, *little* brother? Let's just get it out in the open and resolved once and for all."

She leaned in close, getting into his face, and Terry sunk back against the couch, eyes wide. "I, uh—" He stumbled and stuttered, but eventually, he quit and sat there looking upset.

"You came to my apartment and called me a princess. Well, look in the mirror, little brother. When are you going to quit acting that the world revolves around you? I know it always seemed like it did, but that time is over." Rebecca leaned forward and placed her hands on his knees. "You're my brother and I love you. But I love Shelby, too. And she's not going anywhere. So you're going to have to choose. You want me in your life? Or not?"

"You really do love her?" Greg asked, quietly.

Rebecca looked at her father. "Yes, I do. Will that be a problem for you, too?"

"No." Greg went over and sat in his chair, near the sofa. "All I want is for you to be happy. If Shelby can make you happy, then that's fine by me. It may take me a while to get completely used to it, though."

"That's okay." Rebecca turned her attention back to her brother. "What about you?"

"I still don't like it," Terry snapped. "You weren't gay before you went to the rodeo. It's all her fault."

Reaching toward her brother, Rebecca said, "That's not true. I've always been gay, it just took my time at the rodeo to help me understand that."

Terry pushed her hands away. "Keep your hands off me!"

Rebecca leaned back, hurt by his outburst. "I'm still the same person I've always been."

"No, you're not. You've changed," he accused. "All you can

think about is her."

Greg had heard enough. "Becca, why don't you go see your mother? I think she's in the kitchen."

Give big points to Dad. "Okay. But call me if you need anything, all right?"

"We sure will," Greg assured her.

SHELBY LOOKED AROUND the old house. The light coming in through the windows was still enough to see by. She wiped at her eyes angrily, mad at herself for getting so upset over a few simple words.

In the kitchen, she located the bucket and other cleaning supplies that Rebecca had left behind, but before she could use them, she teared up again. "Dammit," she yelled, running her arm across the countertop and scattering everything. Her back to the cabinets, she slid down until she was sitting on the floor. She thought back to the argument with Rebecca.

She's right. With my family history, I had no reason to try and tell her what to do with hers. Shelby looked around the kitchen, seeing for the first time how much work Rebecca had put into it. She hadn't noticed how much cleaner it was when she was in earlier, putting the sink back where it belonged. "Why should I care what she thinks, anyway?" *Because you love her completely,* her mind suggested. "No. That can't be. We haven't known each other long enough."

Steeling her mind against weakness, Shelby stood and decided to work next on getting the bedroom in better shape.

The bedroom was a mess. A dilapidated dresser stood against one wall, its matching chest of drawers on the wall next to it. Where the bed used to be was a pile of junk, mostly empty food cans and newspapers. A chirping sound caused Shelby to look up. She saw the foot-wide hole in the ceiling, and a bird stared down in irritation, as if Shelby were in his house.

The roof would have to be fixed before anything else, Shelby decided. She left the room and went back to the living room, to get the tool box. She took the hammer and a handful of roofing nails and went back outside. There was still enough sunlight, so she took some supplies and the old ladder she used in the barn and climbed to the roof of the house. First she brought up an eight-inch particle board to repair the hole, and then returned with a load of shingles over one shoulder.

Carefully she navigated the creaky roof, until she was directly over the hole which she squatted over and examined. The shingles were worn away, and the spot that needed a new board was conveniently between two rafters. "This shouldn't be too hard to fix." Standing up, she headed over toward the ladder where she had left the shingles. She heard a strange groaning sound. Her foot went through the roof, and she began to fall.

    REBECCA PARKED HER car at the motel where Shelby's truck had been the night before. There was no sign of her lover anywhere, and she worried that her words had finally pushed Shelby away. The sun had gone down over an hour ago, so she didn't think Shelby would be able to work on much out at the farm.

They had both agreed that the electricity should stay off until an electrician checked over the wiring. Although Mr. Groves had lived there for years without a problem, Rebecca was afraid the old house would go up like dry tinder with the slightest spark.

Now Rebecca was torn. Should she go ahead and get a room at the motel, hoping that Shelby was just running late? Or should she go back to her parent's house and stay in her old room for the night? Neither option sounded good to her. She decided to drive out to the farm and see if Shelby was still there sulking. *If she is, I'll apologize and ask her to come back with me.*

She backed her car out of the parking space, hoping they wouldn't cross paths and miss each other somewhere in between.

At the farm, Rebecca parked her car behind Shelby's truck. She climbed out of her car and looked around, not seeing Shelby anywhere. "Shelby!" she called out as she walked up to the front door. When she didn't get an answer, she opened the door and peeked inside. "Are you in here?" A muffled sound coming from the bedroom caught her attention, so Rebecca headed in that direction. The room was dark and spooky, and Rebecca could barely see in front of her. "Shelby?"

"Up here," a tired voice said.

Skirting the pile of trash, Rebecca took a few more cautious steps into the room near the wall and ran into something hanging from the ceiling. She screamed and fell backward on her rear.

"Rebecca? I could use a little help here," Shelby yelled. Rebecca's eyes were adjusting to the light, and now she could see that Shelby was hanging part in, part out of the bedroom ceiling along the sloped side near the wall.

Rebecca picked herself up and stared in amazement at Shelby's legs and torso which were dangling from the ceiling.

"What are you doing up there?"

"Just hanging around," Shelby snapped. "Could you please come around outside and help me get out of here? I've been like this for hours."

"Okay, just hold on." Rebecca cringed to herself when she said it, and she was certain that Shelby wasn't too happy about it, either. She went out to the side of the house and slowly climbed the ladder, glad the full moon was giving them enough light to see by.

Seeing her lover trapped up to her armpits made her voice shaky. "How did this happen?"

"The roof fell through. I can't get free without help. The wood is splintered and I'm wedged in here too tight." Shelby had never been so glad to see someone in her life. Her arms hurt from the initial fall, and it felt like she had scratches all down her sides.

"What can I do?"

"Use the hammer," Shelby pointed to where it had fallen out of her reach, "and make the hole bigger so I can slide the rest of the way through."

"Are you sure that's safe? You could hurt yourself falling—"

"There's not much of a better option at this point. I don't think this old roof will hold both of us. " Shelby was tired and achy. "Please, Rebecca. I know you probably don't care for my opinions on a lot of things, but please let's just do this my way, okay?"

"Wait. I do have one idea." Rebecca quickly got down from the ladder and ran back into the house. Shelby shouted, but she disregarded it. In the bedroom, she went to the tall chest of drawers and with some difficulty slid it over under Shelby. The tips of Shelby's boot just barely touched the top surface.

Rebecca ran back out, went up on the ladder. "Okay," she said, out of breath. "When we get you free, you won't fall far. I moved the dresser."

"Oh, good idea. All right, pound away."

Rebecca tried to hammer the area around Shelby, but was not putting much force in her blows.

"You're going to have to really slam that thing down, darlin'. You need a lot more force." Rebecca brought the hammer down as hard as she could, and Shelby fought back a groan when a piece of the board gave way and dug into her rib. "That's it. It's easing now."

"And for the record," Rebecca kept beating on the old wood, "I'm sorry about today. You were right." Her hits were having better effect. "Terry *is* acting like a spoiled brat. Dad almost threw him out of the house again tonight."

Finally enough of the wood was away from Shelby's body, and suddenly she disappeared into the bedroom below. Her voice was muffled, but she called up, "You can stop now, Rebecca."

But Rebecca didn't hear her, and she kept going. "He kept going on and on about it being your fault that I'm a lesbian. Have you ever heard such a ridiculous thing? I wanted to smack him for that." She didn't even notice when Shelby disappeared through the hole. "As if I'm not mature enough to make my own decisions. Especially when I'm older than he is." She stopped and looked around. "Shelby?"

"I'm down here," Shelby hollered from the bedroom. "Be careful coming down. I'm going to have to replace the whole roof, I think."

Rebecca backed up and stepped down the ladder, glad to be on solid ground again. Shelby met her on the front porch, clutching at her sides. "Are you okay?"

"I'm going to have some serious scratches and bruises, I think."

"Let's go back to the motel, and I'll take a look at them," Rebecca offered.

Shelby followed Rebecca to the car. "You don't have to. I'm sure a little soap and water will take care of them just fine."

"Maybe so, but I'll feel better once I check you over." Rebecca felt guilty for Shelby having been in the situation to begin with. *If we wouldn't have argued, then maybe she wouldn't have tried to fix the roof on her own.*

"All right." Shelby climbed in the passenger side of the car. "Thanks for coming out to get me. I wasn't sure if I was going to see you tonight, or not. Can you imagine me hanging there all night? My arms were starting to go to sleep as it was."

Rebecca got in behind the wheel and started the car. "That wouldn't have happened. I would have come looking for you, sooner or later. I was worried when you weren't at the motel. This was the only place I could think of that you'd be."

Shelby smiled. "I'm just glad it was sooner."

ONCE THEY CHECKED into the motel, Rebecca pushed Shelby toward the shower. "Go get cleaned up, then I'll take a look at your scratches." She could see a couple trails of blood seeping through Shelby's shirt, and had a pretty good idea that the injuries were more painful than Shelby let on.

"Yes, ma'am." Shelby followed Rebecca's advice, and a short

time later, stepped out of the steaming bathroom with a towel around her hips, leaving her upper body bare. "Is this what you wanted?"

You have no idea. Rebecca cleared her throat. "Why don't you lie down on the bed, and I'll fix you up." They had stopped at a pharmacy on the way to the motel and picked up a few medical supplies.

Shelby followed Rebecca's advice, and was soon sprawled out on the bed, face down. "I think the worst of them are on my back—at least that where it stung the most when I was in the shower."

Rebecca struggled to keep her libido in check as she stared up Shelby's bare legs to where the towel partially covered her rear. *Take care of the scratches, take care of the scratches,* she chanted to herself, trying to ignore the tight ass so close to her. Then she saw the wounds. "Oh, Shelby. Your poor back." There were several deep scrapes below Shelby's shoulder blades, and a few more along her ribs. None of them looked as if they'd need professional medical attention, but Rebecca felt better by slathering them with antibiotic ointment and covering them with gauze which she gently taped down.

For her part, Shelby lay perfectly still and allowed Rebecca to work, even though each touch brought renewed pain to the burning areas. She put her face down in the pillow she had been hugging and allowed the tears to fall, trying to keep silent.

"There, all done. Let me see your stomach."

"It's all right. I already checked."

Rebecca tossed into the garbage the gauze pad she had used to spread the ointment. She leaned down and placed a light kiss above Shelby's shoulder. "Are you okay?"

Shelby raised her head and wiped at her face. "Yeah. That just stung a little more than I expected." She rolled over and into a sitting position, and the towel that hung around her neck barely covered her breasts. "Thanks for taking care of those for me."

"You're welcome." Rebecca was trying hard not to stare at Shelby's nipples, which had hardened in the cool room. She knew she failed by the smirk she received. "What?"

"See something you like?" Although the movement was painful, Shelby leaned back against the headboard and raised her arms over her head. "It's a bit chilly in here, don't you think?"

Rebecca could only stare. Her mouth practically watered at the sight of Shelby's breasts.

Shelby wriggled a bit, causing the towel around her waist to fall away. She slid one foot up until she was entirely open for Rebecca's perusal. "You still with me, darlin'?"

"Oh, I'm definitely with you," Rebecca scooted up the bed until she hovered above Shelby's face. She leaned down and kissed the other woman with an intensity that left them both breathless.

Shelby pulled at Rebecca's top, trying to get it over her head, as they continued to kiss. They broke apart long enough to take the tee shirt off. "You've still got too many clothes on."

Rebecca ignored her, and instead started kissing her way down Shelby's neck. She sucked on the pulse point until Shelby groaned for mercy, then continued the trail toward her lover's breast. As her mouth found its target, her hand drifted downward, and she was pleased with how vocal Shelby could be. "That's it, baby. Let me hear you," she urged, taking her mouth away from its prize long enough to speak.

Shelby almost flew off the bed when Rebecca touched her. She grabbed Rebecca's head and held it close to her, calling out her name within moments. Unable to speak after the intensity of her orgasm, Shelby sat against the headboard, holding Rebecca and slightly trembling. "Damn, you're good at that," she finally whispered.

"Thanks. It's easy to be good at something that you enjoy doing." Rebecca got up from her position and sat next to Shelby on the bed. "Are you okay?"

"I'm better than okay. I guess I was revved up more than I thought. That was incredible." Shelby looked into Rebecca's eyes, and saw love reflected back to her. "I love you, Rebecca."

Rebecca raised her hands to cradle Shelby's face. "I love you, too."

Chapter Seventeen

REBECCA FOLDED THE jeans precisely, stacking them on top of another pair. She had been at the repetitive job for over an hour and was ready to scream. Normally she didn't mind the small details of her job, but today she would have rather stayed in bed with a frisky lover who had caused her to be a few minutes late as it was. It seemed as if all the stress from the last week only inspired their lovemaking until they were both exhausted from the near all night activities. She was thinking back to the look on Shelby's face when she was in the throes of passion, when a voice behind her caused her to drop the jeans she was folding.

"I'd ask about what was on your mind, but I'm about halfway afraid of the answer," her father commented.

"Dad. What a wonderful surprise." Rebecca embraced her father. "What brings you down here? Is anything the matter?"

Her father took a moment to study her. "You've got a happy glow about you, my dear. Does something have to be wrong for me to come see you? Since you moved out of Lockneer's stable apartment, I really didn't know how to get a hold of you."

"I've got a cell phone, dad."

He smiled. "Ah, heck. I know that. I just wanted an excuse to drop in and see you, Rebecca."

"We've been staying in the Rounder Motel out on highway six, and we've been working really hard on the house that Shelby bought."

His face clouded over a little. "I see. Well, one of the reasons I came by was to take you to lunch, if you haven't already made plans."

Rebecca checked her watch. "No, I'm free. As a matter of fact, I should be getting my lunch break any time, now." She looked around until she could see Regina. "Let me go ask my boss, and then we can go."

A few minutes later, they walked across the street from the

western wear store to the same restaurant she met her mother at, which specialized in home cooked meals. Considering how much grease was usually involved, Rebecca didn't think it was like any home cooking she'd ever had, but it was close to work and they could spend all their time together visiting, not looking for a place to eat. It was packed, mostly with blue collar workers and a few women who looked like office personnel. They grabbed a table being vacated by the front windows and waited patiently for the harried waitress to take their order. She did and quickly brought them their drinks.

"So, you said Shelby bought a house? She didn't seem to me to be the type to settle down."

"Well, she bought an old place that needs a lot of work—I think to give herself something to do until she can figure out what she wants to do with her life."

Greg took a sip of his iced tea, then placed it back on the table. "So, it's more investment property than anything else? She's fixing it up to get capital so she can move on?"

"I don't think so. All I do know is that we're *both* working hard on it." Rebecca felt suddenly defensive of her lover. "It's going to be nice when it's finished."

"Okay, okay." Greg held up his hands in defeat. "I'm sorry if it sounded like I was attacking her. I wasn't." He looked up as the waitress placed plates in front of them. "Thank you."

She moved off to another table, barely slowing down.

Rebecca looked down at her plate. "No, I'm the one who should apologize. You were just making conversation, and I jumped down your throat. I'm sorry."

He held up his tea glass across the table, smiling when Rebecca did the same and the two glasses clinked together. "Truce. By the way, I got a call from Jack Sterling this morning."

"What did he want?"

"Well, it seems there's a playday this weekend. He was wondering if you were interested, especially after your stunning rodeo debut."

Rebecca swallowed her first bite before answering. "I'd love to." Her exuberance turned to sadness almost immediately. "Unfortunately, I don't have a trailer available anymore." She wasn't about to ask her old landlord, since she knew what his answer would be.

"Ah, but here's where it gets interesting." Greg took a bite of his hamburger, enjoying its great flavor. He chewed for a moment, then swallowed. "Jack and I were discussing that, too."

"And?" Rebecca loved her father dearly, but his penchant for storytelling wore thin at times.

Her father finished another bite. "He knows where we can pick up an older trailer, really cheap. All it needs is a new paint job."

"Really? That would be wonderful." Rebecca almost jumped up and hugged her father. "How much is it going to cost me?"

He dipped a french fry into some ketchup and popped it into his mouth. Talking around the food he said, "Would you consider working out a trade for it? Jack needs someone to keep an eye on his mare next week while he's out of town. She's about to foal, and he's worried about her. You'd even be able to stable Patches at his place while you were there."

Rebecca almost choked on her hamburger. "That's it? Watch over a mare for a few days?" She was surprised, but happy. "If you'll give me Mr. Sterling's number, I'll call him and accept his offer. And, I'll be thrilled to be in the playday this coming weekend."

"I can do better than that." He reached for the cell phone that was clipped on his belt. "His number's in my cell. Call him right now, if you want."

"I will. Thanks, Dad." With a large smile on her face, Rebecca took the phone.

"YOU'RE TELLING ME someone actually *lived* here and didn't burn the house down?" The electrician shook his head. "The wiring in the house is original, and I'm guessing this place to be at least sixty years old." He wrote something on his notepad, then looked back up at Shelby. "I hate to do this to you, but you're going to have to rewire the whole place before it'll pass inspection."

"I figured as much. What would that sort of thing run me?"

He wrote some numbers on his pad and did some quick math, then showed it to her.

"Geez! That's ridiculous. Can I do it myself?"

The electrician shook his head again. "Nope. It has to be done by a licensed electrician. But I can send someone over who may be able to give you a better price."

"What's the catch?"

"There's no real catch. The electrician I have in mind has just recently been certified and is looking to get some work." He scratched his beard and grinned. "And I'll bet you two would hit it off just fine."

"What's *that* supposed to mean?"

"Nothing. Let me make a phone call, and we'll see what happens, all right?"

"Might as well. It's got to be done." Shelby could almost hear her money being sucked down a huge drain, and the sound was getting annoying.

PARKING NEXT TO Shelby's truck, Rebecca didn't see the electrician's vehicle that was behind the house. She had taken off early from work so that she could meet Shelby, and had gone so far as to borrow an old basket from her mother and making up a nice picnic dinner. Rebecca climbed out of her car and walked quietly inside, wanting to surprise Shelby. Going into the hallway and seeing a pair of legs hanging down from the entry to the attic, Rebecca grabbed at the boots. "Hello, sexy."

"Hello yourself, sweetie," a woman, not much older than herself, replied. She looked down at Rebecca. "You must be looking for Shelby."

"Oh, God, just kill me now," Rebecca dropped the basket and said, covering her flaming face with her hands.

At that moment, Shelby showed up. "Rebecca? Darlin', I wasn't expecting you until later." She moved until she was standing next to her lover, then took Rebecca into her arms. "Not that I'm complaining."

Rebecca buried her face in Shelby's shirt, so her reply was muffled. "I brought you some dinner."

"Is it that time already?" Shelby checked her watch. "I can't believe how fast time has flown by today."

The electrician swung down from her perch to land softly beside the other two women. "I know what you mean. But I should probably be heading back home, anyway." She waited until Rebecca turned toward her and then held out her hand. "I'm Cassandra, handy dandy electrician, at your service."

Accepting the offered hand, Rebecca couldn't help but smile. "Rebecca. Sorry about the mistaken identity."

"No problem." Cassandra glanced at Shelby. "See you bright and early, okay?"

"I'll be here." She watched the other woman walk down the hallway and waited until she heard the sound of Cassandra's truck leaving before she asked, "What mistaken identity were you talking about?"

Rebecca blushed again. "It's nothing, really."

"No, I'd like to know." Shelby's grin widened as she figured out what caused her lover's embarrassment. "You thought Cassie was me?" She started to laugh. "We don't look a thing alike."

"It's not that funny. All I saw were her legs hanging from the ceiling. How was I supposed to know?"

Shelby couldn't control her laughter. "What happened?"

Looking at the floor, Rebecca answered, "I grabbed her legs and called her..." she mumbled the last word.

"Called her what? I didn't quite get that."

"Sexy." Rebecca stared at the floor as she whispered the word. "I really thought she was you."

Seeing that her lover was upset, Shelby decided to stop teasing her. "I'm sure she didn't mind, darlin'. Probably brought a smile to her face." The electrician wasn't homely, but she was no raving beauty, either. Shelby motioned to the basket that sat at Rebecca's feet. "I take it that dinner's in there?"

Rebecca picked up the basket. "It is. Do you have any idea of a good place to eat it? I'm afraid the kitchen's not quite ready."

Taking the container from Rebecca, Shelby started down the hallway. "Let's spread a blanket out in the bed of my truck. We should be plenty comfortable there."

"Good idea." Rebecca followed Shelby, admiring the view.

After enjoying the sandwiches and chips, Shelby leaned back against the cab of the truck with Rebecca's head comfortably in her lap. Shelby's long fingers stroked absently through her lover's hair, which caused Rebecca to yawn. "If you keep that up, I'll fall asleep out here," Rebecca warned.

"What? Oh." Shelby continued her motion, while looking down into the blue eyes she loved so much. "Would that be such a bad thing? It's nice out here." She'd spent many a night sleeping outside when her trailer had gotten too warm. But Shelby wasn't too sure how Rebecca would take to the great outdoors.

"Mmm." Rebecca's eyes closed again as Shelby's fingers traced gentle patterns on her scalp. "Tell me about your day."

"Not much to tell, really. Found out that all the wiring in the house is ancient, and needs to be replaced. That's why Cassie's here."

Cassie, huh? Rebecca felt jealously rear its ugly head. "You two hit it off pretty quick, didn't you?"

"Well, yeah. She's a nice person." Shelby was oblivious to Rebecca's ire. "The guy I talked to this morning recommended her, saying we'd probably get along. I thought it was mighty nice of him."

I'll just bet he did. Rebecca willed her body to relax as she opened her eyes and looked up into Shelby's face. "She doesn't look old enough to be an electrician. Are you sure she's capable of the work?"

"I think so. She's just been certified. But, everyone's got to start somewhere, right? She seems all right to me."

"Uh-huh. Did you ask for references, or to see her credentials?" Rebecca thought that the tight work shirt that Cassandra had been wearing showed off her "credentials" more than adequately.

Shelby frowned. "No. I just figured if the other guy, an established and experienced electrician, recommended her, it was good enough for me. Is there something wrong that you're not telling me?" She saw the tight set of Rebecca's jaw. Then it occurred to her. "You're jealous?"

"Well, I—"

"Darlin', you'll never have to worry about me going astray. I'm a one-woman woman." To punctuate her words, Shelby leaned down and placed a firm kiss on Rebecca's lips.

Rebecca felt bad for ever doubting Shelby. When they broke apart, she murmured, "I'm sorry. It's just that all of this is so new to me, and you're more experienced. I guess I'm afraid of being too boring for you." She felt tears well up in her eyes and wiped at them savagely with one hand. "God knows I'm not much of a catch." Rebecca sat up and tried to scoot away, but was stopped by Shelby's arms around her.

"Now wait just a damned minute." Shelby waited until she had Rebecca's complete attention. "That's the woman I love you're talking about." She caressed Rebecca's cheek with her hands, using her thumbs to wipe away the tears. "I wake up every morning wondering what I did to deserve you, so don't go knocking your importance." Then she smiled. "Besides, Cassie's married and has two kids. I don't think I'm her type."

"Married? To a man?"

"Yep. But I'm not holding that against her."

Rebecca sighed. "Now I really feel foolish. I called her sexy, and she isn't even gay." She lowered her face, unable to meet Shelby's gaze.

"You have no reason to feel foolish. As a matter of fact, that makes me feel pretty damned good."

"Really?"

Shelby nodded. "Really. I'm glad you think I'm sexy." She leaned forward and kissed Rebecca again, this time with more fervor. She helped Rebecca settle back until she was lying flat on the blanket. Feeling strong fingers pull her shirt out of her jeans, Shelby wasn't surprised when her bra was liberated from her body, and the item found its way to another part of the truck along with her shirt.

Rebecca worked at the button on Shelby's jeans, glad when she got help pushing them down. She allowed Shelby to strip her of her own clothes and closed her eyes in anticipation when bare flesh met bare flesh. She reached up and tangled her hands in Shelby's hair. "Come here," she commanded, before no more words were needed, and the two of them joined together underneath the stars.

WRAPPED IN THE blanket they had lain upon earlier, Rebecca couldn't help but grin. "I guess it's a good thing we're so secluded out here, huh?"

Shelby was busy getting back into her clothes since the blanket wasn't big enough for them both, and she was feeling a bit chilled. "Yeah. I also like when you bring picnic dinners, although I'm hungry again."

"I don't doubt that. We both wore off what food we ate. Unfortunately, our basket is empty."

Shelby tossed Rebecca's top to her. "If you'll get dressed, we can run into town and get a bite to eat."

Rebecca opened the blanket that she wore as a robe. "You mean I can't go like this?"

"Well, yeah." Shelby almost drooled at the sight before her. "But you might get a bit chilly at the IHOP."

"Spoil sport," Rebecca said. "But let's not go to the IHOP. Let's just get something and take it to the motel." When Shelby agreed, she dressed quickly, feeling the nip in the night air.

Once they were in the truck and on their way, Shelby glanced over at Rebecca. "I forgot to ask how your day went."

"Oh, that's right, I didn't tell you, did I? I had lunch with my father today."

"How's he doing?" Shelby kept her eyes on the road, but was truly curious.

Rebecca twisted in the seat so that she could see Shelby better. "He's doing well, and wanted to give me a message."

"What's that?"

"There's a playday this weekend." Rebecca couldn't keep the excitement out of her voice. "And I'm getting my own trailer. It just needs a little work. All I have to do is babysit a mare for a few days. Of course, I'm going to need a truck to pull the trailer."

Shelby smiled. "That's great news. And of course you can use this truck." She pulled the vehicle into the drive-through of a fast food chain. "Would you mind if I watched your event?"

"Not at all." Rebecca studied the menu board. "You can compete, if you want. There are always a lot of different events."

"I might just do that. Any extra money right now would be good."

They ordered their food and took it back to the motel. Once inside their room, Shelby tossed her keys on the dresser. "They don't have bull riding, do they?"

"No. But they have bronc riding, and some different roping events. Would you be interested in any of those?" Rebecca asked, following Shelby into the room.

"I haven't tried bronc riding in years," Shelby admitted. "That could be fun."

Chapter Eighteen

SHELBY PARKED THE truck beside a new Ford F-150 and turned off her engine. "There's quite a crowd here." She didn't know what she had been expecting, but counting the trailers, the day would rival the rodeo she had just competed in.

"Isn't it great? People come from counties all around to participate. Are you still going to try your hand at bronc riding?" Rebecca scanned the different trailers to see if she could recognize anyone. "Hey, there's Tammy. And Rudy, too. I haven't seen them in ages." She opened her door and jumped from the vehicle, rushing off to meet with old friends.

Shelby also exited the truck, but at a more leisurely pace. She studied the old trailer, which they had picked up that morning. It indeed needed work, mostly cosmetic. *A little sanding, a few cans of spray paint, and it'll be good as new.* She was surprised at what Rebecca would have to do for ownership. Obviously the man was a friend of Rebecca's father and had no use for the trailer anymore. Still, it was a nice gesture. She was about to help Patches from the rig when she saw Rebecca and her two friends head back in her direction. *This ought to be fun.*

The three women were walking arm in arm, laughing at something while Rebecca chatted away. They stopped at the trailer and Rebecca broke rank to stand beside Shelby. "Girls, I'd like for you to meet my—" she stumbled, then recover to go on and say, "my friend, Shelby Fisher. We met at the county rodeo."

"It's nice to meet you, Shelby," the short, dark-haired woman said. "I'm Tammy Sanchez, and this quiet one next to me is Rudy." As she pointed to Rudy, the woman blushed.

"Nice to meet you," Rudy quietly acknowledged. Her brown hair hung down in her face, almost hiding her light brown eyes. She stepped back, as if she were afraid Shelby would bite.

Shelby looked at Rebecca. A part of her was hurt that Rebecca hadn't recognized their true relationship to her friends. *Well, maybe it's for the best. Small towns normally have small minds, and she has lived here her whole life, after all.* "It's nice to meet you both." Shelby pulled her hat down a bit more. "If you'll excuse me, I really need to get Patches out before she melts in this trailer."

"I'd better help. Will I see you both later?"

"Count on it," Tammy assured her. "We really need to talk more. Come on, Rudy. My brother should have the horses all groomed by now."

Rebecca waved to them as they left. By the time she turned around Shelby had brought Patches out of the trailer and almost ran face first into the horse. "I could have done that."

"No need, I had it handled. How do we sign in for this shindig?"

Rebecca looked uncertain, and for a moment Shelby thought she was angry, but then she said, "Are you mad at me?"

"Why should I be?" Shelby ducked down and walked under Patches neck so that she was on the same side as Rebecca. "We *are* friends, aren't we?"

Rebecca stared down at her boots. "You noticed that, huh? Yes, we're a lot more than that. I'm sorry."

"Don't worry about it. You probably did the right thing, anyway. I'd hate for you to lose any friends because of me." Shelby took a step forward so that she was within inches of Rebecca. "Just remember I love you."

Rebecca stepped forward and was about to wrap her arms around Shelby's neck when a loud voice interrupted them.

"Damn it, Becca. Can't you at least *try* to look normal?" Terry grumbled. "Some of these people are friends of mine. Don't embarrass me." He was dressed in starched denim jeans and shirt, and his pointed-toe boots were brand new. The hat on his head was tilted in an awkward manner, as if he had never worn one before.

"You're asking *her* not to embarrass you?" Shelby laughed. "At least we're not dolled up like some folks."

Terry took a menacing step forward. "Shut up, you queer bitch. It's your fault she's like this, anyway."

Rebecca put her hand on her brother's chest. "Stop it. We're not doing anything wrong."

"Yeah, well only because I stopped you." Terry pointed his finger at Shelby. "What are you looking at, dyke?"

As much as she wanted to knock some sense into Terry, Shelby took a step back. "Nothing. I'm not looking at anything." *That's right, kid. You're just a bit of nothing. No better than the stuff people step in around here.* She leaned up against the trailer and allowed a slight smirk to appear on her face.

"What?" Terry glared at her. "What's so funny?"

"Terry, hush. You're starting to make a scene," Rebecca said. She stepped between her brother and Shelby, obviously afraid that Terry would do or say something that would cause Shelby to go on the offensive. Shelby watched as her lover tried to distract her brother. "What are you doing here? Dad didn't say anything to me about you coming out today."

Her brother straightened the oversized hat on his head, causing another near-burst of laughter from Shelby. "Dad mentioned you'd be here, and I wanted to watch, since I missed you at the rodeo." He glared at Shelby, as if to say he could have kept them apart had he been there. "He didn't know I was coming, either."

"Ah. That's fine." Rebecca wrapped her arms around her brother's waist. His body went rigid at the contact. "It's great to see you."

Terry finally relaxed and put his arms awkwardly around Rebecca. "Mom and Dad will probably be here too, although I think they plan on staying in the stands."

Rebecca smiled. "Really? That would be wonderful." They heard an announcement over the loudspeaker, and she stepped away from her brother. "Would you excuse us? We've got to get signed in."

"I guess I need to go find a good seat before they're all taken, anyway. Good luck, Sis." Not bothering to give either of the women another look, Terry walked away, his gait showing his discomfort with his footwear.

"That went well," Shelby commented dryly.

"Yeah, right."

"What are you going to do about him?"

Rebecca shrugged. "What *can* I do? It's one of those things — kind of like your mother coming to see you when you were in the hospital. We just deal with our relatives the best we can."

"I guess you're right."

Rebecca checked the lead rope that was clipped to Patches halter, assured that it was tied to the trailer properly. "Come on, we really do need to get signed in." She took Shelby's hand without thinking.

Shelby allowed Rebecca to pull her along. *I wish little brother could see this. He'd probably shit his new jeans.* The thought caused her to laugh.

"What's so funny?"

"Nothing. Lead on, darlin'. Let's get this playday started."

Diving into the Turn

REBECCA SIGNED UP for barrel racing and pole bending, the latter being something that Shelby had never seen before. Shelby followed her back to the trailer, slightly confused. "Tell me again what you do?" Shelby asked.

"There are six poles set in a straight line, twelve feet apart. Patches and I zigzag through them, then once we get to the end, spin and zigzag our way back. It's pretty simple, although it takes a really talented horse." They were back at the trailer, and Rebecca patted her equine friend's side. "I'm really lucky that Patches does most of the work. I just hang on."

"I'm sure you do more than that." Shelby went around to the side to where all the gear was stored in the trailer, gathering up what Rebecca would need.

Rebecca took the blanket and saddle from Shelby's hands, and quickly saddled her mount. She then removed the halter and replaced it with a bridle, scratching Patches behind the ear after doing so. "You ready, girl?"

Shelby watched as Rebecca prepared and was impressed by her attention to detail. Rebecca checked and double checked all the fittings, and smoothed her hand across the horse's flank after she did so. "So you do the pole thing first, right?"

"Yes." Rebecca put her left foot in the stirrup and swung her right leg over the saddle, easily mounting Patches. She looked down at Shelby and held out her hand. "Would you like a ride over to the arena?"

Shelby accepted the hand. "Sure." She waited until Rebecca removed her foot from the stirrup, then put her left foot in and allowed herself to be pulled up behind her. "I think I like riding horses better this way," Shelby whispered to her lover, wrapping her arms around Rebecca's waist.

"I thought you would." Rebecca lightly tapped her heels to Patches sides, and the horse started a slow walk toward the arena.

REBECCA'S TURN AT the poles was fourth, so she waited patiently with Shelby next to Patches while the other three contestants rode. The last woman knocked down one of the poles, which cost her penalty seconds and Rebecca released a sigh of relief.

"What's up?" Shelby asked.

"Her horse was about the only one that could outrun Patches. If we keep our heads about us, we should place pretty well."

Shelby understood. "No matter what, I think you'll do

great." She wanted to pull Rebecca into her arms and give her a kiss for good luck, but didn't think it would be wise. She settled for putting her hand on Rebecca's arm and giving it a light squeeze. "Go get 'em, tiger."

Rebecca took a deep breath and climbed aboard Patches. "Thanks. I've just got to clear my head and concentrate." She tipped her white western hat to Shelby and was gone.

Shelby had to admit that Rebecca looked great in her rodeo wear: emerald green Rocky jeans that hugged all of her curves, a green and white striped shirt, and black boots. She'd seen too many other women "make themselves up" just for the rodeo, but Rebecca's clothes were worn enough to show that she dressed this way normally. Of course, part of it was her job, but another was just Rebecca's love for the style of clothes. *And she looks damned good in them, and out of them, too.*

The closer Rebecca and her horse got to the arena, the more Patches began to prance. By the time they got to their starting point, Shelby saw that Rebecca could barely keep her still. Rebecca hunched down and patted the horse, and Shelby could tell she was saying soothing things to calm her. Finally, at the signal, Rebecca leaned over the saddle and dug her heels into Patches, giving the horse its head.

Shelby looked on nervously, as horse and rider became one. They moved through the poles quickly and efficiently, and by the time they were through, Shelby released the breath that she had taken before Rebecca had come into the arena. "Wow." She couldn't wait for Rebecca to return so that she could compliment them both on their ride. The voice over the loud speaker told her what she already knew: Rebecca was in first place.

Rebecca climbed off Patches and led her back to where Shelby waited. Not caring who saw, she rushed into the other woman's arms. "You're my good luck charm."

"Nah," Shelby deferred. "You two did it all on your own. That was amazing, darlin'. And I thought you were fast on the barrels."

"It just looks faster because of the weaving in and out, I think."

Shelby stepped back and held Rebecca at arms' length, aware of the way some of the people were looking at them. She didn't want to cause a scene, especially since Rebecca was so happy. "Well, whatever it is, congratulations. That was a great ride."

"Thanks." At that moment, Shelby's stomach grumbled loudly. "Sounds like you're ready for a bite."

"I'm always ready," Shelby teased, waggling her eyebrows,

which caused her lover to blush.

"For food, you heathen." Rebecca poked Shelby in the arm. "Come on. We'll go get a hot dog or something, so you don't collapse."

"Gee, thanks." But Shelby enjoyed the banter, and was glad to walk next to Rebecca, no matter what.

"ARE YOU SURE you want to do this?" Rebecca asked, as they headed toward the chutes for the women's bronc riding. "You said yourself it had been a long time since you'd tried it."

Shelby tried to ease Rebecca's fears. "I'll just think of the horse as a skinny, hornless bull. No problem." Her spurs jangled as she walked, and she was already wearing her chaps.

"But you said yourself it was completely different."

"It is. But I can handle it. I used to do it a lot when I was younger." Shelby was surprised that they had women's bareback bronc riding as an event, with as much testosterone as she had witnessed around them today. As it was, there were only four women competing, so she had a good chance of placing, at the very least. She had been very lucky that Rebecca knew someone who loaned her the necessary gear which consisted of a special kind of rigging. It looked like a heavy piece of leather with a suitcase handle, and that was all she had to hang on to the bucking animal, while trying to "mark out" the horse—spurring the horse from shoulder to rigging, back and forth to make a qualified ride. Shelby had already introduced herself to the pick-up men, riders whose job it was to swoop in and pick up the rider after the ride was complete. She was truly looking forward for the opportunity to compete in a new event.

They arrived where the other three women who were to compete in the event were getting ready. All were bigger than Shelby, and Rebecca leaned in and said, "That one looks like she could bench press a school bus."

"What makes you think I can't do that?"

"I'm afraid you could get hurt."

"There's always a chance of that, no matter what. But I do know what I'm doing, and if the first ride doesn't feel right to me, I'll quit." Shelby noticed where Rebecca's eyes were. "She is a big gal, ain't she?"

The woman in question noticed they were looking at her. She excused herself from the people she was standing with and headed toward the two women. "Becca?"

Rebecca stared at the well-built woman for a long moment, then broke out into a huge smile. "Dawn? Oh, wow! I haven't seen you in ages." She immediately embraced the other woman, while Shelby looked on, confused.

"In the flesh." Dawn pulled back from the hug. "Although, I'll admit to having a bit more flesh than I did in high school."

"You look great," Rebecca assured her, still not acknowledging her lover. "I didn't know you were involved in the rodeo."

Dawn flexed her arms. "I picked it up in college. But you look fantastic. Looks like the years have been especially good to you."

Rebecca blushed. "I don't know about that, but thanks." Shelby shuffled, and Rebecca turned. "Oh. Dawn, I'd love for you to meet my very good friend, Shelby Fisher. She'll be competing against you."

Shelby held out her hand. "Dawn. Good luck to you." She still didn't like the hungry look the other woman was giving her lover, but decided to let it go for now.

"Nice to meet you, too." Dawn gave a quick glance Shelby's way, then her eyes were back on Rebecca. "Are you doing anything after the rodeo?"

Rebecca was about to answer, but was stopped by hearing Shelby's name over the loud speaker. "I think they're calling your name."

"Yeah." Shelby slowly made her way to the chutes, Rebecca and Dawn's voices fading as they kept up their conversation behind her. She couldn't make out the words, but felt resentful anyway. *Guess the best way to show up that hulk is to beat her.* Now all she had to do was get her mind set on the ride ahead.

AFTER TALKING TO Dawn for a few more minutes, Rebecca realized that Shelby was nowhere to be found. She politely excused herself and hurried over to watch the bareback riding event. One woman was already in the arena, struggling mightily to stay on. Unfortunately for her, she didn't last the allotted time and picked herself up from the loose dirt. *Woohoo. If Shelby can stay on, she'll at least get third.*

Shelby was next. When the gate opened and the horse leapt out, her hat immediately flew from her head, and even from the distance, Rebecca could see her squinting in the afternoon sun. Using spurs, Shelby marked out the horse perfectly. The ride was going well, until a pained look crossed Shelby's face. She hung on, barely, until the pickup men drew her from the back of the still bucking horse.

Rebecca felt the butterflies in her stomach grow until she

thought she'd be ill. Something was wrong. She could almost sense Shelby's pain. She raced from her vantage point to watch Shelby walked from the arena. She held her right arm against her body, doing her best to appear nonchalant.

Shelby's face gave her away. It was shades lighter than normal, and beads of perspiration that hadn't been there previously dotted her forehead. As Rebecca hastened her way, Shelby slowly lowered her arm to her side. A young boy, no older than ten, raced to her side and handed her the brown Stetson she always wore. "Thanks." He hustled away, and Shelby used her left hand to place the hat back on her head.

Rebecca stopped Shelby in mid stride. "Are you all right?"

"Never better," Shelby ground out. "Made the ride, didn't I?" She took in a deep breath, and slowly released it. "Don't you want to go see how your friend does?"

Rebecca's eyes narrowed and she examined Shelby's face. "No, I'd rather be here with you. She asked me out to dinner tonight."

Shelby swallowed hard. "I see. Well, I'm sure you two have a lot of catching up to do." She started to walk around Rebecca, but was stopped by a hand to her left arm. She spun and looked at her lover.

"Oh, please," Rebecca said sarcastically. "She was practically undressing me with her eyes. I didn't feel like a wrestling match tonight, unless it was with you. Besides, you're the one I love." Rebecca studied Shelby's face carefully. "Now, no more lying to me. What's wrong?" She waited a moment, then said, "Come on, you know I'm going to find out sooner or later."

Shelby's face went through a couple incarnations before finally settling on resignation. "I'm not sure. I either messed up some muscles in my shoulder or arm, or something's out of place."

"What's it feel like?"

"My right arm and shoulder feel like they're on fire, with a hot stake poking through." She looked around, but no one was paying either of them any attention. "Is there a medical station here? Maybe they can tell me."

"I don't think so." Rebecca settled against Shelby's left side and placed her arm around her waist. "You're going directly to the hospital." Rebecca walked her on a path toward the truck where Patches was tied to the trailer.

Shelby balked. "What about your next event? You're doing too well to leave, now."

"You're more important than a stupid playday. Shelby, you could be seriously hurt."

"Nah. I can't let you do that. I'm just a little banged up. Let's wait until your part is over, and then we'll go. It's already easing up some. We can even sit up with your folks, if you want."

Rebecca *did* want to compete. Just not at the expense of Shelby's health. She stopped and surveyed her lover's face. "Well, you are up and walking on your own. Okay, but you do promise to tell me when you need to leave? If we need to head to the hospital, you'll let me know, right?"

"You bet."

The rest of the playday went well. They decided against sitting with Rebecca's family, since Terry was sitting there, his ridiculous outfit causing him to stand out in the crowd. Instead, they milled around with the other contestants.

Shelby walked next to Rebecca and Patches, who were up soon for the barrel racing event. The pain was making her sick to her stomach, but she was determined to ride it out so that Rebecca could win the two events she led in. "Looks like it's about time for you to finish off these other gals."

"I sure hope so." Rebecca held Patches reins in one hand, and longed to hold Shelby's right hand with her other. "It's the last event for me, and then we can get you checked out."

As bad as she felt, Shelby was in no condition to argue. "What about Patches? Shouldn't we take her out to the farm, first?"

Rebecca had forgotten about that. Her mind searched for an answer. "After this ride, let me talk to my dad. I've got an idea." They were at the edge of the arena, so she gave Shelby's good arm a gentle squeeze before swinging up into the saddle. "Wish me luck."

"Darlin', you don't need it. You and Patches make a perfect team." Shelby reached up and patted the horse's neck. "But, good luck, anyway." She stepped back from the horse.

"I love you," Rebecca leaned down and whispered.

Shelby reached up with her left hand and ran her finger along Rebecca's jaw. "Me, too. Now go out there and show these folks how it's done."

"You got it." Rebecca nudged Patches forward.

AFTER HER WINNING ride, Rebecca's family met her at the trailer. Her mom was the first to embrace her after she dropped down from the saddle. "That was wonderful, Becca!"

"Thanks, mom. I think Patches did most of the work, though." Rebecca searched the group for Shelby, but she was nowhere to be seen. "Have you seen Shelby?"

Her father also gave her a hug. "Not since seeing her ride today. I didn't even know she was a bareback rider."

"She told me she did it sometimes when she wanted to try for an extra purse. I'm really proud of her."

Terry snorted. "Yeah, she's so good she scratched from the steer wrestling. Probably got scared."

Rebecca stepped up to her brother and poked him in the chest with her finger. "For your information, *little brother*, she injured her right arm. I'm the one who asked her to drop the event."

Kathy stepped in between them. "Let's all calm down." She gave Terry a look, which caused him to sigh heavily. She then directed her attention back to Rebecca. "Is Shelby's injury serious?"

"No, ma'am." Shelby had been resting in the cab of the truck when she heard the voices, and came out to investigate. "Nothing a little rest won't cure, I'm sure."

Not caring what it looked like, Rebecca hurried to Shelby's side and gently wrapped her arms around Shelby's body. "I hate to tell you this, but you look horrible."

"Thanks."

"We need to get you to the emergency room, and have that arm checked out." Rebecca looked at her father.

Before Rebecca could say anything, he held up his hand. "If it's okay with your mother, why don't you use her SUV to take Shelby to the hospital, and I'll take Patches out to Jack's place. We can trade later, back at the house."

Kathy agreed. "That's a wonderful idea. I'll ride with your father, and Terry can take his own car home."

"I really appreciate your thoughtfulness, but—" Shelby was silenced by Rebecca's hand covering her mouth.

"Thank you. We'll be back to your house as soon as we're done." Rebecca stepped away from Shelby to give her parents quick hugs.

THE SMALL HOSPITAL'S waiting area wasn't overly busy, but Shelby and Rebecca still had to wait to see a doctor, since there was only one available. The longer they sat, the more antsy Shelby became. The hours dragged by. "We could always just wait until Monday, then make an appointment with a regular doctor," she huffed. She didn't care for hospitals, and the pain she was in was only making her grumpier. "Let's just go."

"Oh, no. Not after all the time we've already spent waiting."

"Ms. Fisher?" An older woman wearing green scrubs put a halt to their argument. The doctor will see you now."

Shelby slowly got to her feet, no longer trying to hide the pain she was in. She held her right arm gently across her body and followed the nurse. "Thanks."

Rebecca thought about staying where she was, but she wanted to be there for Shelby. Her boots clomped loud on the clean linoleum floor as she hurried to catch up. "I'm right behind you, Shelby."

They were led to a small room off the hallway. The nurse, whose nametag read Linda, popped on latex gloves. "Ms. Fisher, if you'll just climb up on the examining table, I'll get all your vital signs checked."

Shelby looked at the high, paper-covered table, then back at the nurse. "I hate to admit this, ma'am, but I don't think I can manage with this bum arm."

"Stupid me." Linda glanced over at Rebecca. "Do you think the two of us can toss her up there?"

"Of course." She got on Shelby's injured side, and cautiously wrapped her arm around Shelby's waist.

The nurse did the same from the other side, and between the two of them, they easily lifted Shelby to the examination table.

Although the other two did all the work, Shelby felt as if she would collapse from the pain. She sat by quietly as the nurse did her job, checking everything from her blood pressure to her temperature.

"That's all I need, Ms. Fisher. The doctor will be in to see you shortly." Linda left the small room and closed the door, allowing the two women the first bit of privacy they'd had all day.

Rebecca immediately stepped between Shelby's legs and placed her hands on her lover's thighs. "You look miserable, honey. Is there anything I can do for you?"

"You're doing a pretty good job right now. I just can't wait until the doctor tells me to go home and take some aspirin for a few days, and we can get out of here."

The door opened, and a kindly older man stepped into the room. "Trying to take my job away from me, young lady?" He barely noticed when Rebecca stepped back out of his way. The doctor looked at the nurse's notes. "So, you're one of those rodeo people, are you? Pretty rough on the body, isn't it?"

"It sure was this time," Shelby said. She bit her lip to keep from crying out in pain when the doctor gently raised her right arm.

"I'm sorry about that. I think before we go any further into this exam, we'll get some X-rays taken of your arm, shoulder and back. There's no sense in you being in needless pain."

Rebecca stepped forward and rubbed Shelby's lower back in an effort to help her relax. "Thank you, Doctor—"

"Anderson. I'm not usually here at the hospital, but a friend asked me to help out. I have a private practice here in Somerville. Let me go get a nurse to help you to the radiation department." At that, Dr. Anderson left the room.

SHELBY'S X-RAYS ALMOST beat her back to the room, where the doctor was waiting. He and Rebecca were carrying on a quiet conversation, which stopped when Shelby was wheeled into the examination room by the nurse. "Am I interrupting something?"

"Not at all." Dr. Anderson waved off the nurse, who was about to help Shelby get back up on the table. "That's not necessary, Linda. We're only going to be in here for a few more minutes at the most." After Linda left, he clipped the X-rays up on the lit board. "I'm no orthopedic physician, but from what I can tell here, you've messed things up pretty well, Shelby. It's a soft tissue injury, but my best guess is that you've torn your rotator cuff, and have some possible damage to your ligaments and nerves in your arm. You'll need an MRI to verify, and that's not something we'd do here at the emergency room. The best thing I can prescribe for you is some painkillers for now and have you set up an appointment with our sports doctor, who happens to have an office in the building across the street." He gently slipped a sling on Shelby. "This should help, at least a little bit."

"Do you think I'll be able to compete again?" Shelby asked, fearful of the answer.

Dr. Anderson shrugged his shoulders. "I'm no expert, but since what you do puts such a strain on that arm, I'd have to say no."

She was so stunned that she didn't know what to say. She dropped her eyes to the floor, feeling his gaze upon her.

"I'll have Linda give you the orthopedic surgeon's card, and you can contact him on Monday."

Rebecca saw that Shelby was in no shape to answer the doctor. "Thank you. We appreciate all your help."

"I just wish I could give you better news." Dr. Anderson tapped Shelby on the leg. "You hang in there, kid. I'm just an old general practice doctor, so I may not be up on all the new technology available to make you better."

Shelby tried to look more cheerful than she felt. "Thanks, doc. Even if you're right, it's not the end of the world, is it?"

"Exactly. You're young, and there are a lot of things you can still do besides the rodeo." He wrote out a prescription and handed it to Rebecca before leaving the room.

Rebecca helped Shelby out of the wheelchair. "Come on. Let's get you home. We can stop off at a twenty-four hour pharmacy on the way."

Shelby wanted to yank away from Rebecca, but knew the movement would cause the pain in her arm to become worse. "In case you've forgotten, I don't have a home."

Startled at the harsh tone in her lover's voice, Rebecca stopped in the hallway and removed her grip. "Of course you do, it just needs—"

"Work that I'll probably never be able to finish. And I certainly can't afford to fix it up or live in a motel indefinitely. Damn, I was stupid to sell my trailer."

Rebecca followed Shelby outside, moving around in front of her to cause her to stop. "You weren't stupid at all, Shelby. That trailer, no matter what kind of personal value it held for you, was no place for you to continue to live. You need a real place, with running water and a toilet that works."

"And how am I supposed to pay for someplace like that? You said yourself I'm going to need a high school diploma before I can get a decent job." Shelby felt her hopes falling down around her. "Maybe I'll just go live with my aunt for a while. That is, if she'll still have me."

Rebecca felt the blood rush from her face. "You'd leave me?"

"I'm sure not taking any charity from you. Please don't ask me to do that." Shelby brushed by Rebecca and walked toward the parking lot.

"Is that what you think it would be, charity?" Rebecca asked, when she caught up to Shelby, who stood next to the Tahoe. "I happen to love you, you know. Can't I help you without having an ulterior motive?"

Shelby wanted to slam her hand against the SUV, but held her temper in check. It wasn't her vehicle, after all. "That's not the point. I know you love me, and I love you, too. But I can't just sponge off you like some laze-about."

"Then we'll find you a job, and we can live together. It won't take much more work to get the farm livable. You can tell me what to do, and we'll do it together." Rebecca unlocked the SUV and they both got inside. "Would that be okay? This is not about *you*, Shelby. It's about *us*. It's about our life together. Forever. Don't you understand?"

It was quiet while Shelby thought about Rebecca's comment. Could they live together? Was it possible to think of forever? Their relationship was still so new, and the thought of living in one place, with one person, terrified Shelby. She looked across at Rebecca, and time seemed to stand still. Her heart beat loudly in her chest, and she felt a little faint. But then a realization came to her. *There's really no contest, is there?* "You think we can really do it, that we can make it?"

Rebecca nodded solemnly. "I really think so."

It didn't take long until they pulled into the Starrett's driveway. The lights were still on in the house, and Rebecca was surprised to see her father step off the porch and jog to the car.

He waited until she stepped from the vehicle. "How's Shelby?"

"Not good." Rebecca looked into the car where Shelby appeared to be resting. "The doctor we spoke with thinks she may have torn her rotator cuff and damaged some ligaments and nerves, at the very least."

"Ouch. I'm sorry to hear that. It sounds like she's going to need a place to recuperate."

"I'm afraid so, and the house she's been working on isn't even livable, yet. I'm not sure what we're going to do."

"Funny you should say that. We had a long family meeting this afternoon about that very subject. Or, at least, about where you might be able to stay." Greg looked extremely pleased with himself.

"Really? I'd gladly accept any ideas. I've been thinking about it since we left the hospital."

Greg took his daughter by the hand and led her to the unattached garage. They went up the outside stairs to the second floor, which they had always used as storage. He opened the door and flipped on the light switch.

What had once been cluttered with a lifetime of junk, was now a one room apartment. An older, but well-maintained sofa sat against the far wall, its flowery design blending in nicely with the overstuffed chairs around it. On the other side was a door, which Rebecca had never seen before. "Where does that lead?" Rebecca asked.

"Believe it or not, it's a bathroom, complete with tub and sink. As long as I could remember, I thought this was just a big storage room. But at one time, it was an apartment. We thought that the two of you might be comfortable here until you can find something else." Greg pointed out the sofa. "That turns into a bed. I know there's no kitchen here, so you'll just have to have meals with the family, if you'd like."

Rebecca was shocked. "I can't believe you did all of this."

"Believe it. I even got your brother to help."

"How did you manage that? I know he hates me right now." Rebecca lowered her head. "Are you sure it's not going to cause problems around here if we move in? That's the last think we want to do. I'll live in a roach motel, first."

Greg put his arm around her shoulder. "That won't be necessary. After the little talk I had with Terry, he's promised to be civil. And believe me, he doesn't hate you. He's just really confused right now."

"All right. Let me see what Shelby says."

"What I say about what?" Shelby stood on the landing near the door. "What's going on?"

Greg moved aside to allow Shelby access to the apartment. "Come in and see for yourself." He made eye contact with Rebecca. "Why don't you two join me for some hot chocolate when you get the chance?"

Rebecca hugged her father. "We will. Thanks." She waited until he left before turning back to Shelby. "What do you think?"

"About what?"

"We've been offered the use of this apartment until we can get the house fixed up enough. There's a bathroom, but no kitchen. Think we can make do?"

The hopeful look on Rebecca's face made up Shelby's mind. "I think it's a wonderful idea. Let's go thank your folks. But first," she stepped closer to Rebecca and kissed her gently. "I think it's going to be a great life, no matter where we spend it."

Rebecca leaned into Shelby's good shoulder. "I completely agree." She kissed her lover's chin and backed away. "Now, let's go tell my parents. I hear some hot chocolate calling our names." She took Shelby's left hand and guided her down the steps, and into their new life.

Other Carrie Carr titles published by
Yellow Rose Books

LEX AND AMANDA SERIES

Destiny's Bridge - Rancher Lexington (Lex) Walters pulls young Amanda Cauble from a raging creek and the two women quickly develop a strong bond of friendship. Overcoming severe weather, cattle thieves, and their own fears, their friendship deepens into a strong and lasting love.

Faith's Crossing - Lexington Walters and Amanda Cauble withstood raging floods, cattle rustlers and other obstacles to be together...but can they handle Amanda's parents? When Amanda decides to move to Texas for good, she goes back to her parents' home in California to get the rest of her things, taking the rancher with her.

Hope's Path - Someone is determined to ruin Lex. Efforts to destroy her ranch lead to attempts on her life. Lex and Amanda desperately try to find out who hates Lex so much that they are willing to ruin the lives of everyone in their path. Can they survive long enough to find out who's responsible? And will their love survive when they find out who it is?

Love's Journey - Lex and Amanda embark on a new journey as Lexington rediscovers the love her mother's family has for her, and Amanda begins to build her relationship with her father. Meanwhile, attacks on the two young women grow more violent and deadly as someone tries to tear apart the love they share.

Strength of the Heart - In the fifth story of the series, Lex and Amanda are caught up in the planning of their upcoming nuptials while trying to get the ranch house rebuilt. But an arrest, a brushfire, and the death of someone close to her forces Lex to try and work through feelings of guilt and anger. Is Amanda's love strong enough to help her, or will Lex's own personal demons tear them apart?

The Way Things Should Be - In this, the sixth novel, Amanda begins to feel her own biological clock ticking while her sister prepares for the birth of her first child. Lex is busy with trying to keep her hands on some newly acquired land, as well trying to get along with a new member of her family. Everything comes to a head, and a tragedy brings pain - and hope - to them all.

SOMETHING TO BE THANKFUL FOR

Randi Meyers is at a crossroads in her life. She's got no girlfriend, bad knees, and her fill of loneliness. The one thing she does have in her favor is a veterinarian job in Fort Worth, Texas, but even that isn't going as well as she hoped. Her supervisor is cold-hearted and dumps long hours of work on her. Even if she did want a girlfriend, she has little time to look.

When a distant uncle dies, Randi returns to her hometown of Woodbridge, Texas, to attend the funeral. During the graveside services, she wanders away from the crowd and is beseeched by a young boy to follow him into the woods to help his injured sister. After coming upon an unconscious woman, the boy disappears. Randi brings the woman to the hospital and finds out that her name is Kay Newcombe.

Randi is intrigued by Kay. Who is this unusual woman? Where did her little brother disappear to? And why does Randi feel compelled to help her? Despite living in different cities, a tentative friendship forms, but Randi is hesitant. Can she trust her newfound friend? How much of her life and feelings can Randi reveal? And what secrets is Kay keeping from her? Together, Randi and Kay must unravel these questions, trust one another, and find the answers in order to protect themselves from outside threats—and discover what they mean to one another.

ISBN 1-932300-04-X

"An excellent story about two women who've gone through the School of Hard Knocks. You can't help but root for Kay and Randi as they try to make sense of their lives. This is Carrie Carr's best novel yet!"
~Lori L. Lake, author of *Gun Shy* and *Different Dress*

FORTHCOMING TITLES

published by
Yellow Rose Books

HEART TROUBLE
by Jane Vollbrecht

Heart Trouble chronicles Jackie Frackman's journey through a tumultuous romance with the enigmatic Beth Novatny. The story is told from Jackie's first-person perspective. Lesbians of any age who have ever loved someone so right — who sometimes is someone so wrong — are sure to recognize themselves in the portrayals of Jackie and Beth as they struggle to come to terms wiht themselves and each other.

SOLACE
by Jennifer Fulton

Rebel Monroe is a Californian yachtswoman sailing solo around the world. When her yacht - Solace - capsizes in a perfect storm near the Cook Islands group, she puts to sea in a lifeboat expecting she is not going to make it. Eventually she washes up half-dead on the shores of Moon Island, where she is found by ex-nun Althea Kennedy.

Althea, who entered a Poor Clare order at 20, has recently turned her back on religious life after a traumatic experience in Africa. Questioning both her faith and the church, she is on Moon Island recuperating from malaria and pondering her options.

Rebel, considered a hero by the island's owners, is invited to stay a while and she forms an unlikely friendship with Althea. When this blossoms into something more each woman must rethink her identity, her demons, and her life choices before she can find real happiness.

OTHER YELLOW ROSE TITLES
You may also enjoy:

INFINITE LOOP
by Meghan O'Brien

When shy software developer, Regan O'Riley is dragged into a straight bar by her workmates, the last person she expects to meet is the woman of her dreams. Off-duty cop, Mel Raines is tall, dark and gorgeous but has no plans to enter a committed relationship any time soon. Despite their differing agendas, Mel and Regan can't deny an instant, overwhelming attraction. Both their lives are about to change drastically, when a tragedy forces Mel to rethink her emotional isolation and face inner demons rooted in her past. She cannot make this journey alone, and Regan's decision to share it with her has consequences neither woman expects. More than an erotic road novel, *Infinite Loop* explores the choices we make, the families we build, and the power of love to transform lives.

ISBN 1-932300-42-2

THE BLUEST EYES IN TEXAS
by Linda Crist

Kennedy Nocona is an out, liberal, driven attorney, living in Austin, the heart of the Texas hill country. Dallasite Carson Garret is a young paralegal overcoming the loss of her parents, and coming to terms with her own sexual orientation.

A chance encounter finds them inexplicably drawn to one another, and they quickly find themselves in a long distance romance that leaves them both wanting more. Circumstances at Carson's job escalate into a series of mysteries and blackmail that leaves her with more excitement than she ever bargained for. Confused, afraid, and alone, she turns to Kennedy, the one person she knows can help her. As they work together to solve a puzzle, they confront growing feelings that neither woman can deny. Can they overcome the outside forces that threaten to crush them both?

ISBN 978-1-932300-48-2

Other YELLOW ROSE Publications

Georgia Beers	Turning The Page	1-930928-51-3
Georgia Beers	Thy Neighbor's Wife	1-932300-15-5
Carrie Brennan	Curve	1-932300-41-4
Carrie Carr	Destiny's Bridge	1-932300-11-2
Carrie Carr	Faith's Crossing	1-932300-12-0
Carrie Carr	Hope's Path	1-932300-40-6
Carrie Carr	Love's Journey	1-930928-67-X
Carrie Carr	Strength of the Heart	1-930928-75-0
Linda Crist	Galveston 1900: Swept Away	1-932300-44-9
Linda Crist	The Bluest Eyes in Texas	978-1-932300-48-2
Jennifer Fulton	Passion Bay	1-932300-25-2
Jennifer Fulton	Saving Grace	1-932300-26-0
Jennifer Fulton	The Sacred Shore	1-932300-35-X
Jennifer Fulton	A Guarded Heart	1-932300-37-6
Jennifer Fulton	Dark Dreamer	1-932300-46-5
Anna Furtado	The Heart's Desire	1-932300-32-5
Gabrielle Goldsby	The Caretaker's Daughter	1-932300-18-X
Melissa Good	Terrors of the High Seas	1-932300-45-7
Maya Indigal	Until Soon	1-932300-31-7
Lori L. Lake	Different Dress	1-932300-08-2
Lori L. Lake	Ricochet In Time	1-932300-17-1
A. K. Naten	Turning Tides	978-1-932300-47-5
Meghan O'Brien	Infinite Loop	1-932300-42-2
Sharon Smith	Into The Dark	1-932300-38-4
Karen Surtees and Nann Dunne	True Colours	978-1-932300-52-9
Cate Swannell	Heart's Passage	1-932300-09-0
Cate Swannell	No Ocean Deep	1-932300-36-8
L. A. Tucker	The Light Fantastic	1-932300-14-7

About the Author:

Carrie Carr is a true Texan, having lived in the state her entire life. She makes her home in the Dallas/Ft. Worth metroplex with her wife, Jan. She's done everything from wrangling longhorn cattle and buffalo, to programming burglar and fire alarm systems. Her time is spent writing, traveling, and trying to corral their two dogs - a Chihuahua-mix named Nugget, and a Fox Terrier named Cher. Carrie's website is www.carrielcarr.com. She can be reached at cbzeer@comcast.net.

VISIT US ONLINE AT

www.regalcrest.biz

At the Regal Crest Website You'll Find

- The latest news about forthcoming titles and new releases

- Our complete backlist of romance, mystery, thriller and adventure titles

- Information about your favorite authors

- Current bestsellers

- Media tearsheets to print and take with you when you shop

Regal Crest titles are available from all progressive booksellers and online at StarCrossed Productions, (www.scp-inc.biz), or at www.amazon.com, www.bamm.com, www.barnesandnoble.com, and many others.